THE TAPES

BOOKS BY KERRY WILKINSON

Thriller novels

Two Sisters

The Girl Who Came Back

Last Night

The Death and Life of Eleanor Parker

The Wife's Secret

A Face in the Crowd

Close to You

After the Accident

The Child Across the Street

What My Husband Did

The Blame

The Child in the Photo

The Perfect Daughter

The Party at Number 12

The Boyfriend

The Night of the Sleepover

After the Sleepover

The Call

The Missing Body

Home Is Where the Lies Live

My Son's Girlfriend

Your Husband's Fault

ROMANCE NOVELS

Ten Birthdays

Truly, Madly, Amy

THE JESSICA DANIEL SERIES

The Killer Inside (also published as *Locked In*)

Vigilante

The Woman in Black

Think of the Children

Playing With Fire

The Missing Dead (also published as *Thicker than Water*)

Behind Closed Doors

Crossing the Line

Scarred for Life

For Richer, For Poorer

Nothing But Trouble

Eye for an Eye

Silent Suspect

The Unlucky Ones

A Cry in the Night

THE ANDREW HUNTER SERIES

Something Wicked

Something Hidden

Something Buried

WHITECLIFF BAY SERIES
The One Who Fell
The One Who Was Taken
The Ones Who Are Buried
The Ones Who Are Hidden

SILVER BLACKTHORN
Reckoning
Renegade
Resurgence

OTHER
Down Among the Dead Men
No Place Like Home
Watched

KERRY WILKINSON

THE
TAPES

bookouture

Published by Bookouture in 2025

An imprint of Storyfire Ltd.
Carmelite House
50 Victoria Embankment
London EC4Y 0DZ

www.bookouture.com

The authorised representative in the EEA is Hachette Ireland
8 Castlecourt Centre
Dublin 15 D15 XTP3
Ireland
(email: info@hbgi.ie)

Copyright © Kerry Wilkinson, 2025

Kerry Wilkinson has asserted his right to be identified
as the author of this work.

All rights reserved. No part of this publication may be reproduced, stored in any retrieval system, or transmitted, in any form or by any means, electronic, mechanical, photocopying, recording or otherwise, without the prior written permission of the publishers.

ISBN: 978-1-80550-063-6
eBook ISBN: 978-1-80550-062-9

This book is a work of fiction. Names, characters, businesses, organizations, places and events other than those clearly in the public domain, are either the product of the author's imagination or are used fictitiously. Any resemblance to actual persons, living or dead, events or locales is entirely coincidental.

TUESDAY

ONE

It's underneath a rusty power saw that I find the cassette player. Dad's inability to throw things out has led to a garage cluttered with everything from used sandpaper – better known as 'paper' – to a Danish butter cookies tin filled with small light bulbs he'd labelled 'dead'. No wonder he always left his car parked on the driveway: the garage is landfill.

Except for the tape player.

It's about the size of a Kindle, or a mini iPad, though much heavier. There's a built-in speaker and something delightfully satisfying and retro about the chunky buttons and the way the lid flicks open with a substantial *pop*. Now with Siri, Alexa, and all the touchscreens, it's such a novelty to be able to push things.

A shoebox marked 'cables' sits underneath and I remove the lid to find a mangle of spaghettified cords woven into one another. There are the obligatory SCART leads Dad kept, presumably in case they ever returned to fashion, but also the short black lead for the cassette player.

Before he died, when Dad did one of his annual clear-outs that's not really a clear-out, he gave me an old rotary landline phone. My daughter is seventeen, a child of the noughties, who'd never known a world that wasn't wireless. When I took the phone home for her, she stared at it, baffled by the ancient tech, unsure how it worked.

I *really* want her to see this.

The cassette player goes into the very small 'keep' pile and then I continue rummaging.

It's going to take a while to clear Dad's house, to the point that I'm thinking it might be wiser to get the bulldozers in. My father was many things and borderline hoarder was definitely one of them.

God forbid he throw out anything himself.

After a few more minutes of sorting and clearing, I find a box with 'Ange' written on the side in faded felt tip. I'm about to dispatch it to the bin, except the name has me momentarily frozen.

Angela was Mum's name.

Was...

The box has the dust-crusted look of something that's not been moved in a very long time. I'm half expecting old photographs inside – but the contents are even more of a treasure trove. An old corded microphone has the wire wrapped around the handle – and then, underneath, are two long rows of cassette tapes.

I'm falling through time: sitting on my bedroom floor, a tape in the hi-fi, trying to press play and record and the exact time to cut out the DJ's voice as I record songs from the radio. There was a time when I'd carry my own mixtapes in my schoolbag and listen to them on my knock-off Argos Walkman while walking to school. As I stare at the tidy stack of tapes, it's so close, even though it's thirty years ago.

At first I wonder if some of my old tapes survived, except these all have tidy handwriting on the sleeves.

Mum's handwriting.

There's another moment in which I'm blinking my way into the past. It's such a long time since I saw such neatly capitalised letters. Mum once told me she won a handwriting competition when she'd been at school and, when I was eight or nine, I had been so desperate to be as good as her. It's impossible not to feel those ancient tugs.

I choose a cassette from the middle of the row: one marked by a simple 'September 1987'.

The tape inside is a translucent brown, with 'C-90' on a thin label that's slightly peeling from the plastic. I fumble the cassette into the player and push the lid closed with a gratifying *clunk*. There's a plug socket hidden behind something that looks like an old lawnmower engine, so I slot it in – and then press play.

A momentary silence is followed by a *thunk* from a microphone, a gentle clearing of someone's throat, and then more silence.

I realise I can hear my own heart walloping its way through my chest. As soon as the woman's voice says *'Hello...'* a shiver flashes along my spine and I instinctively check over my shoulder, as it suddenly feels as if I'm no longer alone.

I am but I'm not.

Joining me is a voice I haven't heard in thirteen years.

'It's Saturday today and we've been at Hollicombe Bay for a week now. The caravan's kind of small but it's only Bruce, Eve and me here. Bruce made friends with the couple next door, mainly because he's found someone who is also happy to talk about motorbikes for hours. I've been taking Eve for walks around the campsite. She met her first puppy yesterday. I thought she might be a bit too young but—'

I stop the tape because it's too much. I'd have very recently turned two years old in September 1987. The talk of being walked around a campsite and seeing my first puppy...

The last time I heard my mother speak was over a decade ago. If anyone had asked, I don't think I would have been able to describe her voice – and yet it feels so familiar now. There's a little more youth than I remember, and it's perhaps slightly higher pitched – but it's unquestionably Mum.

She sounds so young.

There's a lump in my throat, which is gulped away while I remove the tape from the player. I return it to the case, then the box – where there are so many more.

It's only now that vague memories swirl of Mum sitting at the dining table with a cassette player and microphone. I'd forgotten that there was a time in which she used to record her thoughts as some sort of diary. Like everything as a child, people assume your mum and dad are normal and everyone else's are strange. It's only now I realise most grown-ups weren't sitting down to record themselves.

I think I even remember the caravan park: not from the year on the tape, but we visited the same place every August until the early-nineties. There's a clear memory of being six or seven, complaining about Mum dragging me up a hill, or round a lake on one of those trips. She was always more outdoorsy, while Dad would sit by himself and read the paper.

Dad's garage still needs clearing but I'm almost paralysed by the box of tapes. Almost all sleeves have identical type, with the month and year. Everything's out of order but there's a couple from the early 1980s, before I was born; then a good half-dozen from the 1990s. Even as the world shifted to CDs, Mum was apparently recording the earliest of podcasts for an audience of only herself. I find myself wondering whether she ever listened back to the recordings, or if it was simply a way of getting the thoughts from her head.

I almost return the lid to the box. This is something for another day.

Almost.

Because tucked at the bottom of a row is a cassette that doesn't have a month and date. Instead, there's one simple word.

Eve

My name written by Mum's hand. Another shiver rips through me and, before I know it, the tape is in the player. There's that gentle *thunk* of the microphone being picked up, and then:

> *This is my second go at this. My name is Angela and I've been murdered...*
>
> *...*
> *...*
> *Well, I think I'm going to be murdered.*
> *...*
> *...*
> *I don't know. It's just... I don't think I'm a good person. I did something. I've done lots of things...'*

There's a crackle and a click that makes me wince, then the voice cuts to something different. Mum is there again but her voice is younger, happier.

> 'Can you count to three, Eve? We start with one, don't we? One...'

I listen to a me of the ancient past repeat *one-two-three* in time after my mother, as she calls me clever. She says I'm going to grow up to be an astronaut or a brain surgeon, except I'm still frozen from the first part. I rest a finger on the stop button, ready to rewind and listen again, except there's another crackle and click.

'... if this is Eve listening, I just want you to know I'm sorry. If they say I'm missing, I'm not. I've been killed – and I need you to know that I love you.'

TWO

I can't stop shivering, even though the day is warm. When I stop the tape and press rewind, the machine squeals. The mechanism swirls until there's a harsh click when the cassette reaches the beginning.

The second listen makes slightly more sense than the first, though not by a lot. Mum must've recorded me as a child. My babbling, chirpy voice is there as she tries to teach me to count. I must've been two or three at the time. Except, at some point, she tried to record over our little lesson. Perhaps because of the quality of the tape, or any number of other technical reasons I don't understand, her attempt was only partially successful. There was some sort of cross-contamination between timelines.

That's not all, of course.

'I think I'm going to be murdered... I don't think I'm a good person. I did something. I've done lots of things... if they say I'm missing, I'm not. I've been killed.'

She *disappeared* thirteen years ago. Except... was she *actu-*

ally murdered? Was she predicting the future? When did she record this?

And what does she mean when she says she did something?

I listen a third time as Mum's voice intertwines with the infant me. It's been such a long time since cassettes were part of my life that I can't fully remember how they work. There was definitely a thing where you could sometimes hear what was on the other side if the tape itself got damaged.

'...I need you to know that I love you.'

I should be focusing on the other stuff, I know, yet I rewind the tape a few seconds, and then press play to hear it again, then again. Five times in a row. Ten.

It's been so long since I heard her voice.

Instinctively, I want to ask Dad about the tape. About Mum being murdered or missing, about not thinking she's a good person. Did she really think that?

I always knew she was... *different*.

I want to ask Dad about it. But a moment after thinking it, the memory dawns that he's no longer around to answer.

It hasn't sunk in yet. Dad and I would talk a couple of times a week and he was always there for the little pieces of handyman stuff. When I needed shelving for the spare room, Dad put them in.

'...I need you to know that I love you.'

I try to remember the last time Mum actually said that to me but it's blank.

As I rewind and listen to the first part again, I wonder whether Dad ever listened to these. Chances are he simply piled the box in among the rest of his stuff he wouldn't throw out.

There's no date on the tape, though a clear difference in Mum's voice between the two timelines. When I'm a toddler, she'd have been in her early to mid-twenties; though it's hard to know about the second. There's a slight croak, and her tone is definitely deeper. If it was recorded at around the time she disappeared, she'd have been close to fifty.

'...I need you to know that I love you.'

There's an ache in my side that wasn't there before. I rewind to listen again, knowing I need to get on with what I was supposed to be doing. There's nobody to ask about any of this, so what am I supposed to do with it?

Except, before I can press play, my phone begins to ring. 'Faith' is on the screen. I almost hang up by accident because my daughter *never* calls. I'm lucky if she replies to texts.

'Hello?' I say, somehow still expecting it to be someone else.

'Mum?' There's a quiver of worry in her voice.

'I'm here.'

'Can you come? I need you.'

THREE

I can't remember the last time my daughter said she needed me, if she ever has. I nearly forget to lock Dad's garage as I barrel out of his house, then I realise I've left my car keys inside and have to dart back to grab them.

Faith said she was at her friend Shannon's. She had started to add something when a muffled voice I couldn't make out said something to her. She said she had to go – and that was it. Click. *I need you.*

Town is a blur, except for the obligatory traffic lights that always seem to be on red. Buildings soon become countryside, with the narrow, crumbling roads, tall hedges, and distant fields. The houses are no longer in rows; instead separated by large plots and ploughed pastures. I'm on autopilot, thoughts of Dad's garage and Mum's voice replaced by the very present worry that Faith needs me to such a degree that she actually asked.

And she called me, not her father. Maybe a tiny part of me is glad about that.

I try calling my daughter from the car but it rings off.

Another shiver takes me as I round a bend to see a pair of police cars parked half on the verge. I pull in behind one, and almost fall out of the car as I head for the gate of Shannon's house. A uniformed officer is standing tall in front of a sign that says 'Collins Farm'. When he spots me, he holds out an arm to block the way.

'You can't come this way,' he says.

I point past him, towards the house. 'My daughter's in there. She called me.'

He pauses a moment, slightly raising an eyebrow and not appearing convinced.

'What's going on?' I add.

He chews the inside of his mouth for a moment, before unclipping a radio from his belt. Before he gets a chance to do anything more, there's a sharp call of 'Mum!' from behind him. Faith has emerged from the front door, Shannon at her side.

Thank God.

The two teenage girls beckon me towards them and, as the officer turns between us, he sighs silently to himself, before opening the gate.

I meet my daughter halfway along the path. My instinct is to hug her tight but she's not that sort of person.

'We found a gun!' Shannon says, excited, and apparently keen to share this information with anyone and everyone.

'What do you mean?' I reply, talking to my daughter.

'We found a gun,' Faith repeats, as if this is a normal occurrence. She points past the house, towards the back and the woods beyond. It's not quite clear why she didn't say this on the phone, other than that she sounds a lot calmer now. I suppose the twenty-five minutes or so it took to get here has changed things.

'It was a *real* gun,' Faith adds.

'A pistol, or...?'

'I guess. One of the handgun things. I don't know what sort.'

The girls turn, wanting me to follow as they head around the side of the large house. At some point, this was a farm.

There's an old cowshed near the front that's never been demolished, while the main building is for an extended family of three or four generations.

It's summer and the heat prickles as I trail my daughter and her friend towards the patch of browning grass at the back. A large shed sits at the end of the property, trees beyond, thick with green from the season, no fence separating the woods from the house.

Hardly anybody lives out here and it's a good half-mile to the next house. A police officer is hanging around the treeline, typing something on his phone, and doesn't notice as we stop next to a patio heater. 'We were in the woods,' Faith says. Any shakiness to her voice has gone.

'There was some sort of noise,' Shannon adds. 'I think there was a squirrel.'

'I thought it was a bird,' Faith says, as they talk over one another. There's a hint of giddy excitement from the pair, which is rare from my daughter nowadays.

'Did you see it first?' Faith asks.

'I thought it was you.'

'I guess we found it together,' my daughter adds. 'We sort of looked towards the squirrel, or bird – and there was a gun on the ground. It wasn't hidden, or anything. Just right there.'

'What did you do with it?' I ask.

The two teenagers look to each other, as if trying to remember. I know it's because I'm her mum but, sometimes, Faith seems so young. Not the person a year or so away from leaving school and heading into the huge, wide world; but that uncertain girl who objected to needing a car seat all the way through until she was twelve. She's that little girl now, face riddled by bemusement and, perhaps, a tickle of fear.

'Did you pick it up?' Faith asks.

'No, you said we should call the police, in case there were fingerprints.'

Faith nods, though seems unsure. It can't have been more than an hour ago.

'I think I'm going to be murdered...'

The tape and its contents had disappeared as I raced across town to my daughter but, as I picture this gun, Mum's voice is back at the front of my mind. If she thought she was going to be killed, did she mean she was going to be shot? How would she know ahead of time? Was she scared?

'... Mum...?' I blink back as I realise Faith has been talking to me. 'Are you OK?' she adds.

'Sorry, I was thinking about something else.'

The two exchange a silent sideways glance but I know that look. I was seventeen once and there's an assumption that everyone over the age of about thirty is senile and on the brink of being packed off to an old people's home.

'You don't really see guns around here,' I add quickly, trying to prove I'm somewhat in control of my senses.

'Except for that time at the cinema,' Faith replies.

I nod along, unsure what to add – because that's the only time I've ever been in the vicinity of a gunshot. It's not so much that I'd forgotten, more that I try not to think about things too much.

The police officer at the treeline looks up from his phone and squints towards us, probably wondering who I am. Before he can object or say anything, the back door goes and Shannon's mum emerges. Nicola wipes her hands on her jeans, and nods towards the main gate. 'I didn't know if they'd let you past,' she says. 'I was going to have a word with the police guy but you're already here.'

Before I can reply, Faith skips around me, Shannon at her side. 'We've a few things to sort out,' Faith says, unprompted, before they disappear into the house.

Nicola nods towards the house as well, silently beckoning me inside, until we end up standing at opposite ends of her kitchen. There's a large Aga, and those sorts of thick wooden cupboard doors that catalogues describe as rustic. Nicola's house, but the kitchen in particular, has always felt very farmhouse chic. There's a clatter of footsteps on the ceiling above, then quiet, as Nicola and I watch the police officer through the window. He's pacing in a circle, still at the treeline, either talking on his phone or a radio.

'Is Faith OK?' Nicola asks.

'I think so – but I can't remember the last time she actually called me.'

That gets a short nod. 'The girls were a bit freaked out when they got to the house. They were both talking at the same time, trying to tell me they'd found a gun. I thought it was a weird joke, maybe a mistake. Something like that. They took me into the woods – and there was a gun on the ground. I think it was Faith who said we should call the police.'

I consider that for a moment, proud my daughter had the foresight of what to do. When I next look up, the police officer is bounding towards the house with purpose. Nicola spots him as well and opens the back door, waiting in the frame as he stops a pace or two away.

'The team's got the gun,' he says, poking a thumb over his shoulder. 'They'll be out in a minute.'

'Is it real?' Nicola asks. 'I didn't know if it might be an airgun, something like that.'

'It *looks* real. I'm sure they'll test it. You were definitely right to call. Did one of our lot ask you for more details?'

'Not really.'

There's an eyeroll that's not quite complete. The sense that the officer is used to working with people he considers to be idiots. 'Is the gun yours?' he asks.

'No. I wouldn't know where to get one, even if I wanted one.'

'Have you ever seen it before?'

'No.'

He pokes another thumb towards the woods. 'Is that your land?'

Nicola takes a moment. 'I don't actually know who owns it. It might be the council. We get dog walkers out there sometimes who accidentally end up in our garden. I could probably find out... I've got the deeds somewhere.'

The officer shakes his head. 'It might not matter. Either way, you did the right thing by calling 999. We'll take the gun and someone will be in touch if we have any other questions.' He waits a moment, then adds, 'Looks like it might've been dug up.'

Nicola puffs out a breath. 'We do get foxes around here...'

The officer nods, then turns to head back towards the woods, leaving us alone in the kitchen. We wait in a stilted, bemused silence for a few seconds, before Nicola motions upstairs.

'Do you want a tea? I think they'll be a while up there.'

There's something unsaid in the sense that the girls are quiet. I figured Faith was going to grab her things so we could go home. But perhaps my presence was requested only for those few minutes of uncertainty. Now the police have turned up, I am no longer required.

Faith and Shannon are on the same drama course and have been friends since they were little. They've always been able to sit in one of their various bedrooms and make hours disappear.

Either way, I'm here now – so I tell Nicola I'll have a tea, and then take a seat at the kitchen table.

This is a semi-regular occurrence, although it *is* the first time there's been a collection of police officers outside. Nicola sets the kettle boiling and then leans on the counter, watching the window.

'How'd a gun get into the woods?' I ask, which I realise is somewhat rhetorical.

Nicola doesn't turn from the window. 'Dunno...'

I watch as Nicola stares through the glass towards whatever's going on beyond. A few seconds pass.

'How are the plans for Friday?' she asks, as I realise I've been daydreaming again. It takes a second to remember what she's talking about.

'I think everything's good,' I reply, though I know I don't sound certain. 'I've never planned a funeral before.'

'Mum and Dad both say they're going,' Nicola replies. 'I've taken the morning off, so I'll be there as well.' I nod along, unsure what to say. 'Mum's got Dad eating salads,' Nicola adds. 'Reckons it's about time he sorts himself out.'

She laughs and I know she means well but I can't bring myself to join in. Dad was in his mid-seventies and never the sort who was desperate to get old for the sake of it. He liked his fry-ups, days in front of the TV, and probably even the general grumpiness he allowed himself once he became a certain age. He had a heart attack last year and, once he got home, I always had the sense he wasn't entirely delighted about coming through it all.

By the time a police officer knocked on my front door, there was a looming inevitability to losing him, even if it somehow felt sudden too.

'I've been clearing out his house,' I say.

'What's it like?'

'Cluttered. I don't think Dad ever threw anything out.'

'I think I'm going to be murdered...'

I'm back in Dad's garage again, listening to the tape. Why

did Mum think that, let alone record it? *When* did she record it? My name was on the sleeve, so was it supposed to be for me? If so, why was it in a box so long?

So many questions.

'I've been thinking about Mum a lot lately,' I say, out of the blue, even if the 'lately' only refers to the last hour. Nicola is still at the window but turns to take me in.

'Because of your dad...?'

I nod. It's sort of true. The reason I'm thinking of Mum is because I was clearing out his garage. With all of that, I give into the pull and take out my phone. It's rare that I allow myself to scroll to the bottom of my messages, where Mum's final text still sits, etched digitally in time. When I got a new phone, I refused to turn off the old one until I was certain it had copied across.

It had, and it's still there.

Are you coming over for tea on Sunday? Lamb's on offer at Asda

I read her words again, as I have hundreds of times. I went to my parents' house for Sunday lunch once a month or so, ever since leaving home. Nicola asks if I'm OK, so I pass her the phone, allowing her to read the message. She scans the screen and nods, before giving it back.

'Mum still texts when she's in Waitrose and there's something on offer. I think she misses the Aga.'

I look to the oven and try not to sigh.

'She sent that on a Tuesday,' I say. 'She was gone the next day.'

At some point, I stopped believing she would come back.

Nicola knows this already, of course. Faith was only four when her grandmother disappeared, and she wasn't friends with Shannon back then. I've definitely told Nicola what happened in the years since.

'Do you... want to, uh... talk about it...?'

There's an implied, possibly accidental reluctance. Nicola doesn't want the conversation, even as I consider telling her about the tape.

Except I want to listen to it again before asking anyone else's opinion. Not only that, hearing my mother's voice after so long feels intimate; not yet something to talk about.

Nicola is still half-distracted by whatever's going on outside the window. I don't blame her as she picks up her phone from the counter, checks the screen, then puts it face down again. 'Are we still on for lunch tomorrow?' she asks.

We usually meet once a week for lunch and a catch-up while I'm on a lunch break at work. I missed last week because it was shortly after Dad had died.

'I think so,' I say, slightly surprised by the gear shift. 'Where do you want to meet?'

She catches my eye momentarily and I know what's coming. 'Is it all right if Mum comes along? She says she'll pay.'

I know Nicola's already told her it's fine but she needs to justify it. 'She thought Dad would spend more time with her after retiring but he goes golfing most days. She says he's home even less than he used to be.'

I want to say no but obviously can't.

'Well if she's paying,' I reply, with a laugh, pretending it's all fine. She's done this before – and anyone who's met Nicola's mother isn't desperate to go for lunch with her a second time.

Nicola picks up her phone again, looking at the screen, sighing, then returning it to the counter.

'Everything all right?' I ask, likely knowing the answer to that as well.

'Ethan normally texts when he finishes with a client,' she says – and there's an edge that explains her distraction. She catches my eye again, and it's not the police at the back of her house about which she's concerned, nor my father's death.

Her husband is a personal trainer and, as well as working from a gym in town, he goes into people's homes for private sessions. Nicola's always been a little funny over this.

She sighs theatrically and glances to the clock on the wall.

I suppose this is the sort of friendship Nicola and I have. We each want to talk about our own issues, while not listening to the other. Just like me and Mum, I suppose. She asked if I wanted to visit on Sunday – and I never even replied.

'...I need you to know that I love you.'

FOUR

Dad's house feels different when I arrive back. Nobody's been inside yet the ghosts of conversations and past events breathe from the walls. There's the hallway where Dad's guitar sits resting in a corner. He bought it for thirty quid on a whim from a car boot sale, with the astonishing confidence that he'd somehow be able to teach himself through sheer will. When truth dawned later that same day, the instrument was abandoned, never to be touched again.

The kitchen counter still has the dual olive oil set I got him the Christmas before last, unopened, untouched, gathering dust. It was at a time when Dad insisted he was going to get into cooking healthily for new year; a fad that didn't even make it to the first of January. There's the old plasticky toaster that he'd complain about endlessly, though wouldn't throw out, even though it cost less than a tenner. The giant tub of gnarly instant coffee that he claimed was indistinguishable from anything that could be bought in a shop.

A stubborn man to the end, who went on his own terms.

I'm supposed to be clearing all this and, even though it's already been more than a week since he died, I've not quite got to it. The old toaster did need two goes at actually browning some bread – but there's something about it that feels undeniably Dad.

Maybe it's me who's the hoarder.

I use the terrible instant coffee granules to make myself a drink, knowing it's too late in the day for caffeine and that I'll regret it. Before returning to Dad's house, I dropped off Faith and Shannon at another of their friends – which also had me thinking of Mum. She used to complain that I used her as a free taxi service, which I guess proves everything's circular, because here I am doing the same for my own child.

That initial concern Faith had over the weapon they'd discovered had evaporated by the time I dropped her off, replaced by a rising giddy excitement that there's an overseas drama trip for everyone on her course in a few weeks.

Back in Dad's kitchen, the coffee is bitter but I drink it anyway, thinking of him, vaguely amused that he'd force down this stuff to prove a point to nobody but himself.

Did Dad ever listen to Mum's tapes? The box still sits in the garage, gently crusted by a coating of dust that would indicate it's not been touched in a long time. I try to remember the things he said when Mum disappeared but I was probably too self-obsessed to see past myself back then.

'If they say I'm missing, I'm not. I've been killed – and I need you to know that I love you.'

I drift through to the garage and listen to that part of the tape, then rewind and replay it five times in a row. A part of me wishes I'd never pulled out the box of tapes. With neither of my parents around to ask, there's nobody to offer an explanation.

I let the tape run this time as Mum's voice finishes with a click of the microphone before it cuts back to an infant me. I realise now that the reason my name is on the tape sleeve isn't because Mum was leaving me a message, it's because there was this ancient recording of my voice. This tape had probably been stored for almost forty years. I wonder if it was meant to be a gift for me at some point, or maybe something Mum would listen to by herself to remember old times.

Or perhaps it was simply forgotten?

Nobody to ask.

While infant me struggles with the alphabet, I flit through the rest of the box. It's around the size of something that might've once stored wellington boots. The row of tapes are neatly lined bottom to top. I start removing the cassettes, lining them up by date. The earliest seems to be the September one from the caravan. There are others from November and December of 1987, then four from the year after.

It's as I'm sorting the tapes that something shiny catches my eye from the bottom of the box. It was buried among the tapes and almost slipped through a small hole in the corner.

I hold the necklace in my hand and run it through my fingers. It's that sort of cheap white gold that came from a catalogue, or one of those places that littered the high street in the 1990s.

I know because it's mine.

I bought it when I was seventeen, possibly with various savings from birthdays or Christmases, or maybe with some of my first pay cheque. It was a little under fifty quid, reduced from eighty, and I can't quite remember why I wanted it. The small engraved leaf that dangles in the centre means it is pretty but largely unremarkable. It's difficult to remember who I was at that age because so much has passed. I wore that necklace every day for months, maybe even a year and then, one time, it was gone. I thought I remembered leaving it on my side table while I slept but it wasn't there the next morning. I checked behind the unit and underneath the bed. I looked under my pillow and pulled out the sheets. Neither Mum or Dad had seen it, which left me questioning whether I really *had* left it on that side table. Perhaps I'd lost it during the day?

Seeing it in the box all these years later, alongside Mum's things, gives me the answer. It was never *lost*, and maybe I suspected it at the time.

Mum stole it.

Because that's the other thing about her disappearance. It wasn't *completely* out of character. Mum did unexpected things – like steal from her own daughter.

I run a thumb across the leaf and consider putting it on, before deciding against it and putting the necklace in my bag instead. It's no longer a symbol of my youth and that first pay cheque; it's Mum's dark side.

The tape has been playing while I've been sorting and reminiscing but I suddenly realise it's back to Mum's voice. The older Mum, not the one trying to teach me the alphabet.

'... suppose that's what I'm worried about. I don't want Eve getting involved. I can't keep it to myself, though, which I guess is why I'm recording this. I have to get it out, even if no-one's listening. Even if I'm already dead. I've been telling myself it's not real but if you're listening to this, the reason for all this is because I know who the Earring Killer is.'

JANINE

Extract from *The Earring Killer* by Vivian Mallory, © 2015.

The wooden deck is soft from rain, like treading across the surface of a trampoline. I half walk, half bounce across to the bench as a man stands to shake my hand. The lush emerald of the field stretches towards the distant fence, where a woman wrapped in an ankle-length coat is being dragged by a pair of scruffy grey collies.

The man and I sit on the bench watching the dog walker as the gentle sound of rain tickles the roof above.

'It's a lot different in summer,' he tells me. 'We have families who come down and watch. It's not really about the cricket, it's more a community place. Kids play on the boundary and the mums might have a book to read. The dads have a pint of cider, something like that. There's nowhere like it.'

I ask him how long he's been coming and the man stares momentarily towards the horizon, where a newish housing estate sits: all red-brick and skylights.

'Since I was ten or so,' he says. 'I met Janine when we were both about eighteen. She got a job working behind the bar…'

He tails off and it's hard to blame him. The bar is in the clubhouse behind us.

'Nothing felt rushed,' he says. 'After Janine's first shift, I helped her clean the clubhouse and we ended up talking until about two a.m. I walked her home and, after that, we sort of ended up doing things together. We'd go to the cinema, or bowling. Sometimes we'd just sit here, on this deck, and we'd talk. We'd listen to the rain. I never asked her out, or anything like that. We were boyfriend-girlfriend and that was that.'

Harry Bailey and Janine were living together within a year; married within three. They were talking about saving for a week or two in Cyprus and then, ultimately, children. It was a small-town love story, even as Janine moved on from working behind the bar at a cricket club.

'That was just a summer thing for her,' Harry remembers. 'She was still at college, doing business studies, and then got a job with a recruitment agency. She did that for a bit, which is when we ended up moving into our flat and then getting married. We always came to the cricket on a Saturday, partly through habit, I suppose. I'd play sometimes but, others, we'd put down a blanket on the grass and lie in the sun.'

There's no sun in Sedingham now. The grey wash stretches deep into the distance and the rain starts to clatter harder on the roof above. The dog walker is long gone, with pools of water starting to form on the far side of the field.

Harry fidgets on the bench, standing and readjusting his jeans, before sitting and scratching his head. He's six foot and a bit, a gentle giant sort with big hands and a deftness when he speaks. The sort that doesn't have a lot to say but, when he does, it's probably worth listening to.

'It had been so busy because we got married three or four months before,' Harry says. 'Janine had just got a new job and it felt like a lot was happening at the same time.'

I ask about the new job and Harry smiles with his lips closed. There's a sigh that's impossible to miss. 'It was essentially the same job in recruitment but she was making a bit more. She didn't really want to move but her old place never gave pay rises, so she didn't think she had much choice. She was trying to work her way up. She'd got through her first week and was enjoying it in the way you do when there are new people. I think it was probably Thursday night when she said some of the girls were going out after work on the Friday. She asked if I minded her going along, and of course I didn't. We weren't clingy like that. I would go out with my friends; and Janine did the same with hers. I do think about that sometimes.'

The Friday morning was the last time Harry ever saw his wife. This was before the days of text messages but Janine sent him an email from her work computer at three minutes to five, saying she'd see him later. She logged off and headed the short five minutes into town with her workmates. They hopped around a few pubs, danced in a place named Reflex, and then headed out to get taxis at around eleven o'clock.

It is there where that part of the story ends. One new friend got into a taxi on the corner opposite the town post office, leaving Janine to walk the short two-minute trip to the actual taxi office.

Except Janine never made it.

It was Harry who identified her body four days later, after she'd been dragged out of the canal.

'It was her but it wasn't,' Harry says, as his voice cracks. 'Before I went into the room, one of the officers said that I should brace myself, that it wouldn't be what I thought. I remember thinking it was such an odd thing to say, because my wife had been missing for four days, and I was now in a morgue ready to identify her body. I obviously wasn't going to be ready for it. I'd never seen a dead body before, for one. I was almost angry at him. But then I went into the room and I knew what he meant. It was Janine but it wasn't. Her skin was this sort of grey colour and parts of her hair weren't there. The guy asked me if it was her and I had to turn away. I can't even remember saying yes.'

It was outside the room, away from Janine, that the officer asked the question that would come to define Harry's life.

'They wanted to talk about Janine's earrings,' Harry says. 'It was such a strange thing given everything I'd just seen – and the four days before. I was a mess and couldn't understand at first. They wanted to know if Janine usually went out with only one earring. All I could say was that I didn't think so but that I didn't know. I didn't get what it all meant at the time.'

It wasn't long before it became very clear why the police were interested. Four months before Janine was murdered, another dead body had turned up. Police had struggled to find a motive for that killing, let alone the killer, but they had been taken by a peculiar detail in that the victim was only wearing a single earring.

'They told me later that they thought whoever killed Janine had taken one of her earrings,' Harry says. 'Some sort of trinket or trophy. He'd done it before and they were worried it was linked. With that first killing, it might have been an accident that she only had one earring but, because there were two, suddenly there was this pattern.'

A 'pattern' is one way of putting it. From one victim killed in mysterious, unsolved circumstances, there were suddenly two. Not only that, there was a calling card in the form of those missing earrings.

'The first time anyone mentioned "serial killer" to me was a day or two after I identified Janine's body,' Harry says. He's shrunken into himself while we've been talking, knees to chest, his large feet perched on the tip of the bench. I have to lean closer to catch what he's saying, with the thunderous patter of the rain almost drowning out the placidity of his voice.

'The thing is, as soon as someone said "Earring Killer", that was it. Janine was no longer her own person, she was "victim number two". I tried not to read too much, or listen to any of it, but it was impossible to ignore. People wouldn't use her name, or talk about who she was. She was just "the second victim", or "number two in a series..." It felt like it was this big competition, like how many could he kill. They became numbers, not names, and I found it so hard to deal with. Even now, you get the odd thing and they'll put up the victims like it's a league table.'

Harry says he was unsure of talking to me for this reason – and it's hard to blame him. As with seemingly any serial killer, a borderline glorification grows. Society's obsession is as gleeful as it is morbid. It would be wrong to pretend to be above any such things, given the existence of this book. I admit as much to Harry, while insisting that I do want to tell the story of the victims. He's right that they've largely been forgotten in all this. They do have names, and Janine Bailey deserves to be remembered.

'It's not that I was desperate to move on,' Harry says quietly. 'But I'm defined by this as well. I'm not trying to be a victim in any of this but it's true. I went on a date about four or five years after what happened and I thought I should be honest. I told her that my late wife was a victim of the Earring Killer and she just stared. We didn't go out again after that, and I don't really blame her. It's been years and I'll always be the person whose wife was murdered. I do want people to know Janine's name, and to remember her – but this is so much bigger than that. All the people over all these years. I'm one of the lucky ones in that I'm still here – but it's a part of everything I am and everything I'll ever be. I still talk to Janine's mum and dad and they've never had answers. There's all these people left with this big gaping question, because none of us know what happened, or why.'

Harry lowers his feet and rubs his forehead. We sit quietly together for a moment, before he nods behind and asks if I want a coffee. He has a key for the clubhouse, and so we head inside. There's a pastoral, slightly rundown feel to the space, but charm as well. Photos line the walls of cricket teams from years and decades past. Young men – and, in one instance, young women – with lives ahead of them.

Nineteen years ago, there was one more person here who might have appeared in these photographs.

Janine Bailey is not a number.

She was twenty-two years old, with a life ahead of her – and she deserves to have her name remembered.

FIVE

Chairs scrape across the already scuffed wooden floor as everyone stands as one. Three or four head directly for the exit, not wanting the chit-chat that often marks the end of these support sessions. As soon as the doors open, a draught of icy air blisters the space.

The hall is a cliché, but so am I.

There's still tea in my mug and it isn't as if I have a lot to race home for. I drift across to the radiator and stand, cradling the cup and using it to warm my fingers.

Liam spots me and nods an acknowledgement. He's in conversation with one of the newer alcoholics, who has a lot of questions. Liam shows great patience as he explains a few things about our group, before swapping numbers with the man. They shake hands and then the newcomer heads for the exit, before Liam joins me at the radiator. His fingers are wrapped around his own mug.

'I've never got to the bottom of why it's so cold in here?' he says, with a smile.

'This hall has its own microclimate, where the temperature never changes. Freezing in summer, freezing in winter.'

There's a nod of agreement and then we each take a slurp of tea. Liam started this AA group twenty years before. I've known him for seven years, one hundred and thirty-one days, and around forty-five minutes of those two decades.

Not that I'm counting.

'I was sorry to hear about your dad,' he says. 'I know I sent that text and it was a bit of a worry when you weren't here last week. I'm glad you're OK.'

'The funeral's on Friday,' I reply. 'Things are more or less set but there's a lot to do at his house. It's going to take a while.'

'How's Faith taking things?'

'She wasn't that close with her granddad. I suppose we're not that sort of family. She's been fine, though. She's tight with her friends.'

My response has me wondering whether she is *actually* fine. It's true that she and my dad didn't spend much time together – but they're still related. It's still the first proper death of someone in her life. I've asked if she wants to talk but there was only the teenagery shrug. Everything's great until it isn't. There was still that twinge to her voice earlier when she found the gun, and now I wonder if there was more to it.

'And you...?'

It's a question within a question. Liam's sort of asking how I am but there's a reason I know it's seven years and one hundred and thirty-one days since we met in this church hall. We love to count at Alcoholics Anonymous. Or I do.

'I've been coping,' I say. 'I've been too busy.'

'Is that a good thing?'

I think on that for a moment. 'I guess I never realised how much paperwork there is. There's the death certificate and the official stuff, then the funeral director needs instructions and more paperwork. It all has to happen immediately. It's not like you can put it off for a month, then come back to it.'

Liam's nodding along but I've seen this face. This is him being polite, even while it's clear to anyone who knows him that he wants to move on. More people are saying their goodbyes, leaving only five of us in the hall. Liam will have to lock up, and it's often the two of us who leave last. Luckily, one of the regulars is pouring herself a new tea from the urn as she chats to someone else on the far side of the hall. We've got a few minutes, except I can't quite think of a way to twist the conversation in the way I want.

'I was sort of prepared for it,' I add, trying to keep things going. 'Dad had that heart attack last year. The doctor said he'd have to start walking every day and cleaning up what he ate. I don't think he changed a thing.'

Liam nods along, not prepared for the grenade I'm about to hurl. I've been practising this conversation ever since I heard Mum mention the Earring Killer on that tape.

'I guess it wasn't a shock for me,' I add. 'Not like with you...?'

I know it's a terrible thing to do; an awful segue to make with someone I actually like. Except I'm not sure what else to do. Who else is in my life to direct questions at?

Liam blinks with surprise but it's just about a natural enough transition that it doesn't feel forced. He's focusing on me again.

'Sorry,' I add.

He shakes his head. 'No, it's fine. It was all a long time ago now. I never mind talking about it.'

'Do you still think about it?' I ask.

Liam takes a moment. He's spoken about this sort of thing frequently in the meetings, because it was ultimately what led to him forming this local group.

'Probably not as much as I once did. The last murder was twelve, thirteen years ago – so it's not constantly in the news any more. For a while, it was like I couldn't escape it. There was basically a seventeen-year spree and it felt like it would never end. Then it just did.'

I googled the Earring Killer when I was at Dad's house but it's difficult to figure out fiction from fact. The line from news to opinion to speculation feels ever blurred. I know what people call him, of course, but it's not as if I've followed every facet of our area's resident serial killer. If anything, I've gone out of my way to avoid the grisliest details – but I know Liam's mum was one of the early victims; possibly the third. I know that's what led to him starting this group.

There was maybe a time I thought Mum's disappearance could be linked – except there was never a body with her. She wasn't part of the pattern. Plus, she had her own issues anyway. For most, utterly disappearing would be out of character. For her, it wasn't a complete stretch.

Liam glances across to the trio on the far side who are talking near the tea urn. He never ushers people out, and I know I'm taking advantage.

'Does that mean that he hasn't killed anyone since?' I ask.

'I guess not.'

'If they say I'm missing, I'm not. I've been killed…
I know who the Earring Killer is.'

Two separate lines from Mum's tape. Can it really be a coincidence that she disappeared – and there hasn't been a single killing since? As Liam said, a spree that went on for a decade and a half that simply… stopped.

It's only now I see the link in the timing.

'Is there a chance he might've carried on – but he stopped stealing earrings?' I ask.

Liam is still looking across the hall as he answers, 'I had a check-in with the police about five years ago. They said Mum's file was still open but there were no new leads. I asked if the

Earring Killer might still be going but that he could be hiding it better. They said they couldn't rule it out but they didn't think so. All the victims had their throats cut in the same way. They were all women with long, dark hair. No bodies have been found like that this entire time. If he's still doing it, it would have to be completely different.' He pauses for a moment, then adds, 'I think he just... stopped.'

We're in now: a conversation I don't want, but instigated, and somehow need. Liam is so used to talking about this sort of thing in front of people that it doesn't occur to him I might have ulterior motives.

'Do serial killers stop?' I ask.

Liam stiffens a fraction and then turns back to me with a blink. 'I don't know,' he says. 'Do you remember the book that came out a few years back?'

'I don't think so.'

'Written by Vivian something. She emailed about a year ago, saying they were going to make a documentary about it all. I'm not sure how far it all got but I've not heard anything since.'

I think on that for a moment, already picturing the drone over the main street, then somebody sitting in a chair asking, 'Are we running?' to a person off-camera. Every one of those true crime things come out exactly the same.

But then there's Mum's voice, saying she knows who the Earring Killer is. I listened on, but the tape blended back to me as a babbling infant. From what I can tell, that's it – except it feels as if there's a lot of the recording missing. Perhaps she named the person earlier, but it was lost to the poor quality of the tape?

Maybe it's on one of the many other tapes in the box?

I almost jump as Liam touches my shoulder. 'I know it's hard after the death of a parent,' he says. 'Even if it's somewhat expected.'

I'm almost overwhelmed by the guilt of making him talk

about this under some false pretence of struggling with my father's death. The whole point of this support group is honesty and I've managed to obliterate that by not telling him about the tape.

'You've got my number,' he adds, which is about as brutal a nudge as he's going to give that he wants to lock up. 'Are you sure you're OK?'

I tell him I'm fine, then grab the final chairs that haven't been packed away. I add them to the stack and then wave a goodbye to the trio across the hall.

Except, as I head to the car, I realise the talk with Liam has only strengthened the thought I first had when I heard my mother's voice mention the Earring Killer.

What if the final killing wasn't the one they all think? What if there *was* one more? What if that person *also* had long, dark hair?

What if she was my mother?

SIX

Music bleeds through the wall from Faith's room. There's a pounding beat for a few seconds, then something more melodic, then back to a *thump-thump-thump*. She's scrolling on her phone, her attention span such that she's swiping from video to video while – I assume – barely watching them.

It's easy to get all *kids today* about this sort of thing but I suppose every generation has this. My mum said I watched too much television – but then perhaps her mother told her she listened to too many cassettes. Each new set of parents is convinced their children's minds are being rotted.

Faith is used to me being late home on a Tuesday. I've not hidden the AA meetings from her, even when she was younger. That's another thing about today's generation: none of them seem to think talking to one another about their problems is strange. The fact I head off to a church hall once a week or so to listen to alcoholics tell their stories isn't a great source of shame for my daughter. If anything, the opposite is true. Even when she's busy with school or her friends, she'll find time to ask how my Tuesday night went.

It went fine, I told her – and then we were back to our own

rooms and our own lives. If the discovery of that gun affected her, she isn't showing it any longer.

For me, the large box of tapes from Dad's garage is on my bed. I filter through the rows one by one, still partially obsessed by my mother's handwriting. It would never have occurred yesterday that I'd be so hung up on such a thing but now I'm obsessed with the way she drew the letter 'M' with such rigid precision.

Almost all the tapes have months and years on the sleeve and I've tidied them into date order – but there are a few that are different. One is mine, of course: the perfectly printed 'Eve', cataloguing my early attempts to count and learn the alphabet, intermingled with Mum saying she was murdered.

Another simply has the word 'Sorry' written with letters so neat it's almost as if they've been printed. I almost don't want to listen to the contents, dreading to think what could be on it, except it's an easier choice than randomly choosing a month and year.

The cable for the cassette player is short, so the device ends up balancing half on the bed as I try to get comfortable. I have work in the morning and should be trying to sleep – but it's difficult to think of that when there are hours of my mother's voice nestling in the box at my side.

It's so satisfying to put a tape into the player with the *clunk* and *click* as it slots into place. I revel in that for a second, then push play. The now familiar microphone pops and then, again, my mum's voice seeps from the speaker.

'I went to the library today. I couldn't find my card but the woman on the desk typed my name into the system and found me. She gave me a new card but said it costs two pounds if I lose it again. I think I went to school with her but can't remember her name and she didn't seem to know me.

The psychology section has moved. It used to be across from the kids bit, where there are always lots of parents with children. It just means there are always people watching. I went there but it's books on tape now and the woman said that's the new trend. I joked that I've been putting things on tape for years but she didn't get it.

She said the psychology books were upstairs – and I found them near the back wall where nobody ever goes. I already had an idea what I was looking for because I'd started reading it in the bookshop – but I suppose it was the first time I was able to admit to myself that I actually am a kleptomaniac. It's such a fun word. Klepto. Kleptomaniac.

I suppose I proved the point because I kinda, um, borrowed the book. I want to tell Bruce about the irony of it all. That there's a book that describes how I lack impulse control, and the reason I have it is because I wanted it. It's funny, isn't it? But I don't think he'd get it. Actually, I know he wouldn't. He'd much rather it all went away. He wants to pretend it isn't real. I do get it. It'd be easier if it wasn't but at least I have a name for it now. I'm klepto. I'm a kleptomaniac. I sort of like the label. I'd consider going to the doctor to ask for a proper diagnosis. Maybe there's help? But I don't want to risk them taking away Eve. She's only nine and her dad left last week. It's all been a bit—'

I stop the tape, largely because my mother's voice saying my name is too much. The calm is so unnerving that goosebumps ripple across my arms.

'Her dad left last week.' But my parents were together my whole childhood, weren't they?

The older I got, the more I realised something wasn't quite right with my mother. By the time she disappeared, I was past my mid-twenties and it was obvious. I never heard her use the word 'kleptomaniac' to describe herself, and wonder if this tape was her way of getting it all out without actually having to tell anyone.

I google the word, and, suddenly, a lot makes sense. She was admitting to herself that she couldn't resist the urge to steal things she didn't need. The library book for one; plus my necklace. So many other things, too. She stole from me because she couldn't stop herself. Not only that, she says I was nine in this tape, meaning it was a good ten years before she took my necklace. Mum had known for a long time what she was and yet, when I went to her, asking if she'd seen it, she still said no.

My thoughts are jarred by a gentle knock on the door and I jump, instinctively, suddenly back in the present as I realise it can only be Faith.

'Are you OK?' she asks through the door. 'I heard you talking to yourself...?'

It takes a moment to realise my daughter thought the voice on the tape was my own. She was only four when her grandmother disappeared and doesn't remember her. I wonder whether this means I sound like my mother.

I'm up off the bed and open the door, to where my daughter is on the landing. Her hands are tucked into her armpits as she holds herself.

'Are you OK?' she asks again.

'Just a lot going on, with Dad and all.'

'Is there anything I can do?'

'I don't think so. It'll be better after Friday.'

I keep talking about my father's funeral, even though it isn't really in my mind. It's my other parent I can't stop thinking about.

'Can I get a yoghurt?'

'You don't have to ask if you're hungry.'

'I didn't want to wake you if you were sleeping, but then I heard you talking to yourself...'

I don't deny it, because the truth of torturing myself with my mother's voice is so much more complicated.

'Thanks for checking,' I say.

Faith hovers for a moment, considering whether to say more. I'm almost always asleep before her and she's concerned that I'm sitting up, chatting to myself directly after the AA meeting. All that not long after Dad died.

'I'm honestly fine,' I say. 'I promise.'

She waits a moment and then nods, apparently satisfied, before heading downstairs to grab her yoghurt. I move back into my room and close the door, then sit on the bed, listening to Faith make her way back upstairs. She very much keeps her own hours, although I was no different at that age. I could sleep for twenty-four hours, or for two, with seemingly little warning or preparation for either.

When Faith has settled, I return to my own bed and lower the volume on the player.

'...she's only nine and her dad left last week. It's all been a bit—'

I listen to Mum's voice again, but only briefly, because I'm struck by the realisation that memories simply don't work the way everyone assumes. The way *I* assumed. Everyone thinks it's a binary black-and-white thing, where a person either remembers or they don't, except my mother recorded these tapes in real time. This is an accurate on-the-day version of how she saw things, yet, even from the snippets, I'm realising how much I've forgotten.

I don't recall Dad leaving – but I *do* remember the time when Mum told me he had to go away to work for a few months. All that time, I was going to school, visiting friends' houses, or going to clubs – then returning to a home where I only had one parent. I took it in my stride, as a child. It wasn't worth remembering.

It seems so obvious now that he *wasn't* working somewhere for that length of time; he'd simply walked out. Was it because of Mum? Me? Was he having an affair?

But that sparks another thought, because Dad was gone during a winter and I remember telling Mum I liked a coat I'd seen in a shop window. When I got home from school the next day, it was on my bed waiting for me. I assumed she'd bought it because I needed a winter jacket. Now, having heard my own mother describe herself, and perhaps even without that, there's such clarity to what actually happened.

All memories that are now so perfect and yet, an hour ago, didn't exist.

I listen to more of the tape, where Mum continues to explain her problem. The pilfered book about kleptomania has clarified things for her and she says it's like reading a biography of herself.

> *'...I once stole hiking boots from the outdoors store in town. I'd seen them in the window the week before and couldn't stop thinking about them. I went in to look at them and there was a second pair at the back of the store, near the counter. They had a left foot on the rack, then a row of boxes underneath. There was only one person working there, this university kid, maybe twenty, twenty-one, something like that. I knew where to look for security tags by that point, so I'd already ripped them off and left them in a different shoebox. Then I waited until he was helping someone over by the coats, and just put the boots on and walked out. I actually felt sorry for him because I wondered later if he might get charged for them. Stupid thing was, I already had a new pair of boots because Bruce had bought me some for Christmas. They were so much better than the ones I took, and I'm not sure I even wore the stolen ones in the end.'*

I stop the tape again, partially because there's a shuffling from the other side of the wall as Faith settles for the night. The other reason is that it's not easy to hear that voice speaking with such clarity about her own failings. Is the self-awareness better or worse?

It's hard to stop listening for long, though.

'...there was this checked red and black pet coat that looked cute. We don't even have a dog, so I left it on next door's porch. It might make up for the time I took their car. That's the thing because the book says that things escalate. I went from boots, to dog clothes, to their car, to robbing the bank. I stole a million pounds just to show I could, then gave it back and the manager thanked me for helping. That's the thing with—'

The obvious lie has me stopping the tape, simply to take it in. The mistruth is so clear and unbridled that I listen to it again, just to assure myself she said what I thought. Mum never stole next door's car and she definitely didn't rob a bank. Even if she somehow had, there's no way she simply gave it back, no harm done.

But who's the lie for? Was she kidding herself, trying to pretend her problem wasn't so big? Except it occurs that being a serial thief means being a serial liar. It would be impossible for so many items to simply show up without explanation. She would've had to claim she bought things.

We weren't rich, but I had new school shoes every year, a new uniform, new bag. There was nothing I ever needed that I didn't have. It didn't occur to me then that any of this was strange. Now I wonder how much of that was taken from various shops, then left on my bed. Perhaps all of it.

It's impossible to know for certain, because there's nobody to ask. Dad could not have been so blind to it all. He must have known.

Maybe that's why he disappeared for those months? I think maybe I knew as well. Deep down. But it's not an easy thing to keep at the front of your mind when you're thinking about your own mum.

I can't listen to any more of the apology tape, so swap it for a random one with a month and year. It's late, so I undress and lie under the covers, listening to my mother talk about her book club. She had a large disagreement with someone named Viv about the meaning of a Stephen King novel that apparently split the group. She spends a good fifteen minutes explaining why she's right and Viv is wrong.

Perhaps she really *was* a podcast pioneer?

I'm still not asleep, and another dated tape has Mum whispering about a long hot summer and how the plants in the garden are wilting. There is still so much more content and it feels as if they'll end up being a dizzying mix of heavy confessionals blended with banal musings about books and weather.

I definitely prefer the latter.

Except I still cannot sleep.

I retrieve the first tape and skip through the first part.

'... and I need you to know that I love you.'

I listen to it over and over, wishing I didn't need the affirmation, yet addicted to it. It's impossible not to see my mortality, especially as my own daughter is sleeping on the other side of the wall. Perhaps I should record a video for her, saying I love her, just in case? She would likely think it strange in the present but, one day, she'll be me – and I'm certain she'd want to hear this again.

'... and I need you to know that I love you.'

I close my eyes and listen to my mother tell me she loves me one more time, although it's hard to sleep as the tape skips back to the infant me, and then onto my mother saying she knows who the Earring Killer is. I know I should stop it entirely but I've been denied this voice for thirteen long years and the one taste now feels like an addiction. Not only do I want to hear more – but I already have a plentiful supply in the giant box under the bed.

I'm an addict.

Except my eyes close and I let my thoughts drift and swirl and...

'... that's why it's my fault. I found a jewellery box.

...

OK, I didn't find it. I just... couldn't help myself. It was so pretty with the flowers engraved on the side but then, when I had it back home, there was something about the light and the colour. It didn't seem that nice at all. It was ugly, really – scratched, too. I couldn't figure out why I'd taken it but that's what my book says. I keep reading the same bit about impulse control. It says you want something, so you take it, even though you don't necessarily need it, or even want it. I know I shouldn't, I know I don't really want these things, but I can't stop myself.

...

That was the thing with the jewellery box. It was empty, and ugly, but there was also a rattle. Like there was something in it, even though there wasn't. I became obsessed with it after that, until I found a catch that opens a secret bottom. That's where I found the earrings. They were—'

I stop the tape. I must have been drifting, asleep for maybe ten or fifteen minutes. The tape is much further on now and it's entirely my mother's voice. I had never let it get this far before, assuming the rest of the recording was the infant me learning numbers and letters.

I sit on the edge of the bed, wide awake, and rewind the past few seconds.

This is why Mum knew the identity of the Earring Killer. She stole a jewellery box, filled with stolen earrings.

> '...I found a catch that opens a secret bottom. That's where I found the earrings. They were all singles, not pairs. It took a couple of seconds but I knew I'd seen them before. Then I realised they're from the photos, the news reports. It's all the single earrings he took from those women. There's one that has a peacock dangly bit and it's so unique.'

There's a near-silence in which I can hear my mother breathing steadily into the microphone. A few seconds pass as the hairs on the back of my neck flare.

> 'I can't go to the police, not after everything. Maybe that's why I'm recording this. I don't know what to do, or who to tell. He's going to know I took the box, and then he's going to kill me.'

LAURA

Extract from *The Earring Killer* by Vivian Mallory, © 2015.

I'm on the canal bank when the pair of lads call across from a slowing narrow boat. They're sitting on the edge, legs dangling, each wearing tracksuits, baseball caps and bright, white trainers. The sort of teenagers certain tabloids insist are running around stabbing one another in absence of anything better to do.

'You got a light?' one of them asks. He can't be older than seventeen or eighteen and it strikes me I've never associated canal boats with young men in tracksuits.

When I first got into reporting, an old editor told me I should always carry three things: a notepad, a pen, and a lighter. 'You never know the conversations you'll get into with people who need a light,' he said. I always took the advice to hand, so, back on the canal bank, I fished around before tossing the lighter across the small gap in the water to the boat. It only occurred to me later that the boys might have been too young to smoke but the pair of them each lit a cigarette. Then, with a grin that I found impossible to resist, the taller of the two asked if he could keep it. The cheek of it all was enough for me to tell him it was fine – and off they went in their boat, chugging along at a few miles-per-hour as I trailed on the towpath.

I had long since improved my old editor's advice by always carrying *two* lighters.

The Sedingham Canal runs almost through the centre of town, with the path providing something of a shortcut to get from one part to another for anyone not in a vehicle. I joined the path at the back of the cricket club where I met Harry Bailey. It's a nicer day today: crisp in the morning but warm by the afternoon. The sky is a perfect, endless blue. As I follow the canal, I'm passed by couples on bikes, kids on BMXs, plus that curious breed of people in hiking boots who chug along at a serious clip, while never seeming to draw breath.

The Sedingham Canal is a mix of tracksuited teenagers on canal boats, bumming a light with a cheeky smile; plus middle-aged men in expensive boots barrelling along as if they're training for the Olympic towpath-walking competition.

It wasn't always like this.

Laura March left work at a couple of minutes after six on a spring evening where the sun was low and the shadows long. The police later followed her route via a series of shop CCTV cameras, which is why they know she stopped to talk to a *Big Issue* seller at 6:11 p.m. He told the police she asked whether he was hungry, before volunteering to pop into the Tesco Express to buy him something. He insisted he was fine, so, instead, she gave him a fiver and said she didn't need a magazine.

There's a moment in which the cameras catch Laura stop on the corner of the high street, look both ways, and then make a decision that cost her life.

If it had been a little wetter, or a little colder; if she'd been in more of a rush, or got trapped at work for longer than expected, she would have almost certainly turned left. That would have taken her down the hill, towards the bus stop outside the Ladbrokes bookmaker. There, she would have caught the number nineteen bus, and taken the twenty-three-minute ride back to where she lived on the Glenhills Estate.

It was the same bus she caught every day that week.

Instead, Laura paused. Even from the CCTV, a viewer can sense that indecision. She glances up, then looks to her watch, before making her choice.

Laura waited for a silver Toyota to pass, and then crossed the road. She's next seen by a jogger who was doing laps of the cricket club field. She watched Laura head around the back of the clubhouse, following the trail down to the canal.

From there, it was a forty-minute walk in something close to a straight line until she'd reach the Lock Inn pub, where she'd follow a gravelly path to the Glenhills Estate.

It's a different time of day and year as I follow that same route. If anyone was asked whether they'd seen me, there would be those two lads on the canal boat; the couples in their walking gear; those on bikes. The path is a vibrant part of town life.

Only one person saw Laura on the towpath that day. Alan Ilverston lives in a cottage that overlooks the canal. For large parts of the year, the trees at the back of his property are a vibrant green, teeming with life that obstructs any view of the water. On the day Laura passed, the branches were in the early stages of returning to their summer glory.

'I keep trying to think whether I saw someone else behind or in front of her,' he told me from the bench at the back of his house. He's made a pot of lemon tea and we sit together, drinking from dinky china cups and saucers that he says only come out for visitors. 'I think about Laura probably every day,' he adds. 'I wish I had a better answer, that my memory was clearer, or that I'd had some sort of camera back then. All I know is that I was in the kitchen doing the washing-up. The window overlooks the back and I watched a woman in a green coat walk along the canal path. She must have noticed a flicker of movement, something like that, because she turned towards me and we sort of nodded to one another. You know, like you do when you catch a stranger's eye. Just a way of saying "hello". That was it. A second, two at the most. I didn't know then I'd be the last person to ever see her.'

Laura's body was found three days later in a drainage ditch at the side of a crumbling unremarkable country road that leads into town. The town had a problem with fly-tipping in the area, and a driver stopped, thinking her body was a dumped bin bag.

Except it wasn't.

Laura March was forty-three years old. She was found with her throat slit and a single peacock-shaped earring in her ear. At that time, it was 1998 and the World Cup was beginning. David Beckham was about to be sent off and become a national figure of hate. But as football fans burned effigies, here, in Sedingham, the police had far bigger worries. Laura was the Earring Killer's fourth victim in three years – and if there had ever been any doubt, there wasn't any longer.

The town had a serial killer.

WEDNESDAY

SEVEN

I can never watch mystery shows on television.

It's mainly because I'm always stuck wondering why nobody ever has a job. There'll be these allegedly normal people going about their day, getting involved in scrapes, never once going to work. I wonder how they pay their rent or mortgage, how they can afford things; where all the free time comes from.

That's the thing with death, with mysteries: life goes on. I've slept barely three hours, yet I'm behind a desk, trying not to yawn, pretending to focus on a computer monitor. It's my father's funeral in two days and I've been up most of the night listening to the ghost of my mother tell me how she found a jewellery box filled with earrings of murdered women.

All I want to do is look for that box.

After being awoken by Mum's voice, I listened to the whole of that tape for the first time, then turned it over and listened to the second side. Of the ninety minutes, around an hour is my infant self, struggling with letters and numbers; fifteen to twenty is either blank or fuzz; and the rest is my mother talking about how she fears being murdered because she knows the identity of the Earring Killer.

If Mum names the person, it's lost among the tape glitches.

It's hard not to think on that, but I did fall asleep with the sound of my mother's voice in the background for probably the first time in four decades.

I found a tape with her talking about a Sedingham summer fête. There were camels on the high street, and a dancing elephant – which reinforces, as always – that the 1980s were a very different time.

Another yawn. I'm the office manager of a landscaping company and, in the two hours I've been at work, I've deleted a few emails, had a conversation I've already forgotten, and three mugs of bad coffee.

I'm checking a work order against the inventory log, but the information isn't going in. Usually, I could do this sort of thing on autopilot but the tiredness and the bright white strip lights are not a good combination.

As another yawn is fought away, the door opens and a pair of the gardeners come in. Dina's one of the few women who work for the company, though she's the most competent person by a long way. Owen's not long out of college and likely has a crush on his older workmate, based on the way he constantly tries to look at her in a not-looking-at-her way.

'Is the van booked in for its MOT?' Dina asks, not one for small talk. I click between spreadsheets, trying to appear as if I'm awake until I find the correct page.

'Friday,' I tell her. 'I'm not going to be here but there shouldn't be any issues.'

'You off on holiday?' Owen tails off as it's impossible to miss Dina's very raised eyebrows.

'It's my dad's funeral,' I reply, trying not to be too harsh with it. Owen has the look of a person who wants the ground to swallow him up.

Part of being the office manager is essentially doing a bit of everything. I book jobs, assign teams, order supplies, plus arrange maintenance for the equipment and vehicles. Owen is saved by Dina taking over and asking what she should do with the paperwork. With that sorted, they turn to leave for the day's tasks, before I remember that it was me who went through Owen's CV when he applied for the job. He's almost out the door when I call him back, asking if I can have a word. He tells Dina he'll be right with her, then returns to the desk.

'Sorry about the, um... funeral,' he says, avoiding eye contact.

'Can I check something with you?' I say. 'Is it right you do audio editing on the side?'

He brightens at this. 'There's a podcast studio in town. I help out on weekends and edit at home as a bit of a side hustle.'

'Do you know much about cassette tapes?' I ask.

He laughs, presumably considering this a joke before his features become more serious. 'Oh, right... yeah. I mean, I know what they are. I've got a degree in multimedia production, and we covered tapes.'

He laughs again, though there's an edge. He's probably had a conversation or two with his parents about why he spent three years doing a degree in multimedia, only to end up at a landscaping company.

'I might know someone who can get old tapes, if that's what you want,' he says.

'I was wondering if you've got the equipment to digitise a recording.'

'Oh... I mean, probably.'

I remove the tape from my bag, and place it on the counter between us, knowing this is potentially dangerous territory. 'Could you do this?' I ask. 'I can pay whatever it costs. It cuts in and out. I think they've tried to record over something but the old audio comes through underneath...?'

He nods along, though it's unclear if he knows what I mean. 'I don't know a lot about cassettes,' he says. 'I think that can happen if the tape is thin? Maybe if it's damaged? You can hear what's on the other side...?'

Owen sounds unsure, though it's hard to blame him. By the time he was born, CDs were on the way out, let alone tapes. I might as well be asking about typewriters or leaded petrol.

Still, I'm already in too deep.

'Have you got any machines that might be able to salvage the audio? Even if it cuts out?'

'So you could have it on your phone?'

'Exactly.'

He shrugs. 'Probably. If not me, there's a guy in the studio who's really old. He knows all about this stuff.'

There's no malice, but the 'really old' feels particularly brutal. Owen reaches for the tape and picks it up. 'Is this it?'

'My mum's voice is on there,' I reply. 'She's been gone a long time, so it's quite important to me...'

He nods, then opens the case and removes the cassette, twisting it in his hand as if he's an art collector who's heard all about the wonder and mystery of the *Mona Lisa*, but is only now seeing it in person.

'It might take a few days,' he says. 'I don't want to promise, but it's probably OK.'

He turns the tape around, and then returns it to the holder. I wait until he looks up at me.

'My mum says some strange things on the tape,' I tell him. 'She was ill towards the end, so if you could keep them to yourself, I'd be really grateful.'

Owen's confused for a moment but I can see him turning things over in his mind. 'Um... sure. Is it, like... illegal, or something...?'

'She had a bit of dementia at the end, so wasn't always sure what was real.'

It's a lie and I'm not sure whether it's a good one. Owen's too young to remember my mother disappearing and I've phrased things in such a way that it sounds like she simply died.

Recording from analogue to digital means the audio will have to play all the way through – so someone could potentially listen to it all the way through. I figure it's better to warn Owen ahead of time. If he knows about the Earring Killer, perhaps he'll put it all down to the fake dementia.

'Uh... sure,' Owen replies, slipping the cassette into the pocket of his hoody. He glances backwards to the door, and Dina who'll be beyond, ready to leave. 'I think I've got your number,' he adds. 'If I don't see you before, then good luck with Friday...'

I thank him for listening and then he spins and charges out of the office and into the waiting van. As soon as he's out of the door, I pull my phone from my bag and place it on the counter, then load voice notes, before playing back the most recent clip.

'... I need you to know that I love you.'

If something happens to the tape, I could probably live with it – but I couldn't face losing those few seconds. The quality is washed out from the cassette recorder's speaker, and my phone's microphone – but it's enough. Regardless of whether Owen can clean up the original recording, I'll always have this.

As I listen a second time, something prickles the back of my neck and I glance sideways to realise I'm being watched. The company owner, Mark, has an adjacent office that's been empty all morning. He must have entered via the other door, because he's now perched on the corner of his desk, watching me not work. There's a frown and I wonder how long he has been there; whether he overheard me asking Owen for the favour. He says nothing but he's one of those men whose faces do enough talking without the mouth ever having to open. There's a *less chat-more work* look about him, which has me silencing my phone and returning my attention to the monitor.

All is immediately explained when I see the email at the top of my mailbox.

> Eve. I'm not paying you to chat. Next door have been waiting for an engineer for over an hour. I thought you were on this?
> Sent from Mark's iPhone

Oops.

I thought my tiredness wasn't affecting my work – but the moment I see the word 'engineer', I remember what I didn't do. As well as owning the landscaping company, last year Mark bought the storage centre on the adjacent plot. The previous owner had a heart attack and I think it might have been an impulse buy. Either way, I somehow ended up with a doubled workload more or less overnight.

This is what I mean about a job getting in the way. Because I want to be at my father's house, rooting through that garage, looking for the jewellery box Mum was talking about on the tape. If it's not there, is it somewhere else in Dad's house? The only thing I have to go on is that Mum said there were flowers engraved on the side. If I can find that, I'll actually have something to take to the police.

Except, I have to work.

So I make the phone call to the engineer needed next door, I double-check the MOT appointment for the work van, I reply to a couple of emails, answer a call from someone who's waiting for one of our teams to turn up, check the company's credit card statement for anything untoward… plus all the other mundane parts of the job that somebody has to do.

As I work, I continue to feel watched, as Mark's presence looms in the adjacent office. He's one of those who only knows how to use a computer keyboard in one way – banging the keys one at a time until they submit. My actual work is punctuated by the rhythmic *thump-thump-thump* of whatever he's doing in the next room.

I still find a bit of time to google the Earring Killer. I know the name, of course, because I grew up with it. The Earring Killer is like quicksand – one of those things I heard a lot about as a kid, but something that's not affected my life as an adult.

He's blamed for killing nine women, although, from the Wikipedia page, it doesn't seem as if there's been a single attack in thirteen years. That's what Liam said, although it's a stark number.

I never really connected Mum to the Earring Killer, and nor did anyone else. A body wasn't found and disappearing always felt like something of which she'd be capable. If not that, then harming herself. That darkness was within her – and even she knew it.

Except… thirteen years is the same amount of years that Mum has been missing.

EIGHT

Whenever I tell Mark I'm off to have lunch with my friend, he puts on a high-pitched voice and says, 'Oooh, you're one of those ladies who lunch.' Every time he does this, I have to fight the urge to put a brick through the window of his BMW. This happens once a week.

Nicola's mother picks me up in her Range Rover – then immediately proves it's too big for her. She almost barrels into a pair of parked cars while trying to figure out how to reverse, then shoots forward, almost hitting a bollard. Nicola is in the passenger seat, knowing when to be silent, as I sit in the back, like a kid waiting for Mum and Dad to start fighting in the front.

Lucy Parris drives us out to the golf club, taking three attempts to reverse park, before breezing through the main doors into the restaurant.

It's a different world as someone in a suit greets her as 'Ms Parris', before guiding us onto the veranda. There's a table already waiting, with a view overlooking the lush valley of greens and fairways. Nicola's mother doesn't *play* golf – but she enjoys the facilities. Less than a minute after being seated, there's a large glass of red wine in front of Lucy as she tells her daughter she'll have to drive us back.

As I watch Nicola's mum gulp a large mouthful of wine, I wonder if Mark had a point back at the office. Perhaps I *am* a woman who lunches, albeit against my will. My usual weekly catch-up with Nicola involves a sandwich in the pub at the end of the road and a general gossip about anyone we know who's had a recent Facebook meltdown. This is the unwanted exception.

'Eve's been clearing out her dad's garage,' Nicola says, after her mum's downed another mouthful. 'She says he's a borderline hoarder.'

Now she's settled with her wine, it's clear Nicola's mother would've been happy to be here alone, were it not for the way the staff would look at her. No free ride home, either.

'Mum's always going on at Dad to tidy the spare room,' Nicola adds, trying to involve her mother in the conversation.

'Maybe all dads are like that,' I reply. I've known Lucy Parris for years, though I don't think we've ever quite got on. We come from the same place – but it can be very different.

'Maybe you can help sort out our place when you're done with the garage?' Lucy says, and it feels half-serious. 'I found a bag of coat hangers in our spare room the other week. Kieron said you never know when you might need them. I wouldn't mind, except he got a storage locker when we downsized.'

There's a side glance of disapproval towards her daughter, followed by another swig of wine. When Nicola said her mum missed the Aga, she was speaking specifically about the one in her kitchen. Her parents once owned the farmhouse, though downsized to an apartment a few years back. My dad reckoned it was probably some sort of inheritance tax scam thing, though I've never asked.

One thing's for certain: I don't think it was the idea of Nicola's mother.

'Thanks for the RSVP for the funeral,' I say, unsure what we should be talking about.

'Oh, that's all Kieron. We wouldn't miss it for the world.'

There's a flourish of the hand as she beckons across a waiter, though the sarcasm was impossible to miss. When the waiter arrives, she orders seared scallops for the three of us, not bothering to ask if that's OK. I guess she is paying, after all.

As she stares across the course towards some golfers in the distance, Nicola locks eyes and mouths 'I'm sorry' at me. We swap a smile but this isn't the first time her mum has gatecrashed one of our lunches. They always go the same way.

'What are you doing with the house?' Nicola's mother asks. It's so out of the blue that it's only when she turns that I realise she's talking to me.

'It was left jointly to my brother and me, so we're waiting for the probate and then it'll be sold.'

That gets a tight nod. 'What will you do with the money?'

'I don't know. Dad only died a week ago.'

'I'm surprised he left anything, to be honest.'

I open my mouth to say something, though I'm not sure what. Nicola's mother is the sort of person who can make anything sound like a personal insult. 'Hello' comes off as 'I am demeaning myself by even acknowledging you exist'.

She's been in my life to some degree for around two decades. When Mum got herself into trouble with the police one time, there was a pilot scheme where officers would act as mentors in an attempt to stop reoffending. Mum got her conditional discharge, but had to check in with a police officer once a month. For some time at least, that meant Nicola's father. A year or two on, Nicola and I ended up in the same pre-natal classes and we realised the connection.

With her barb going unanswered, Lucy swivels back to me. 'I could probably put in a word if you want to hold the wake here,' she says. 'Alain is a personal friend of mine.'

'We've already booked Dad's social club,' I say.

'Which one?'

'The Labour Club in town. He still went once or twice a week.'

Lucy looks to me blankly, as if she's never heard of such a place. 'Surely, it's nicer here? Don't you think guests would appreciate the view...?'

'Maybe – but I've already sent the invites. The Labour Club is more him.'

That gets a pouted bottom lip. 'Yes, I suppose it is.'

I sense Nicola tensing a little across the table as she wonders if this will be the time that I finally break. Every minute I spend in her mother's presence pushes me closer to the very sweary meltdown that's surely going to come one of these years.

Not today.

Lucy slips from her chair and says she'll be back, before strolling off towards the toilets.

Her daughter lets out a long breath. 'I'm so sorry,' she says. 'She's being a bigger bitch than usual.'

'I thought she was actually being nicer.'

Nicola laughs, though not really. Before she can say anything else, the waiter reappears with a trio of plates. He places them around the table, pours more water for Nicola and I, and then leaves us to it.

'I don't know why she ordered for us,' Nicola says. 'She does this all the time, like it's some sort of power play. She'll say she wants to take me out for dinner, then we'll end up in some high-end place where she'll get lashed on the wine, while insisting I eat whatever she does.'

'It looks like three small severed thumbs in congealed snot,' I reply, eyeing the plate.

Nicola pokes at one with a fork, before eating the scallop in one.

THE TAPES

'Have you still been thinking about your mum?' she asks, after swallowing.

It takes a moment to realise that's what I told Nicola at her house yesterday. I'd only just found the tape and struggled not to talk about it.

'Sort of. Dad, too. You do miss them when they're gone.'

Nicola stares towards the bathroom for a moment. 'Do you ever think she could come back?'

I'm slow today and it takes a while more to realise she's talking about my mother.

'Not really,' I reply. 'Maybe. Mum's friends all said the disappearance was out-of-character. She'd not talked to any of them about a fall-out, or wanting to leave. Nobody at her work knew anything about her being unhappy.'

I dwell on that a moment, because all it really made me think was that her friends didn't know her *that* well. But then I have been listening to her tapes, so perhaps I'm seeing things with retrospective eyes.

'What did your dad say?'

So much has happened in the last thirteen years that it's hard to answer. Those confusing few weeks after Mum disappeared blended into each other. There were sightings that weren't real; rumours that weren't true. I always assumed she'd return home, even when days turned to weeks to months. I'm not sure when I stopped believing.

'Dad had gone to the Labour Club at lunchtime,' I say. 'He got back about two hours later and she wasn't home. By the time it got to about half-four, he was calling, asking if I'd seen her. I'd not heard from her since that text about Sunday lunch. None of the neighbours had seen her, none of her friends, not me. Her bag was on the side, her phone was in the living room, her keys were on the hook, passport in the drawer, car in the garage. She'd just gone.'

'...if they say I'm missing, I'm not. I've been killed.'

How did she know? Why didn't she simply tell me – or anyone? Why the tape?

'Wasn't it the week of the floods...?' Nicola says – and she's right. It's one of the reasons Mum's disappearance never quite got the attention some do. We'd had three months of rain across a weekend and the river had burst its banks. Hard for people to care about a single missing person when hundreds were being evacuated into hotels, unsure when or if they'd be able to return home. The police were never going to prioritise a missing middle-aged woman when they'd been roped into building emergency sandbag barriers on the riverbank.

'There were no cash withdrawals,' I reply. I'm back in that week now. I think of Mum's disappearance and I think of rain. It's impossible not to. The unrelenting wall of water. 'The police did check in the end. They asked the taxi companies but there were no pickups in our area during that time. They said they looked at the CCTV from the shops at the end of the road but she didn't go past. There was no sign of an attack, and we never got a ransom. After a week or so, we asked, "What now?" and they sort of shrugged. They told us it's not illegal for an adult to disappear.'

I'm not sure I ever quite got over that. It's perfectly legal for a person to walk away from their life and never look back. Given what Mum was like, me and Dad never pushed for more. What were we supposed to do? Stand outside the police station with a giant sign? Being a victim of the Earring Killer was never really a suggestion as she didn't fit the bill.

We don't get a chance to say any more, because Nicola's mother is striding back from the toilets. She slots back between us and has a drink from her glass before clicking her fingers at the waiter. A moment later, and he's returned with the bottle and a polite 'madam', as he pours for her.

She urges us to dig in, and then eats one of her own scallops. I do the same and, luckily, it tastes better than it looks.

'How's that husband of yours?' Lucy asks, talking to her daughter.

'Busy,' Nicola replies.

Her mother points towards the wall near the toilets. 'I saw his flyer on the board. You know my friend Annie says he's a miracle worker.'

Nicola eats her final scallop and takes her time chewing. 'He could just work at a gym,' she says eventually.

'Oh, don't be so silly. I don't know where this jealous streak of yours comes from.'

The daggers Nicola stares at her mother are impossible to miss as I chew another of the scallops. I've often thought Nicola's jealousy of her husband was a little silly – but this is the first time I've heard anyone else saying as much. I don't think it's the personal training with which she has a problem, it's that he visits people in their houses. Or, more specifically, *women* in their houses. It feels like a non-issue, but Nicola did once tell me that Ethan was engaged to somebody before her. Even though *they're* now married, it doesn't feel as if she's ever got over that.

'Who's side are you on?' Nicola replies, and there's spite in her tone.

'Sanity's,' her mother replies, deliberately stoking the fire, having already tried to wind me up.

Just as it feels as if Nicola might go off, my bag begins to buzz. I ignore the disdainful look from Nicola's mother to grab my phone. Usually, I would ignore a call from an unknown number – but it could be the funeral director ahead of Friday, plus I could do with an out anyway.

'Is that Eve Falconer?' a voice asks after I say hello.

'Yes...?'

'This is Detective Sergeant Zoe Cox. Can I just check it was your daughter who reported finding a gun yesterday?'

There's a chill and I stand, moving away from the table towards the window, keeping my back to Nicola and Lucy.

'Is Faith OK?' I ask, suddenly worried.

'Yes. Sorry. I didn't mean that. There's no problem with your daughter. It's about the gun itself.'

'What about it?'

'This is sort of complicated. We were hoping you might be able to come to the station…?'

'What's happened?' I ask.

There's a humming from the other end, a smidge of uncertainty. 'We tested the gun for fingerprints,' the officer says. 'We got a match.'

She waits, taking a breath, but there's something in her voice that I know means she can't explain what she's about to say.

'The fingerprints belong to your mother.'

NINE

It's been a while since I was in a police station. I've seen the TV shows, too, with grotty corridors and solid metal tables bolted to the ground. The two-way mirrors and the whole good cop, bad cop thing. I always assumed it was a bit of a cliché – and perhaps it is.

Sedingham isn't big enough to have its own police station, so Nicola dropped me back at the office, then I had to drive half-an-hour to the next town along.

On arrival, Detective Sergeant Cox – call me Zoe – took me through to a small canteen area. There's a large tub of instant coffee on top of a humming fridge, plus a microwave that doesn't look as if it's been cleaned since the millennium bug was a thing. A page of A4 has been taped to the fridge with, STOP STEALING MY MILK, YA THIEVING SHITES written in large capital letters.

Zoe asks if I want a tea, then sets a kettle boiling as we sit around a small table. The chairs have a school staffroom vibe, with metal frames and soft padding poking through holes in the fabric.

'I didn't want to do this in an interview room,' Zoe says as she stands next to the kettle. 'It can feel a bit formal in there.'

She waits as if to see whether I have any objections. She must know I spent the drive here wondering what this could all mean.

'Obviously I know this is a shock for you,' Zoe says. 'We were stunned, too, if that's any consolation. The sarge actually called to double-check there hadn't been a mistake.'

'It's definitely Mum's fingerprints on the gun?'

'We're as sure as can be. Do you know if your mother ever owned a gun?'

'I don't think so. She never mentioned it if she did.'

Even as I say such a thing, it's impossible not to think of her tapes. Mum's idea of ownership was... fluid, at best.

'Was she ever interested in shooting?'

'Maybe when the Olympics was on? I've been trying to think but I can't remember a time she ever talked about guns. It wasn't part of our life.'

Zoe nods along as the kettle clicks off. She raids the cupboard for a pair of teabags from a giant PG Tips box, then drops one in each of two mugs, before filling. Milk comes from the fridge, although it's unclear if this is of the 'thieving shites' variety, and then Zoe sits across from me.

'Are you *sure* they're her fingerprints?' I ask again.

'We had them on file after one of her arrests. I think she got a conditional discharge – but everything was kept.'

That must be the other reason Mum never called the police when she realised what she had found with that jewellery box. She and the police have history.

Had history.

Of course, so do I.

Detective Sergeant Cox has no notepad, no recording device. To all intents, we're having a cosy chat over a cup of tea – except it's never been quite so simple to shake off the vision of police given to me by my mother. She said they could, and should, never be trusted. That they were an instrument of the state, there to put down the working man – and I only had to look at the miners' strike to see proof. I didn't know what any of that meant for a long time, but the suspicion stuck.

Zoe sips her tea and then puts down the mug. One of her colleagues has entered the canteen. He strides to the fridge and removes a yoghurt, before making brief small talk with Zoe about one of the cars being on the blink. A couple of minutes pass and then he heads back the way he came, leaving us alone again.

'I've been reading the files this morning,' Zoe says. 'Your mother was reported missing thirteen years ago – so this is going to sound like an odd question – but have you heard anything from her in that time?'

It's impossible not to think of the tapes. Does that count?

'No,' I say, and then: 'You?'

She shakes her head. 'We'd have been in touch. Her file is open but inactive. Sometimes people come back and it's never reported to us. That's why I asked.'

Zoe is staring now and I have the sense that there's been a long conversation in which I was mentioned.

'I've not heard anything new in thirteen years,' I repeat.

Zoe pauses with the mug part-way to her mouth, before she sips and nods. My tea remains untouched.

'There are ballistic tests ongoing but nothing available yet,' she says.

'What does that mean?'

'We're trying to find out whether the gun's ever been fired. Whenever we recover bullets from a crime scene there's a sort of signature that allows us to trace it back to the weapon that fired it. It's standard when we recover a firearm.' There's a pause and then she adds. 'I can count on one hand the number of times this has happened since I started working here. We don't really get guns around here.'

I think for a few moments, unable to explain why Mum's fingerprints are on a gun. I can't imagine her ever holding one, let alone firing.

'There are other partials on the gun,' Zoe says.

'I don't know what you mean.'

'Sorry, fingerprints. Your mother's prints are a complete match, but there are other partials on the weapon. Parts of a finger or thumb, but there's no match to anyone in our system. It means somebody else held the gun at some point, but we don't know who.'

Oh. I now see where this is going. The next question feels so obvious that I'm annoyed at myself for not seeing it coming.

'Have *you* ever owned a gun?' Zoe asks.

Detective Sergeant Cox asks. I remind myself she is not my friend.

'What do you mean?' I ask.

'It's just... with your previous issues and the record you have...?'

It's not quite a question, but perhaps it is. When DS Cox checked my mother's file earlier, she also had a look at mine.

'That was a long time ago,' I say. This is so out of the blue, it feels as if I've been walloped in the chest.

'I know,' Cox replies, although it doesn't feel as if she does.

'I've been clean for over seven years,' I add. 'You can ask my sponsor. You can test me.'

'We don't need to do any of that,' she replies – but there's a coldness there now and I'm furious at myself for not realising this is how things would go.

'I needed to ask,' she says.

I can't stop talking, even though I know I should. 'I've never even held a gun, let alone owned one,' I'm saying. 'I wouldn't know where to buy one.'

Cox catches my eye, holds it for a moment, and then nods. I don't think she believes me.

'My fingerprints are in your system. If those partials were mine, you'd have a match.'

The officer's lips are pressed together as I realise – again too late – that she already checked the prints against mine. I've been such an idiot. Despite everything, I somehow walked right into this. Even bringing me to the staff canteen was part of it. Nothing's recorded, and I'm not under caution – but that doesn't mean a person can't say something stupid.

Cox waits, likely expecting me to talk myself into trouble because, for some reason, I apparently lack the will to keep my gob shut. It's closed now, though.

'Is there anything else you want to ask?' she says.

It feels like a loaded question now – but DS Cox doesn't know how much I might have. There's a tape from my mother in which she admits she's a serial thief, who stole a jewellery box that contains the missing earrings taken by a serial killer. Oh, and that person *might* have killed her, although those murders stopped at the exact time Mum disappeared.

I'd have struggled to say all that, even if it wasn't for the other obvious lies and brags on the tape. Mum never robbed a bank, she never stole next door's car – and, maybe, she never found that jewellery box, either. Maybe she made up *all* of it.

I *could* say all that, except: 'I don't think so,' I reply instead.

Cox waits a moment, then sips her tea. Mine remains untouched. 'There's no rush,' she says, nodding to the mug. 'I can show you out when you're ready.' She has another mouthful and then adds: 'We might need to talk to your daughter at some point – and her friend.'

'Why?'

'We got a brief statement from them yesterday about where they found the weapon – but the fingerprints might change things. You have to admit it's quite the coincidence that your daughter found a discarded weapon that somehow has the fingerprints of her missing grandmother.'

I'd somehow missed that but Cox is correct. No wonder the police invited me for a face-to-face talk. Faith is underage and would need a parent to be present for any questioning. None of that applies to me, except it wasn't me who found the gun, nor my prints. They're confused and fishing. They think I know more than I do.

If Mum was reliable and honest, this would all be so much easier. I swing from believing she found that jewellery box, to thinking it a flight of fancy, just like the claimed bank robbery. Except, if I can find the box, it'll at least prove part of what she said on the tape happened. Perhaps it's at Dad's house, somewhere among the rest that needs to be cleared.

Perhaps.

I don't know where to look – but as I sit, wilting under Detective Sergeant Cox's gaze, it occurs I might know someone who does.

TEN

Dad's house feels different in the afternoon. There's something about the direction the sun rises and passes through the sky that means the house is enveloped by shadow after lunch. My father was never a fan of having the big light on, and I don't think he ever quite came to terms with the fact that leaving something plugged in wasn't going to lead to a bankruptcy-inducing electricity bill. Either way, the various rooms are speckled with dim lamps that leave large parts of the house coated in pervasive gloom.

A bit like me.

I searched through the garage as best I could but there was no sign of a jewellery box of any sort, let alone something with engraved flowers around the side. Mum was a liar – but was she lying about the box?

Then there's the gun.

How could Mum's fingerprints possibly be on it? And how did it get into the woods at the back of Nicola's house? It's been thirteen years since she disappeared and a long time since I last thought she might turn up. But is she somehow out there, keeping an eye on us? I can't make sense of it all – and it's no wonder the police can't figure it out, either.

So I wait, the curtains open, half-watching the street until the shiny black car glides into view. It looks new, and, as the suited man slips from the driver's seat, I wait for him in the doorframe. He's wearing sunglasses, and blinks into the daylight as he removes them to take me in.

'You look good,' I tell him as he stops in front of me, gaze sliding across the house.

'Thanks,' he replies, no hint of returning the compliment because, let's be honest, my brother is a complete nob.

'How's the funeral looking?' Peter asks. He has a way of taking in a person while seemingly looking right through them.

'You could be involved.'

'I'm busy.'

'So am I.'

He snorts a fraction at this and there's a hint of an eye roll. His job is more important than mine, obviously. His life. He holds up a hand, wafting it in the vague direction of the garage. 'If this is about the house, I told you to do whatever. Let's get it sold. The sooner, the better.'

It's true that he said that – in an email. That's the level of relationship my brother and I have. The house will be sold, with the value split fifty-fifty between us. Our father has no other dependants.

'It still needs clearing,' I tell him.

'So clear it.'

'I've been trying. The sofa, chairs and table all went to someone on Facebook Marketplace. People will take *anything* on there if it's free.'

Peter's gaze flickers towards the neighbour's house and the car that sits on the driveway. There's moss growing around the window edges and the bonnet is a different colour to the rest of the vehicle. That'll definitely drag down the house's selling price.

'Why am I here?' he asks.

'I was wondering if there's anything of Dad's you might want?'

'Is that why you had me drive all the way out here? I thought there was something wrong with the house.'

'I made a pile.'

I nudge open the front door and hold it wider. There's a moment in which it feels as if Peter might huff and walk off – except he's come this far, so he sighs his way inside instead. I take him through to Dad's kitchen, where our father's watch sits on the counter. I found it in his bureau a few days back, and hand it across to Peter.

'I thought you might like that,' I say.

He flips it over and squints at the writing on the back, before sulkily returning it to the counter. 'It's fake,' he says. 'Trash.'

'Yes, but not everything's about money. I thought you might want it because it was Dad's...?'

My brother lets out something that sounds like *yuck* but then snatches the watch back. 'Fine, I'll have it. Is this all? I've got stuff to do.'

I more or less hold in the sigh. I can't remember the last time my brother and I got on, if we ever did.

'How are the twins?' I ask.

My brother's reply is a snapped 'They're fine' but it's as if he catches himself because he waits a second and then softens a fraction. 'Bridget's mum has taken them to Center Parcs for a few days.'

Someone's earning...

'That sounds nice. Do you know if they'll be back for the funeral?'

Peter frowns and it feels as if this hasn't occurred to him. 'I'm not sure,' he says. 'I'll have to check. I think so.'

'Faith was saying it'd be great to spend some time with them. It's been a long time since we all got together.'

Peter nods along, not asking how Faith's getting on, or suggesting he'd like to see my daughter. To see *his niece*. 'We'll see how things go,' he says instead, before looking to his own watch. It's far chunkier than the one of Dad's that's now in his pocket. 'I'm sort of in a rush,' he adds.

I realise I'm going to have to force the conversation, considering he apparently has no intent of engaging otherwise.

'I found a box of cassettes in the garage,' I say. 'Do you remember when Mum used to record herself...?'

It feels as if there's a battle against the Botox as the gentlest of crinkles appear in Peter's forehead. It's the first time he's been remotely interested in anything since arriving at the house. 'I think I remember her sitting in the garden with a tape recorder and a microphone. She said she was recording a diary.' There's a momentary smile, finally a hint of humanity. 'That's so long ago. I can't believe Dad kept all that stuff.'

'I was listening to a tape where Mum said I was only nine but that Dad "left" last week. I'm pretty sure I remember her telling me he was working away. I believed it at the time – probably because I was only nine – but it doesn't feel right now...?'

It's sort of a question. There's a blink and I can almost see the memory reappearing. Peter is eleven years older than me and had already left home by the time I was nine. Just one of the reasons we've never been close.

'Dad did leave for about three months or so,' he says matter-of-factly. 'There was another woman. Someone he met at work. I thought you knew?' I shake my head and there's something approaching curiosity on my brother's face, as if he'd forgotten about all this as well. 'I think she was married, too, and they both ended up going back to their partners.' He stops and thinks for a couple of seconds. 'Harriet-something. I think she lived up in that cottage by the rugby club. Her family used to run the bar there.'

He runs a hand through his hair and looks to me. There's a second or two of connection that I'm not sure we've ever had, certainly not recently. 'I remember now,' he adds. 'Your mum didn't want you to know...'

He tails off and it feels as if he suddenly regrets telling me. As if he's kept a secret for thirty years and then blurted it out by accident. As well as that eleven-year gap, we have the same dad but different mums. Dad was fourteen years older than my mother, so it all got a bit complicated with the age gaps. There was never really a time in which we all lived as a family. Peter had his mum and dad, then I had mine. It's just that our father happened to be centre of the Venn diagram.

That's probably why I know I can't tell Peter about the 'murdered' part of Mum's tapes, nor the Earring Killer claim. If he ever listened to the tapes, he'd focus on the stolen car part, the bank robbery bit, pointing out that Mum was a liar – and it should all be discounted. Perhaps I'd think he was right.

But I do wonder about that jewellery box.

If I could only find that, it would prove at least some of what she says is true. It wasn't clear from where Mum stole it, but I assumed it was from someone she knew.

'Did Dad ever talk about couples he and Mum were friends with?' I ask.

'From when?'

'Any time through to when she, uh...'

'When yours walked out?'

This is why it's a dangerous conversation. Peter's mother died young of cancer – and he has a very defined sense of difference between his memories of his perfect mother, compared to the train wreck of mine. I never knew his mum, so have no idea how much is real, and how much is rose-tinted.

'I guess,' I reply, not wanting an argument about whether Mum 'walked out'.

'Why?' Peter replies.

'I suppose I'm wondering if there's anyone I've forgotten to invite to the funeral. Someone Dad might've lost contact with...?'

It's a lie but good enough for Peter to think it over. 'You'd know as well as me.'

'I've invited everyone *I* can think of. That's why I'm asking you.'

Despite the fillers and the way my brother's face doesn't really move, I can see him trying to come up with a sarcastic reply. When nothing appears, he huffs: 'Did you invite Kieron and Lucy?'

'I saw Lucy earlier. They're both coming.'

He shrugs a fraction. 'What were our old neighbours called? The Greens?'

'I think they both died.'

That gets a blank look, even though I know I texted my brother to ask whether he knew. That blankness quickly turns to a suggestion of a cruel grin and I know what's coming a moment before it does. 'The Rowetts?'

He makes sure he catches my eye.

'Not them,' I say, as I try to force away a shiver. I don't want him to know that he's got me. I hate that name.

That gets a snort and a shrug. 'I dunno what you want then.' He looks to his watch again. 'I have to get off. I've got work to do, then football later.'

I vaguely remember the LinkedIn post about how he gets up at five every morning for a run; and how he plays football twice a week. Something about keeping himself young, in among all the other nonsense about eating egg whites and #familytime with his #soulmate.

The dig about the Rowetts would usually be enough to end this conversation, except I still need him.

'There's other stuff on the tape,' I say, trying not to sound desperate. 'It's patchy and hard to make out. Owen from work is trying to clean up the audio. Have you ever seen a jewellery box around the house...?'

It's certainly a non-sequitur but I'm hoping Peter doesn't notice. He tries to frown but his forehead fights back. 'Owen...' he says, as if he knows my workmate. He opens his mouth again to add something, closes it, thinks for a moment, and then: 'What kind of jewellery box?'

'I think there are engraved flowers on the side.'

There's a flicker of something, though Peter is increasingly hard to read. 'I didn't really go snooping when I visited Dad,' he says. 'And I don't think that was Dad's sort of thing.'

'I know but maybe it was Mum's. Perhaps he kept it?'

He huffs a dismissive sigh and shakes his head before looking to his watch again. I figure he's about to leave. 'Dunno what you mean.' Another check of the watch. 'Need a slash...' He doesn't wait for a reply, instead bounding for the stairs and leaving me alone.

Except... the floors are thin and the carpets not much better. His footsteps should be heading towards the bathroom, except I hear my brother moving in the opposite direction, into Dad's bedroom.

I'm in the doorframe, half in the kitchen, half in the living room, listening to my brother above when a flicker of movement catches my eye from the front of the house. I drift across the front room to the window. There's someone over the street, partially concealed behind a lamp post. I'm far enough from the glass that she shouldn't be able to see me, but I watch as she holds up what looks like a phone.

I think she's taking photos of the house.

If I wasn't concerned about what my brother was doing upstairs, I'd cross the road and ask. She's wearing black but largely in shadow and it's hard to see much in the way of features. If I had to guess, she's in her sixties but the silver hair could be the light.

There's a creak from overhead as Peter moves a pace or two around Dad's bedroom. There's a muffled thump, as if he's opened a drawer, although it's hard to know for sure.

Meanwhile, as my attention was diverted, the woman across the road is ducking into a small silver car. I shift a pace, trying to get a view of her face but the glare of the car windscreen is too much. Moments later, she's done a three-point turn and headed out of sight. I tell myself it's nothing, except it really did seem as if she was taking photos of the house.

Unless, of course, Mum's tapes have me paranoid.

There's a further creak from above and then the quick movement of feet as Peter moves to the far side of the house. The toilet flushes and the pipes creak as water gushes through the house.

Moments later and Peter is back in the hall. I meet him there, wondering if I should ask what he was doing in Dad's bedroom. I probably would, were it not for the fact that, once the probate has gone through, we'll be the legal owners. If I ask, he'll tell me he has as much right to be here as I do.

'I thought I saw someone watching the house,' I tell him instead.

My brother rolls his eyes. 'Probably a neighbour,' he replies dismissively. Something has shifted in the time he's been upstairs and there's a nastiness that wasn't completely there before. 'Look, I'll be at the funeral but I told you to get this place sold. We don't need to be in each other's lives, especially now Dad's gone.'

It's so direct that I reel away a fraction. 'Oh...'

'I don't mean to be harsh but the women in this family attract crazy – and I don't want that. I don't know what you're on about with all these questions and I don't know what you're on about with someone watching the house. It's all nonsense.'

He mumbles something that might be goodbye, then turns for the door. As he does, he pats a pocket, probably involuntarily. There's a bulge I don't think was there before.

Something taken from upstairs.

ELEVEN

I watch from the front window as Peter disappears off to afternoon football, or wherever it is he's actually going. A part of me always wished we could get on better, but perhaps that's not who we are. We've always been destined to argue because, ultimately, we have nothing in common other than sharing a father. I consider that for a minute or two until I snap back to the present. I bet he's not thinking about me at all as he zooms off.

Upstairs, I head into Dad's bedroom and open a few drawers, then look under the bed. There's still plenty to be cleared, though I figure this will be the last room. I can't quite bring myself to get rid of all Dad's clothes yet, even though they should be some of the easier items. There will be a finality that I don't think I can face before the funeral.

Peter seemingly has no such problems. He was in the room for around five minutes and it sounded as if he was looking for something he knew was in here. If it was a memento – such as the watch – he could have said he was taking it, and the chances of me objecting would be very low.

Reading my brother has always been difficult, and that was before the quarterly Botox injections. There are no signs of anything in particular that's been moved around, and, although the dresser drawer was fractionally open, I think it might have been like that before.

I stand in the upstairs window, looking to the street below, realising how mad I must have sounded when I was talking to Peter about a strange woman watching the house. She probably was looking for her keys, something like that. Since listening to Mum's tapes, I feel more on edge than before – especially at Dad's house.

It's mid-afternoon and I should return to work. Mark wasn't overly happy at me skipping out a few hours ago, but it was hard for him to say no considering the police wanted to talk. I stole another hour and a bit at Dad's house, part looking for the jewellery box, part waiting for my brother and it's going to be pushing my luck to take the rest of the day off.

Except Peter's dig about the Rowetts stuck. He was trying to be cruel and it worked, because Jake Rowett will be on my mind all day now. But my brother accidentally had a point: the Rowetts *were* people that Mum and Dad knew well back then.

And if Mum *did* steal a jewellery box, it could have easily been from someone very, very nearby.

As soon as that idea appeared, I knew I wasn't heading back to the office.

Dad's house is not where I grew up. He bought it years ago with a mix of withdrawing some pension money early, the life insurance from Peter's mum's death, plus various scraps of savings. It's the sort of thing people of his generation seemed to be able to do at will. They wanted a bigger house, so they bought a bigger house.

The road where we lived as a family is around fifteen minutes away by car. The house is in the middle of a long row of terraces. Cars line both sides of the street, leaving a tight gap through the middle, and the parking spot is almost five minutes away, at the back of a pizza shop.

It's been a trippy, time-twisting day or so – and the walk back towards my old house is no different. There's the corner where my old friend, Marie, knocked on a door, then ran – except the person who owned the house was already walking in the other direction and watched her do it. The woman threatened to march the pair of us home and tell our parents what she'd done.

After that, there's the house that always had a pink front door; then the one where the owner used to leave his work van on the street outside, taking up an extra parking space that led to a fist fight with his neighbour. There's Mr Mintrim's house; a man who permanently seemed eighty, and used to sit in a deckchair on the pavement when the sun was out.

The memories flood back as I reach the street where I lived the first nineteen years of my life. There are more cars; more satellite dishes, but so little has actually changed. There are still 'no free papers' postcards in people's front windows; still varying degrees of threats and requests for people not to park in front of the houses. When I pass my old home, the tiny crack in the corner of the downstairs front window is still there. There's tinsel in the upstairs window, even though we're months away from the festive period.

The house directly next door belongs to the Rowetts and my bedroom shared a wall with theirs for those entire nineteen years.

Mum and Dad were friends with them largely by default – and, of every house from which my mother could've stolen a jewellery box, it has to be at the top.

Plus, Jake Rowett being the Earring Killer would make me feel a lot better about a few aspects of my life.

I knock on the Rowetts' door and wait. I would've done this

in years gone by, when Mum sent me round to ask for teabags, milk, something like that.

Such a long time has passed.

There's no answer, so I try tapping the window, before it occurs to me that our old neighbour could've moved. It's possible, even if they were the sort who'd live in the same place forever.

Thirty seconds or so pass and I'm about to try knocking again when the front door opens and catches on the chain. An eye appears, darting both ways until settling on me. 'Who is it?' a woman's voice asks.

'It's me, Allie. It's Eve.'

There's a momentary pause and then the door closes, before there's the scratching scrape of a chain being unlatched. When it's re-opened, a short old woman is standing in front of me, one hand on her hip. I'm a little teapot.

I've not seen Allie Rowett in a good ten years, and she must've shrunk by four or five inches in that time. Her hair is starting to thin; the fuzzy grey curls no longer long down her back as they used to be.

'Eve, love. My God. What are you doing round here?'

'I came to tell you that Dad died. We're having the funeral on Friday.'

She stares, mouth open, until a surprised-sounding: 'Oh...' It takes a second or two for her to absorb the information, until she adds: 'Thanks for telling me.' She asks about the time and place, and, once I tell her, she's already worked it out in her head. There's a bus that connects to another bus, but she'll make it.

'Was he ill?' she asks.

'Sort of. He had a heart attack last year and the doctor said he'd have to change his diet and start walking every day. Dad decided it wasn't for him, so I guess it was inevitable in the end.'

Allie nods along. She knew my father for long enough that the stubborn streak wouldn't have been a surprise.

'You know Jake died a few months back,' she says.

I nod, but it's impossible not to stand a little straighter at the mention of her husband's name. I'm on alert.

Seconds pass but it feels like longer. Allie is probably in her eighties now. She's angling slightly to one side, as if one leg's shorter than the other. Standing up seems exhausting for her but there is still a brightness to her eyes.

Sadness, too.

Because then she says the words I've been waiting more than two decades to hear.

'I always knew you were telling the truth…'

TWELVE

I'm not sure why I came, but maybe it was for this. Maybe this is what I've always been waiting for. There's a lump in my throat and I turn, blinking back the tears. I sense the old woman moving behind me but I can't face her, especially not in this house. She must realise that because she lets the seconds pass until I'm finally able to twist back.

'Do you want to come in?' she asks.

I want to say no but, somehow, I'm inside the living room – and it's the same as it always was. There's the old bricked-up fireplace, with a rickety bookshelf in front; then the row of collectable plates on shelves near the back window. The television is newer, flatter, but still in the corner by the front. It's like stepping into a time capsule – not only because barely anything has changed, but because it's the mirror of the living room in which I grew up. All these houses have the same design.

'Do you want a tea?' Allie asks, bringing me back to the present. 'Coffee?' She's in the doorway behind, leaning on the frame. I tell her I'll have a tea, even though I don't want one. The familiarity is so striking I can barely remember why I'm here. As she shuffles off to the kitchen, I'm left looking at the layer of dust that's crusted to the 1981 commemorative Royal Wedding plates.

Because Allie loved cooking, we'd often have Christmas dinner in this room, with tables dragged together; chairs carried from next door. I'd sit in the cramped corner, staring across to these exact plates, wondering if they were ever used.

Looking around the room I notice that Allie still has a VCR underneath the television, plus rows of video tapes with things like *Taggart* and *The Bill* written on the labels. There are trinkets and tat, plus a pile of blankets on the radiator underneath the front window. I'm transfixed, and still doing a lap when Allie returns with a full tea tray. There are two mugs, a small jug of milk, a bowl of sugar, two teaspoons, and a plate with four pink wafers in a neat line.

We sit, and the sofa padding is barely existent as it feels as if I might fall through it. Allie has her recliner chair and oohs her way down, before picking up her tea. 'Doctor says I'm not allowed sugar any more,' she says. She nods towards the hall, and the kitchen beyond but, as I turn to look in the direction, she adds a swift: 'Oh, Eve, love. I'm so sorry.'

There's a quiet between us; the only sound the distant groan of a knackered car engine.

'I know I should've said something at the time,' Allie says. 'I really wanted to. I almost did a couple of times but Jake… he, um…'

She tails off but there's no need to finish the sentence.

I was fifteen when Jake Rowett pinned me to the wall in the hallway and put his hand inside my top. It was Christmas Day and I was in a green jumper that had white snowballs across the bottom. Mum had given it to me that morning and I'd worn it for her, with the strict insistence that I'd never wear it in public.

I still remember the scratchiness of the fabric as our neighbour's hand groped his way inside.

Every time somebody says something similar nowadays –

#metoo and all that – you get the people who insist it's a lie, because the person didn't speak up at the time. Except I *did* exactly what all those people say. I went into the living room, where my mum, dad, and Allie were eating, and I told them exactly what had just happened. Jake said it was a misunderstanding. We'd passed in the hall and there was nothing untoward.

There were five people in that living room, including me, and everyone knew what had happened.

Everyone.

Nobody did anything.

Instead, the other three adults agreed that it had to be a misunderstanding, because it was easier if they did. We never visited for Christmas again, and I was never left alone with Jake. They all knew, and they all changed the way things were done – but none of them ever did anything in the moment.

I've been waiting twenty-five long years for Allie to finally say she knew I was telling the truth. It took everyone else dying for it to finally happen.

I should tell her it's OK, that I appreciate the words, except I don't think I do. Fifteen-year-old me needed to hear it; forty-year-old me doesn't.

'He deserved what happened to him,' she adds – and I have to remind myself I'm there to ask about a jewellery box.

Not yet, though.

'How did he die?' I ask.

'Heart attack. Ambulance got stuck in traffic and he was gone by the time they arrived.'

I picture him in pain, clutching his chest, waiting for that ambulance, feeling his lungs get tighter and tighter and *tighter*... except it doesn't make me feel any better.

'I've been clearing out Dad's house,' I say, wanting to move on. 'I know this is a strange question but it got me thinking. I was sure I once saw a jewellery box of yours a while back.

There were flowers engraved on the side. I was wondering if you remember where you got it...?'

It's not what Allie expected, likely in more ways than one. She looks to me blankly. 'Sorry, Eve. I don't think I've ever had a box like that. Could you be thinking of someone else?'

I force myself not to react, partly because, as soon as my brother mentioned 'the Rowetts', I'd convinced myself Jake was the Earring Killer. It would make so much sense, for me if no one else. Mum and Dad might have popped round here one evening to share a bottle of whisky and reminisce over past Christmases. Mum had found that box, taken it, then discovered the stolen earrings inside.

So easy.

Everyone would know who he was and I'd be able to talk openly about the way he pressed me to the wall, how his eyes narrowed, how I felt so helpless in those seconds.

But it's not him.

I sit for a moment, ignoring the tea. It's the second one made for me in almost as many hours that I've left.

There's nothing to talk about and, much as I want to go, I can't quite drag myself to the door. Allie perhaps recognises this because we sit in silence, not quite acknowledging the other, not quite ignoring. After a few minutes, my bag buzzes, so I retrieve my phone. A message from Faith.

Can you pick me up after college?

I reply to ask where, and she tells me the theatre that's attached to the college. She sometimes walks, but usually takes the bus. It's only if she's had a long day that she asks for a lift.

I'm about to return the phone to my bag when another message arrives.

BTW, saw someone that looks a bit like grandma

I stare at it for a moment. Faith is too young to remember my mum but there are photos around the house. She's always been somewhat intrigued by the idea of her grandmother disappearing, which is understandable. I text to ask what she means, but get the briefest of responses to say she's heading into lectures and will tell me later. It's such a Faith reply, although not completely out of character. At least twice a year, I'll get a text from her with a photo of an older woman she's seen, asking me if it looks like my mum. I think Faith has the idea that, despite the thirteen years, her grandmother will simply reappear someday.

The only thing I can say about the photos is that there are times when I need to have a second look – but none of them have been my mother.

This time I am expecting that to be it, except a slightly blurry photo comes through. It's been taken from a distance and isn't of an old woman. Instead, it's of woman driving something I've seen very recently.

A small, silver car.

THIRTEEN

With an hour and a half left of the work day, I'm back in the landscaping office. One of the security guys has been answering the phones and my desk is littered with two-dozen Post-it note messages to pick up. I do my best to catch up with everything I missed.

Although 'my best' might not be entirely true.

Faith hasn't replied, although she's likely in tutorials, where phones are supposed to be off. I've zoomed in and out of her photo so many times, and am almost certain it's the same silver car I saw parked across from Dad's house a few hours before. The shadows made it hard to see but I thought the driver was a woman somewhere in her sixties. It was too far for me to make out anything more precise – and I'm assuming Faith sent the photo because there's a blurry shadow of a woman in the driver's seat. Her message said the woman looked 'a bit like' Grandma, which wouldn't bother me if it wasn't for the fact that my mum's fingerprints are on a gun that was discovered yesterday.

Could this woman really be her? *Really?* Why would she have been holding a gun near Nicola's house, much less left it?

Mum said on the tape that she knows who the Earring Killer is, that she thought she was going to be murdered. Except she *also* said she stole the neighbour's car and robbed a bank. She admitted to having impulse control problems, and there's no question she was a liar. Except, where do those lies begin? And is she now driving a small silver car, while keeping an eye on both her old house, and Faith at college?

As I sort of, kind of, get on with work, all that swirls.

How am I supposed to keep going about my life? The clock is ticking as I wait for the time to leave – properly now – so I can pick up Faith and get some answers about the woman she saw. It's three minutes to five when a new message arrives from my daughter.

Sorted now – Dan giving me a lift x

I don't want to be annoyed at her, largely because I *want* to be the backup. I don't ever want her to be stuck, worried about calling me for help in case of a backlash. There's no further information about the woman in the car and I scroll back to six weeks before, when my daughter last sent a photo of a person she said could be her grandmother. It's a woman outside Waitrose, laughing with another woman who's holding a bouquet of flowers. She's wearing a wax jacket my mum would've hated, and is too tall anyway.

There doesn't seem much point in following up until Faith and I are at home later. It shouldn't be too long.

Instead, I reply to say it's fine, and ask if she wants anything in particular for tea. There's no instant response, which I guess means she's getting something with her friends.

At least she's safe.

I'm about to log out of the system when something bangs outside. Mark's voice is unmistakeable, largely because he has no sense of what might count as an indoor voice. He swears loudly, then shouts at someone that they only have a job because of him. A classic way of motivating employees that I've heard hundreds of times. Someone replies meekly, though I don't see or hear who.

Before I close down my computer, I hit the home button, where the browser loads the company website. Mark is front and centre, leaning on the back of a van with a slogan saying the work is 100% guaranteed. In all the time I've worked for him, I've never quite figured out what that means, considering there's usually at least one customer dispute ongoing, and never been a mention of any work assurance.

I click through to the owner section, which never fails to make me laugh. Mark hired a professional photographer to take a series of pictures with him dressed in his work suit for half the shoot; and landscaping work gear for the rest. There's a photo with him in his suit, standing in that politician power pose: legs too far apart, like he's struggling for a poo. He's standing tall with his arms folded in another; awkwardly holding a rake in a third.

Mark left school with no qualifications and, if a person didn't already know that, he'd make sure to tell them within three minutes of meeting. There's a lengthy bio on the website.

> Mark Dixon is one of life's success stories. Self-made and self-effacing, Mark is a dreamer, who started his burgeoning career on a production line at Prince Industries. Having immediately shown his worth, Mark quickly rose to become manager. He soon realised he had the ambition, work ethic, and intelligence to start his own business. For some, this might have been a risk – but that is how Mark came to start the landscaping company entirely by himself. From only one employee, he now has thirty full-time staff, plus contractors, who rely on him for their livelihoods.

Well, someone invested in a thesaurus.

There's plenty more than that. Mark is one of those who, at his core, probably is impressive. Except, because he can't stop wanging on about himself, he manages to annoy and upset essentially everyone that ever comes across him.

It doesn't help that he'll frequently tell his employees that they only have a job because of him.

Mark blusters into the office and does a double take when he sees me. 'Didn't think you were coming back,' he says.

'The police kept me a while.'

Mark chews the inside of his mouth, unconvinced. 'Can you come in fifteen minutes early tomorrow?' he asks.

'Is everything all right?'

There's a leer that reminds me of my brother. 'We'll talk tomorrow.'

'I've got some time now...?'

It gets a shake of the head. 'Not everything's about you, Eve. We'll talk tomorrow.'

He stomps to his office and closes the door – and I know it won't be a fun morning. Whatever it is could've been said now, but this is how Mark manages people. He wants his employees to fall out and fight for his favour. He wants people like me to spend a night stewing.

I finally log out of the system, then wait a minute because Mark is on the phone in his office, arguing with someone that sounds like a customer. No good will come of this, so I head out, waving goodbye to Dina, who's unloading a van, then head out to the road.

The office is a little out of town, buried on one of those soulless trading estates. I head past a row of cars, trying to remember where I parked, before spotting my car underneath a lamp post on the other side of the road.

Except, as I start to cross, a man gets out of the vehicle

parked directly behind. He's tall and broad; shoulders like a rugby player, neck the same width as his head.

I know him, of course – because he's a police officer.

FOURTEEN

The one saving grace for the trading estate, perhaps, is the fact that a pub sits just off the roundabout on the way in and out. There's a large play area to the side and an even larger beer garden at the back. The food is bearable but cheap and it's packed at the weekends.

I've been brought to the pub as a test, of course – not that he'd ever say as much.

Kieron Parris sits across from me in the garden, partially shaded by a parasol, cradling a Guinness as I eye the lemonade he bought for me. There's too much ice and I never really trust anywhere that dumps so much in a single glass. Might as well just order water.

'Guinness Zero,' Kieron says, raising his glass. 'Tastes just like the real stuff.'

I clink his glass with mine and we each take a sip, even though I don't want to be here.

'Nicola talked to you then,' I say.

Nicola's father has another sip of the Guinness, leaving a slim line of foam on his top lip that he licks away. This is what I feared when I was in Nicola's kitchen after the discovery of the gun yesterday. Possibly even from lunch today. Too many gossips in that family, even if one of them is my friend.

No.

Her dad is a *retired* police officer. A chief inspector at that. I don't know all the ranks but I know he was high up.

'She did,' Kieron says. 'But before any of that, I should probably apologise on behalf of my wife. I believe she was quite rude to you at lunch.'

Nicola really has been chatting.

'Sort of,' I say.

'You shouldn't worry too much about her. I've told her she's a snob but she relishes it.' He waits a second. 'But Nicola's worried about you.'

I should've known it would get back to him. I was talking about Mum, on the back of Dad's death. It all sounds a bit depressive; all a bit like I might be considering hitting the bottle. Which is obviously why we're here.

'I didn't specifically come to see you,' Kieron adds, as if reading my mind. 'I was visiting my storage unit, then saw you coming out. I know it's been tough after your dad. I suppose I'm worried...'

He angles himself gently towards the pub, making the point sledgehammer-style. On the other side of the garden a group of five lads are talking loudly as they sup pints of lager. I keep reading that young people today aren't into drink or drugs but I guess there are always exceptions.

'Seven years and one hundred and thirty-two days,' I say. 'I was there last night.'

'I'm not checking up on you.'

'It feels like it.'

Nicola's father takes this in his stride, sipping his drink again with barely a tilt of his square ol' head.

'Do you want to go somewhere else?' he asks.

I almost laugh because we're already here and his intentions are so obvious. Kieron Parris is a man of the old-school parenting and policing. Nicola once told me that he made her smoke ten cigarettes in a row, because he found a packet in her school bag. That really does sum up his approach.

'We're here now,' I say, making a point to drink the lemonade, which is already mainly water. The sun is high and the only shade is the crooked parasol that's barely covering me at all.

'I saw Allie Rowett earlier,' I say, largely because I want the response. I get it, of course, as Kieron tenses, a vein appearing in his neck.

'Why?'

'I invited her to Dad's funeral. We were neighbours for long enough.'

His pint is halfway to his mouth but stuck in mid-air. 'Is that all?'

'She told me she believed me.'

He waits a moment, sips, returns the drink to the picnic table, then nods shortly. We both know what this means. 'People *did* believe you,' he says.

'Mum didn't. Dad didn't.'

Kieron bites his lip, not sure what to say. We both know my parents *did* believe me, but chose not to cause unnecessary trouble. The reason Kieron is aware of all this is because he was the person who interviewed me at the police station after I'd rammed a glass in Jake Rowett's face.

Years had passed, I was drunk in town and saw him in a pub. By that time, Mum had disappeared and Dad no longer lived next to the Rowetts. I watched from across the bar as Jake stared at a young woman further along. She couldn't have been much older than eighteen or nineteen and I knew that look on his face.

That's why Allie Rowett said he deserved it – because he did.

Except you can't ram a beer glass in a man's face while being filmed on CCTV – and then walk away as if nothing happened.

It's been seven years and one hundred and thirty-two days since I last had a drink. Seven years and one hundred and thirty-one days since I sat across from Nicola's dad in a police cell and told him why I ground that glass deep into Jake's skin, enjoying his screams, watching the crimson flow, only stopping because I was hauled away, drenched in blood both his and mine.

I was wild that night.

At those church hall meetings, I'll talk about how it was my lowest moment. It was, of course, and yet there's a tiny part of me that still relishes those few seconds of long-sought revenge. I can lie to everyone else but not myself.

Except, Faith and Shannon were already friends by then. Nicola was in my life. Her father had been a temporary mentor to Mum after one of her arrests. That's why it was him. He asked why I'd done it, so I told him everything. The way Jake had stuffed his hand up my top while pinning me to the wall on Christmas Day when I was fifteen; the way nobody stood up for me, including my parents. The absolute fury with which I'd lived across so many years.

It was Kieron who somehow got me off with probation. He was a respected chief inspector, and he knew me. He got me into AA, so I was clean. There was no prison time. I don't know who he talked to, or the arms he twisted, but it was him – because prison would have been catastrophic. Faith was only ten and would have been taken from me. Both our lives would've been wrenched apart because of those few seconds.

It's a small price, but having to meet with him, to have conversations like this once or twice a year, is worth it – no matter how much I hate it.

Kieron drinks and then his gaze flickers sideways to the

rowdy group of men. He says nothing, not to them anyway. 'Nic told me about the gun,' he tells me instead. 'Then I heard from my old colleagues about your mum's fingerprints. I didn't know what to make of it.'

'Me either.'

'Did she ever own a gun?'

'She never showed even a tiny amount of interest in anything like that.'

'Could she have...? With her history and all...?'

That's the thing with being a self-diagnosed kleptomaniac. Sooner or later, that lack of impulse control is going to get a person noticed by the police. Ironically, Mum's record is nowhere near as serious as mine – but there is that nice string of petty thefts.

'I have no idea,' I say, although it suddenly dawns on me that I can properly ask the question now. 'I was reading about fingerprints. It says they can stay on something essentially forever...?'

Kieron flicks another sideways look at the group, then turns back to me. 'Sort of. You could pick up your glass now and leave nothing, or – if nobody else interferes with it – you could leave a print that's still there in a hundred years. It's a lot less consistent than people might think.'

'So Mum could've held that gun a long time ago?'

'Maybe. The only certainty is that, at some point, she held it.'

I find myself clutching the glass, as if Kieron suggesting it somehow made it happen. The drink is too cold and my teeth tingle. I really want to leave.

'I'm so confused,' I say. I've been desperate to tell somebody the breadth of what's happened in the past day or so, largely to get it out of my head.

'It's been tough with your dad,' Kieron says, but he doesn't get it.

'I found a box of tapes,' I say, staring at the table. 'They were in Dad's garage when I was clearing it. Mum used to record herself on this old cassette player. Sort of like a diary. I picked one at random and she said that, if someone was listening to the tape, then she had disappeared, that she'd been murdered.'

I sense Kieron breathe in but it doesn't feel like a good inhalation. As if he's wondering whether I really am still clean. That Dad's death might have got to me far deeper than I'm saying.

'The tape quality isn't great. It cuts in and out, plus it sounds like she's tried to record over something but the old version is still there. Owen from work is seeing if he can fix it up.'

He waits a moment. 'I'm not sure what you're telling me.'

I can't force myself to look up from the table. I'm so desperate for someone to take me seriously but Kieron is one of those people who's had a real job, lived a real life. He seems so grown up.

'Mum said she found a jewellery box,' I tell him. 'There were earrings inside – but only one of each type. No pairs...'

There's a slight shift as Kieron straightens, then puts down his glass. It takes a few seconds. 'Are you saying what I think you're saying?'

'I don't know.'

My phone is fumbled from my bag and then I lay it in front of him on the table as I press to play the voice note. There's the crackled, fuzzy line that Mum loves me, but snippets of the rest as well. The quality sounds so much worse outside, almost drowned out by the braying men across the garden.

Kieron leans in then asks if it's OK to pick up the phone. He holds it to his ear at my nod. It's then I allow myself to peer up, but his features are granite with concentration. It's impossible not to see that face and not think of the time seven years before when he appeared outside the police cell. I was still caked in dried blood then, reality starting to set in that the few seconds of satisfaction was going to cost me my daughter and freedom.

Kieron eventually returns the phone to the table. 'Did you tell Nicola?' he asks.

'I'd not listened to it all yesterday. And... no. I didn't.'

I'm not sure whether we're friends like that anyway. What kind of friend do you tell this kind of thing to?

'I can ask my colleagues about this,' he replies. 'But we'd probably need the tape.'

'My friend from work has it. He's good with audio and is going to try to fix the quality.'

Kieron nods but I know what's coming. 'I'd love to believe what she's saying here...' A pause. 'OK, that's not quite what I mean. It's just your mother and the truth have a complicated relationship. I'm pretty sure I heard her say she robbed a bank. It's very difficult to take this seriously – especially as she isn't around to clarify any of it.'

It's nothing I don't already know, nor anything I haven't already considered. The whole thing is fanciful, which probably sums up my mother.

'I don't know if it's true,' I say.

'Is there any sign of this jewellery box?'

'I don't think so.'

Another rowdy howl goes up from the group and Kieron pushes himself up almost instantly. 'I'll be right back,' he says.

He strides purposefully across the lawn, although there's a hint of a limp as he reaches the group. Silence clouds them suddenly and there's something almost unworldly as they all look up to the newcomer with deference. I can't make out what he says but, seconds later, one of them shakes his hand. When Kieron walks back to me, the only sound from the group is a quiet murmur.

As Nicola's father sits across from me, I want to ask what he said. It was like a magic spell, though I suspect it was more about him as a person, than any specific words. Kieron has another mouthful of his drink, holds it, then swallows.

'Is there anything else you want to tell me?' he asks – but I suddenly feel as if I've missed something.

'Like what?'

There's a moment of indecision before he speaks, which isn't like him. Then I realise why. 'The voice on your recording, it sounds a lot like you.'

He fixes me in such a stare that I'm frozen. It takes a second or two to realise what he's actually said, because it hadn't occurred before.

'I, um...'

'I know it's hard with your dad and everything. That's why Nicola spoke to me. We're all worried for you.'

'No, it's... that's Mum's voice. It's *her* talking. I have all the tapes.'

Kieron presses back, still examining me, and I so wish the group of men were shouting now. Instead, there's a black hush between us.

He doesn't believe me. At best, he thinks I found the cassette player and recorded this myself for attention.

Nicola's dad reaches for his glass and finishes the drink. He wipes his top lip and rubs his eyes. 'I'll discreetly talk to a few old colleagues and see what they think,' he says.

I want to believe him but it sounds as if he's humouring me, seeing if I'll break first and tell him there's no need. That I *did* record the audio myself.

I was desperate to share and now I'm wondering why I couldn't just shut up.

Kieron stands and waits for me to do the same. 'You've come a really long way,' he says. 'I hear only fantastic things about Faith and how she's getting on.'

It's a compliment, I know, but it doesn't sound like it. I mumble a 'thanks' but there's a croak to my voice: the desperation at wanting to be believed. He takes a step towards the gate and the short walk back to our cars. 'If you have any other questions, you know where I am,' he says.

'OK...'

'If I don't see you before, Lucy and I will be at the funeral.'

We pause at the gate and he looks down on me with a gentle smile that doesn't quite suit his face. 'It's OK to ask for help,' he adds.

I ball my fists, dig the nails into my palms, and just about manage to stop myself telling him to shove his concern up his arse.

OPHELIA

Extract from *The Earring Killer* by Vivian Mallory, © 2015.

A woman in pink fluffy fairy wings jigs past, balancing a takeaway in one hand and her phone in the other. She's simultaneously holding one conversation with the friend at her side, a second with the person on the other end of the phone, plus eating the vinegar-soaked chips.

Who said the British education system wasn't fit for purpose?

Despite my multitasking friend, Sedingham on a Saturday night is a broadly serene affair compared to the hedonism of British town centres from the nineties and noughties. There are no snaking lines outside late-night clubs, nor over-zealous bouncers obsessed with lads wearing trainers. Instead, Tails is a calm, brightly lit bar, half filled with couples drinking fluorescent concoctions, where the manager tells me thirty per cent of every drink sold is non-alcoholic.

'It's not that the night scene is dying,' he adds. 'It's that you have to adapt. People aren't up for massive nights and early mornings any longer. They don't want to sleep on benches and have fights down back alleys. They want a quiet drink or two, and then to get home safely.'

The idea that Sedingham isn't dying at night might be true – but there are signs all over that there are problems. The boarded-up shops are the biggest clue, but also the pair of vandalised bus stops and, perhaps, the fact there are food banks at either end of the high street.

I cross the road outside Tails, to where the old Post Office is covered with boards advertising a café's grand opening with a date that's almost a year gone. A woman is leaning against one of the signs, balancing on her heels, vaping while scrolling on her phone. She looks up as I step onto the kerb, lowering her phone and noticing my unashamedly old-school notepad.

'What you doing with that?' she asks, with what seems like mild amusement.

I tell her I'm in town to research and write a book about the Earring Killer and, unprompted, she touches her own ear. She tells me she's called Kelsey, that her friend is inside the nearby kebab shop, waiting for a burger, because she doesn't like kebab meat.

Kelsey is chatty, first offering me some of her kebab, then saying she wants to sit because she's been on her feet all evening. We end up perched inside the bus shelter, Kelsey's friend standing over us as they both pick at their late-night food.

'We both had the talk,' Kelsey says, before her friend, Adele, continues the sentence. 'We were in year nine or ten and there was this big assembly for all the girls.' It's as if the two women are telepathic. As one stops to eat, the other resumes the memory.

'This was before we ever went out drinking, or anything like that,' Kelsey says. 'But they wanted us to understand how to be safe when we were out.'

'Didn't we have it two years in a row?' Adele asks.

'Definitely two; might've even been three.'

The two women are approaching thirty, something they tell me with a joyous cackle, before teasing one another over who is going to end up with the most exes.

But their ages are crucial, because they would have been in their teens at the start of the twenty-first century. There had been a three-year gap with no deaths attributed to the Earring Killer. It was a strange time, in which newspaper columnists openly wondered whether the police had overreacted. Perhaps there never had been a serial killer? Maybe there was an unfortunate similarity in cases that had people jumping to a false conclusion?

From the wary concern of the late-nineties, the people of Sedingham and area had started to convince themselves that is was safe to walk home alone; that the Earring Killer was a myth.

But then came Ophelia Baron.

Known as 'Oh' to her friends, Ophelia was a county-level hockey player. She had excelled throughout school, before playing her first game for the town's ladies' team while only fourteen. By the time she was seventeen, Ophelia was a regular for the first team. From there, she made friends that helped her find a job with the town council's planning department. The final Saturday night of her life saw her and the rest of her teammates share a drink in the bar that's now known as Tails. Thirteen of them commandeered a booth for much of the night, where they sang, laughed and reminisced over their 4-1 victory earlier in the day. Ophelia had scored one and assisted two.

The next day, she slept off a hangover in bed with her husband, who says he made her toast at around midday. She read a magazine and then had a long nap, before waking up to watch some Sunday evening television. On Monday, she went to work as usual – and then drove straight to hockey practice. Her team trained hard, working off the Saturday night excesses, and then they said their goodbyes in the chilly car park.

Ophelia's car broke down on the way home from practice. It was the early days of widespread mobile phones and hers sat on the passenger seat, with an unsent message, telling her husband that the engine had cut out. There was a single footprint – hers – in the mud at the side of the car but nobody saw Ophelia alive again.

Six days later, her body was found in the woods, around a mile from where her car was discovered. As with the previous four women, an earring had been taken, leaving her with one small stud in her left ear.

It's because of Ophelia that Kelsey and Adele had those school gatherings two or three years in a row.

'It wasn't a usual assembly,' Adele says. 'We didn't have to sit on the floor and they'd set up all these chairs. They broke us off into smaller groups and invited anybody to talk about their worries.'

We're still underneath the bus stop but the laughter has gone from the women, and their food hasn't been touched in a minute or so.

'They talked a lot about safety in numbers,' Kelsey says. 'Find a friend and stick with that friend until you're both in a taxi, or both home – that sort of thing. They told us to guard our drinks.'

'I remember one of the police officers saying we should make proper plans and tell people where we were going and what time we were going to leave.'

The pair exchange a glance and it's easy to see how much this message has stuck. 'They never told us not to go out, or not get drunk, that sort of thing. It was all about staying safe when we did.'

The initiative was a joint plan between the local education authority and the police. Despite criticism that it was glorifying bad behaviour, those safety briefings ran through local schools across six years. A generation of women such as Kelsey and Adele still remember the core parts.

'Have fun,' Kelsey says, with a hint of a smile – and she's not saying what most would assume. The pair repeat back the acrostic in perfect harmony.

'HAVE
A PLAN
VIGILANCE AND
EYES ON DRINKS
FRIENDS LOOK OUT FOR FRIENDS
U FIND SAFETY IN
NUMBERS'

'We thought it was silly at the time,' Adele says. 'But I guess we both remember it, so it did its job.'

As if to reinforce the final line, Kelsey stands and waves towards a passing car. Her boyfriend has come to pick up the pair of them, all in the name of having a plan and finding safety in numbers.

That joint initiative was, in part, put together by Detective Inspector Kieron Parris. He gave the first set of talks himself, though concluded quickly the sessions would be better if they were delivered by women.

'We had a full-time safeguarding officer from the council working with us on the material,' he tells me later in the week. He's a tall man with a presence that's hard to define. There's a calm authority as he speaks, the sort of tone that would easily have a person believing everything is going to be fine, simply because he's said it.

'We wanted input from as many people as possible, so head teachers helped, plus some of my own team. The starting point for everything was that there was no point in trying to teach abstinence. Young people are going to enjoy themselves. It was the same in my day. Pretending that doesn't happen wasn't going to help anyone.'

Statistics can be used to prove or disprove more or less anything – but one thing is abundantly clear. The HAVE FUN seminars did not stop the Earring Killer.

That, in itself, does not make them a failure. The rate of other assaults in Sedingham and the surrounding area fell by around thirty-five per cent across a three-year period. Correlation and causation aren't the same thing – but the plan's architects, such as Kieron Parris, are keen to point to that statistic as proof of the scheme's worth.

And maybe he has a point – except it's hard to declare any sort of success given what happened next.

FIFTEEN

After the talk with Kieron, I return to Dad's house and continue looking for the jewellery box I know isn't there. I wanted to find it before to somehow prove Mum was telling the truth – but now it's about my own credibility.

I sit in the garage and use voice notes to record myself telling Faith that I need her to know I love her. It sounds corny, and I know I won't send it. Except, when I play that voice note and then the one I recorded from Mum's tape, it's hard not to see that Kieron has a point. Or *thinks* he does.

The two recordings sound so much like one another that I have to tell myself I'm not my mother. I thought I was finally unburdening myself by talking to Nicola's dad but there's a decent chance I've made things worse. Kieron will likely check in with Liam to make sure I'm still going to the AA meetings. At the beginning, it was part of my probation. I'm past that now – but, considering he went out on a limb for me, that doesn't mean Kieron won't be checking up.

I fill a couple of bin bags with stuff to take to the tip, although it never quite feels as if I'm putting much of a dent in the mountain of stuff. I do find a couple of my old school folders, that are crammed with various essays and test papers I must have kept. I spend a short while skimming through those, before stumbling across the old HAVE FUN flyer that was given to all girls in my year. That was at the height of the mania around the Earring Killer, a decade and a bit before Mum says she discovered the person's identity.

The folder goes into a black bag but I put the flyer to one side, while I continue emptying more of Dad's junk into the trash pile. It's as I'm questioning why he has kept a bag of sawdust that the doorbell sounds. I head through the house and open up to find my daughter standing there.

'I saw you on Find My Friends,' she says, as I let her inside. 'You said you might be here.'

I close the door and follow my daughter through to Dad's kitchen. 'There's not much in the fridge,' I say.

'I ate already.'

I ask about college, which gets as much of a response as ever. 'It was fine' covers more or less everything. So much has happened in the past few hours, that I forget to ask about the older woman. It's Faith who brings it up.

'Did you see my photo?'

'The silver car?'

'Yeah, there was this weird woman who was following us. It was only when she pulled away that I thought she looked a bit like Grandma.'

I check the photo on my phone but it's blurry and the glare is too strong to make out much of anything.

'You didn't say "follow" in your text,' I say.

Faith is going through the cupboards and pulls out a packet of unopened custard creams. 'I didn't know anyone ever ate these,' she says.

'Good job you already ate then.'

She grins at me. 'Maybe "following" is the wrong word. We were outside the theatre, walking towards the main union building. Then Shann noticed there was this silver car behind us. It was going really slow and Shannon reckoned there was someone inside watching us. We went across the car park but then, when we got to the other side and looked across, the car had parked on the road. A woman had got out and was taking photos.'

'Of you?'

'I don't know. We were a bit far away by then.'

It does sound as if it could be a misunderstanding – except for the fact I also saw an older woman with a small silver car who was possibly taking photos of my dad's house.

'Why did you think it looked like your gran?' I ask.

'Dunno. I was looking through some of those photos you sent me at the weekend, so maybe she was on my mind. We were doing improv in class for how we'd react if a long-lost relative turned up. It was weird.'

After Dad died, Faith asked if I'd send her some pictures of her grandparents, so it does explain that she has a visual reference. That doesn't mean this woman was my mother, though. More likely wishful thinking on Faith's part, prompted by Dad's death and the coincidence of the long-lost relative improv.

I decide not to tell my daughter that I saw a similar vehicle earlier in the day.

Faith continues going through the cupboards, though I've already cleared anything that had been opened.

'Didn't Granddad have any real food?' Faith asks.

'He thought rice was exotic, so not really.'

Faith lives off a diet that mainly seems to be eggs and yoghurt. It feels like the sort of thing someone on social media has recommended.

'Can Shannon come over tomorrow?' Faith asks, as she reaches Dad's largely empty fridge.

'Of course.' I wait, and when the explanation doesn't come: 'Problems?'

'The usual. Her mum's arguing with Shannon's stepdad 'cos he keeps getting home late from work. She's convinced he's having an affair.'

Faith closes the fridge and then props herself on the counter. I think for a moment, largely about Nicola and her jealousy. She scared off her first husband, Shannon's father, for the same reason. She seemingly finds it impossible to trust any of her partners.

'Do *you* know if Ethan's having an affair?' Faith asks.

'How would I know?'

'Maybe Nicola had said something to you?'

'We don't really talk about things like that – but you know what she's like. Probably thinks he is.'

Faith swings her legs and shrugs. 'I quite like him. Shannon does too but she says her mum is trying to get him to give up being a personal trainer and take a proper job somewhere.'

'What does she mean by "proper"?'

'Something that means he's not visiting people in their homes...'

We catch each other's eye because we've had conversations about this before.

'Is there anything I can do around here...?' Faith asks.

I know that type of phrasing, because we've all been seventeen once. Offering to do something with a clear indication we'd prefer not to. But there's something I need to tell her.

'I talked to the police earlier,' I say.

'Why?'

'About the gun you found yesterday. They said your grandmother's fingerprints are on it.'

My daughter's legs stop swinging. 'What d'you mean?'

'I'm not sure. They didn't seem to know what it meant, and I definitely don't. At some point, Mum must've held that gun.'

Faith has a self-confidence I'm not sure I've ever had. It probably comes from having a solid group of friends over a course of years. That, or her father. She's concerned now, as she stares unmovingly for a couple of seconds. 'I don't get it.'

'I'm not sure anybody does.'

'But when would she have left it there?'

'I don't know. Apparently, fingerprints can stay on something a long time. It could've been a while back.'

Faith thinks on this for a second and I know what's coming. 'So maybe I did see her...?'

'I don't think that's possible, love.'

Faith blows a small raspberry with her lips to say that she's not convinced – except I don't know what to feel, either.

Somehow, without much of a conversation, we end up in the garage together, filling bin bags with junk. It's the first time anyone's helped – and there's a few moments of bonding as we laugh about the state of the things Dad kept. There are eight fly swatters, a box of rusting springs, a flattened rugby ball that has a slash in the side. Faith talks about the plans for her course's overseas trip, dropping unsubtle hints that she'd like a few new outfits – but it's nice to have a conversation that doesn't have me second-guessing myself. We fill so many bags that there are too many for the car and, for the first time since I started, it feels as if there's been some progress made in clearing the space.

There are even odd minutes here and there in which I switch off from Mum's tapes. Where I enjoy being a mother, and marvel at how grounded my daughter is.

Faith finds an old calendar from 1996 and asks why 'milk due' is written every other Monday. I tell her we used to have a person deliver milk each day and we'd pay cash every couple of weeks. My daughter is baffled by this and we go through the rest of the months together. As well as milk deliveries, 'Eve badminton' is written in a series of squares from the start of the year until Easter.

It's another memory that had been lost. 'I had badminton lessons twice a week,' I say, remembering.

'Does that mean you were good?' Faith asks.

'I doubt it.'

Except, as I think about those sessions at the leisure centre, the shuttlecocks stuck high in the webbing of the wall, the way most of us could barely get the damned thing over the net, I realise it wasn't my choice to go. It was the time mentioned on the tape, where Dad had left and I was living alone with Mum. She told me I had to get a hobby, so she'd have time to do things around the house. That's why I spent around three months playing badminton badly.

Which means this calendar includes the three months or so that Dad had walked out on us to live with someone named Harriet.

But now I have a year and month, one more thing occurs. I've spent the day reading on and off about the Earring Killer. There were peaks and troughs of attacks: short bursts of a few kills in a row, and then years of nothing.

And the Earring Killer's first murder happened at the exact time Dad had moved out.

THURSDAY

SIXTEEN

I stop on the way into work to talk to Dina for a minute. She looks tired but I don't say as much. She's waiting for Owen to get in and annoyed that he's late. In the office itself, I find Mark sitting in my chair. The company owner is going through the drawers of my desk and doesn't stop when I walk in. He barely even looks up.

'Why have you got so many staples?' he asks.

'What do you mean?'

He picks up a box of staples and places it on the desk between us. 'You've got about thirty of these.'

I'm baffled for a moment, partially because it's so early but also because I don't think I've ever given stationery a second thought.

'I think they all came as a bulk thing,' I say. 'I don't think I ordered them.'

He seems unconvinced but returns the box to my drawer and then leans back in my seat. 'What time do you call this?' he asks.

I look up to the clock above the desk, confused by the question. My day doesn't start for another three minutes, so I'm early.

And then I remember he asked me to come in fifteen minutes ahead of time for a chat.

'I'm so sorry,' I say. 'I've got a lot on with Dad. It's his funeral tomorrow.'

Mark nods along but his gaze is narrow. 'How were the police yesterday?' he asks, although it doesn't sound like a friendly enquiry.

'It's complicated,' I say. 'My daughter found a gun in the woods the day before. She's underage, so they needed to talk to me.'

Mark's still nodding but it's with a clenched jaw and a *we-need-to-talk* face. 'I've been meaning to have this conversation for a couple of weeks,' he says. 'It's never been a good time what with your, uh... issues and everything.'

It takes me a moment to realise that by 'issues', he means my father dying.

'What do you mean?' I ask, hoping I've misread things.

'The mistakes, Eve. That's what I mean. Like yesterday with the engineer you forgot to call. Or last week with the inventory update you forgot to do. The email I sent about a client wanting an extra storage unit. I could go on but this morning is another example of your patchy timekeeping – just like yesterday.'

'I'm not late today,' I say.

'I asked you to come in early.'

'I had to drop off my daughter.'

'You're still late – and that's after taking off most of yesterday.'

'The police *asked* to see me!'

Mark sits forward in the chair, almost overbalancing but just about catching himself. 'It's not just one day.'

'My daughter had pneumonia at the start of the year. I needed that time to be with her.'

'And that meant I had nobody covering the front desk for a whole week. If we survived that, and we got through yesterday, what exactly do we need you for? I need someone who'll come to work, who—'

'I *do* come to work.'

I feel that old anger rising. Faith was on a ventilator overnight and in hospital for two days, before being released. She was fine in the end but that isn't the point. I still returned to work earlier than I should have – largely because of the multiple texts Mark was sending every day. I ended up being forced to take that as holiday – which was my only time off until Dad died, where I had two more days.

Mark is silent but that makes it worse. I can't stop myself: 'It's not my fault you bought the storage place next door, fired the manager, and gave almost all his responsibilities to me.'

It's been on my mind but it's never come out until now. Mark folds his arms and it's so clear where he's going next.

'I took a chance on you,' he says. 'Most people would've written you off after seeing that conviction on your CV. They'd have kicked you while you were down. I'm the one who took you off the scrapheap.'

There's partial truth there. I had to declare my conviction on the job application but the 'taking a chance' part is only true because he offered twenty per cent less than the salary that had been advertised. It was couched under various probation periods as he outright said he'd give me a chance. That was around six years ago and, since then, there have been zero salary increases, despite the extra workload. My history has always been held over me.

'What do you want me to say?' I ask.

Mark uncrosses his arms and holds up a hand, indicating the yard beyond. 'I want to know this is still your priority –

because your attitude is catching. Owen's not turned up today either. I saw you chit-chatting yesterday on work time. Something about a tape.'

So he did overhear. I wonder how much he caught.

'Owen's nothing to do with me,' I say. 'I was asking for some advice.'

Mark rolls his eyes. He's long considered any conversation not directly related to work as needless chit-chat. He waits but I have nothing to add, so he tries again: 'I want to know that this is still your priority...'

I know what I should say. This is where I bend the knee, bite the bullet, apologise. Tell him that, yes, of course *his* business is my priority, no matter how many times he talks down to me.

That's what I *should* say.

Not today.

'My daughter's my priority,' I reply instead. 'She always has been and she always will be.'

Mark chews the inside of his cheek and I get the sense he's not entirely sure what to do. He's used to deference.

'I'm going to mark the engineer thing from yesterday as an official verbal warning,' he says. 'This morning's lateness is a second verbal warning. Anything more will be your first written warning. After that, I'll have no option other than to terminate. I suppose I hoped you – of all people – would have a little more gratitude.'

He moves around the desk about to head to his own office as I stew silently.

And then it's not so silent.

'I'm done,' I say.

Mark's at his door but turns to take me in. 'Done with what?'

'You.'

SEVENTEEN

I regret quitting my job the moment I walk out the gates. I had around thirty seconds of satisfaction at seeing Mark's face until it dawned that I have no easy way of paying the mortgage. I have some savings, but not much. Suddenly, clearing Dad's house so it can be sold has become a necessity – which is not the way I want to think about my father.

I don't necessarily have to declare my past now so much time has gone by – but I've had the same job for more than six years. I'm going to have to explain to any potential employer why I don't have a reference for that time.

What a mess.

I sit in my car for ten minutes, partially hoping Mark will follow me out to ask if I want to change my mind. I know he won't, because it would be too close to an apology, which is something he doesn't do. Not that I can complain, considering *I* could say sorry and ask for him to take me back – but I definitely won't.

Those ten minutes pass but it's impossible not to stop my mind drifting to Mum's tapes and the jewellery box she says she found. I veer from believing her to not. The conversation with my brother still sticks as well. I've not heard a thing from him since the talk yesterday and yet, as well as his dig about Jake Rowett, there was something else he said. Something that's niggling.

With no job, I find myself driving out of town, still considering calling Mark to see if he'll pick up and forgive me. Still not doing it.

The sign for the rugby club is battered and weather-worn. It's advertising the season's start in a few weeks, plus training camps for the next half-term. I pull into the dusty car park, sending a scattering of small stones skittering towards the vast expanse of pitches. Someone's on a ride-on mower in the distance but the area is otherwise empty. There are signs to stay off the pitch, then rows of advertising hoardings for local businesses.

I've been here once before. It would have been someone's baby shower, where they'd rented the function room, or possibly a christening. Something like that.

I head towards the main clubhouse, where a large banner is advertising an upcoming dinner dance. Around the back and a pair of cars are parked by a giant wheelie bin. I ignore those and follow the gravel until I reach a cottage that's largely overrun by a mangled web of ivy.

It's a long shot after so many years and yet, somehow, I know there will be at least some answers here.

A woman is watering a flower bed at the front of the house. She's wearing foam knee pads and gloves, humming to herself with her back to me as I approach. I wait, trying not to startle her – which fails, because, when she turns, she leaps back a step.

'Didn't see you there,' she squeaks.

She pulls off a glove, then lowers her glasses to peer over them.

'Eve...?'

I nod and she puts down the watering can, then takes off her other glove. 'I heard about Bruce,' she says quietly. 'I didn't want to, um… well, bother you, I suppose. I didn't know whether you knew about me.'

My father walked out on nine-year-old me to spend three months living here with this woman. It's thirty years ago and I don't let on that I only found out about it properly the day before. Perhaps it's because I used up my well of anger with Mark but I'm struck by a twinge of pity for Harriet. She must be seventy and I can almost hear the creak as she stands up straighter. She looks exhausted, as if permanently on the brink of a yawn that won't quite come.

'I appreciate you coming,' she says. 'I've been thinking about you ever since I heard.'

She looks at me so earnestly, this complete stranger, yet I know it's the truth.

'It's the funeral tomorrow,' I find myself saying. 'I was wondering if you wanted to come.'

It's not the reason I visited, yet maybe it is.

Harriet glances away and lets out a long huff, before finding a tissue in her pocket. She blows her nose and waves a hand in front of her face.

'Sorry,' she says. 'I didn't expect this. I don't want to impose on anyone.'

'It's fine. I think I've been wanting to talk to you for a while.'

Harriet nods, taking the lie at face value. She gulps, then wipes her hands on her sides, before nodding towards the club house. 'They do lunch every day,' she says. 'I'm life president, and it's not worth having perks unless you use them. Do you fancy something to eat? I know it's early.'

She's right about that but I didn't eat breakfast and my gurgling stomach reminds me as much. Harriet takes a few steps, then remembers the knee pads. She crouches to remove them and then ekes her way up. After that, she leads the way towards the club, then uses a key to open the back door. We end up in a large reception room with floor-to-ceiling bay windows that overlook the pitches. A man is mopping a floor on the far side but he stops and checks his watch.

'You're early,' he says.

'I've got a friend today,' Harriet tells him. 'Is it too early for food?'

He tells her everything's fine, then takes a menu from the bar and passes it across. Harriet tells him she'll have the usual, so he offers an enthusiastic 'of course', before heading to the coffee machine. Meanwhile, Harriet leads me to the small table in the centre of the window, giving us a sweeping view.

'This is the president's table,' she says, and there's a whisper of glee at the pomposity of it all. She waves a hand towards the pitches. 'My dad owned all this land back in the day. He sold it to the rugby club for a pound when they were looking for a site. It was all history for him because he grew up in a Welsh mining town. They made him life president but he insisted it was a hereditary title, which is why this is all mine.'

She laughs a fraction and catches my eye, wanting me to know it's a joke, that she doesn't take herself this seriously. I smile as she points to the menu. 'I always have the club sandwich. Brian's the bar manager and makes it as good as anyone.'

As if on cue, Brian reappears with a black coffee that he places in front of Harriet. He asks what I want, so I say I'll have the same as Harriet – and then he heads back to the coffee machine for round two. We sit quietly for a moment, watching the guy on the mower, who's ploughing a straight line widthways across one of the pitches.

'If it's any consolation,' she says, quieter now, 'I know it probably isn't – but your father and I really did have feelings for one another. Nothing happened the way I wanted it to. I told him not to leave you, or your mum. I kept saying it but him and me weren't this spur-of-the-moment thing. Your dad would say he and Angela were incompatible. She was outdoorsy, he wasn't. Other things too. I said he couldn't walk out on his family. I really did tell him.'

Outdoorsy was the least of it, I'm sure.

Harriet cuts off because Brian returns with a second coffee for me. He almost drops the cup as he lowers it, then apologises, before heading to the kitchen. There's a different type of quiet now because Harriet was right about one thing: it isn't a consolation. Nobody wants to hear their parent walked out on them to be with another person. I'm thinking of Mum and the way she told nine-year-old me that Dad was working away: how she kept that up for months, knowing he was on the other side of town.

'I don't think Mum deserved that,' I say carefully, except there's no disagreement from the other side of the table.

'Neither did my husband from the time. I'm not trying to justify anything – and I would change almost everything that happened. I suppose I wanted you to know that it wasn't a pointless fling. There were feelings.' She waits and there's a mawkish melancholy between us because we've both lost the same person, even though he meant different things to each of us.

'Your mum didn't want to poison him against you,' Harriet adds, even quieter. 'I know he appreciated that. I think we all knew things would go back to how they were after a while.'

If it hadn't been for seeing Mark earlier in the day, I know there'd be a fury I would struggle to contain, but, in the moment, I'm limp and defeated by it all. Dad walking out happened thirty years ago and almost everybody involved is now dead.

'Did you have any kids at the time?' I ask.

'No. I never could. I suppose when I'm gone, the club will need a new president.'

She doesn't laugh this time and the swathe of lush green pitches suddenly has a bleakness that wasn't there before.

Brian is suddenly back, two plates of sandwiches that he places in front of us. He checks that everything else is fine and then returns to mopping the floor in the furthest corner. Neither Harriet or I reach for the food. I still haven't brought up the real reason I came.

Dad walked out at almost the exact time of the first Earring Killer murder. If Mum is telling the truth in her tapes, there's a link from my family to the killer somewhere.

Not that I can say as much so openly.

'What was Dad like when he was with you?' I ask.

Harriet shifts for the first time in a while, probably wondering why I'm asking. She looks to me momentarily but then turns back to the field. 'I think he and I both knew it was a mistake,' she says. 'You don't want to know specific details but it took a bit of time for us both to admit it. He missed you and there were a couple of days he went to the school. He'd watch from a distance as your mum picked you up—'

'Really?'

The older woman catches my eye again, wanting me to know this is true. 'He really did love and miss you. Maybe he missed your mum as well? He used to go out in the evenings and sometimes didn't come back. I wondered if he'd returned to you but then he'd be back the next morning, saying he'd been out walking all night, thinking things over.'

It's not what I wanted to hear and I almost have to tell her to stop. The idea of Dad disappearing for entire nights at the same time as the Earring Killer chose his first victim is beyond comprehension. I figured there'd be a coincidence of timing that could be cleared up with this talk. Instead, everything is much worse.

Harriet notices because she leans in. 'Are you OK?'

I tell her I am but my mind is racing far away from this

rugby club. On the tape, Mum said she found a jewellery box filled with earrings – but it was unclear from where she'd taken it. I assumed she meant somebody else's house but was she talking about something Dad had hidden away?

It's impossible.

'Your brother came over a few times,' Harriet says. 'He'd sit and talk to your dad. I think your father enjoyed the company because he was feeling cut off.'

That explains how Peter knew where Dad had gone. He'd have been nineteen, maybe twenty at the time.

Harriet pauses a moment, perhaps considering whether to say something. 'I asked your brother to leave one time because he was ordering me around in my own house, being really disrespectful.'

'How do you mean?'

'A woman's place, and all that. Seemed to think I should be cooking for him, waiting on him, clearing up after him. That sort of thing. I never saw him after that. Your dad said he agreed with me but he already felt alienated. He didn't say anything to your brother and just let me deal with it. I think that was probably the final straw for us, really. If Bruce couldn't stick up for me, what was the point of it all?'

It's something that feels both surprising and not. Entirely in keeping with my experience of Peter, of course. I've often wondered if he's a nob in general, or only when it comes to women. It's almost heartening that it isn't only me he has a problem with. An equal-opportunity nob.

The sandwich is untouched but I should probably go. I came hoping for some sort of exoneration, or explanation of a timing coincidence. Instead, I have more questions than answers.

There's no ill-will towards Harriet, not really. She's welcome to come to the funeral but, at the same time, I don't think I want to be around her.

The lie is ready and perhaps I should be worried at how easily it comes. 'I found a jewellery box in Dad's things,' I say. 'There are flowers engraved on the side but I don't think it's Mum's. I wondered if it might be yours?'

There's a moment in which I think Harriet's about to say that it *is* hers. That she's been searching for it all these years. That I'll have to admit that Dad took it. Except she shakes her head. 'I don't think I've ever owned one,' she says. 'Let alone lost one. I wasn't particularly precious about that sort of thing.' She holds up her left hand, showing a single ring on her index finger. 'This is the only jewellery I ever wear. I never saw the point – but thank you for thinking of me. I hope you find the owner.'

So that's it. No link between Harriet and the Earring Killer, assuming she's telling the truth.

She reaches for her sandwich as I stare out towards the pitches and the mower once more, trying to think of the politest way to leave.

As if on cue, my bag buzzes, so I retrieve my phone. There's a text from Dina and I assume she's just found out that I quit. She'll be asking what happened, and I'll have to decide whether I want to feed the gossip mill.

Except her text isn't about that at all.

Have you heard about Owen?

My first thought is that he has my tape. I'm halfway through a reply, asking what's happened, when Dina's name appears on screen. I answer the call but barely manage to say 'hello' before her tearful voice cuts me off.

'He's dead,' she says.

EIGHTEEN

Police tape stretches across the gateposts of Owen's house. Neighbours are milling on the pavements and between the parked cars, pointing and talking – which isn't a surprise when a pair of police cars are blocking the street.

That's the thing when something terrible happens in a small town. People do put down their phones; they do gather and talk. Everyone wants reassurance together that only other people can bring.

Dina is sitting on a wall across the road from Owen's place. She looks up as I approach and practically hurls herself at me. This is not the brash, confident woman from the office. 'I didn't know who else to call,' she says. 'I was supposed to be on a job with him today but he didn't show up. He wasn't answering texts, or calls – which is really unlike him.'

She stops and fishes for a tissue to blow her nose. When she can't find one, she stands and heads to the work van that's parked a little further along the street. When she returns, her eyes are dry. We sit and watch as an officer diagonally across the street sits on a wall and stretches blue net covers over his shoes.

He then ducks underneath the police tape, heading towards the house.

'Owen lives in the downstairs flat,' Dina says. 'I've picked him up a few times. I thought I'd come by to see why he wasn't answering his phone but, by the time I got here, the police had already blocked the road. One of the neighbours said they'd found a body and I was talking to the officer, telling him my friend lives in the flat. That's when they said...'

She tails off and I take her hand. She squeezes back, blinking away more tears. I know why she called. Mark is the macho face of the company and he's designed it in his own image. Dina has to be tough on the surface, or he'd walk all over her. But this is the real her – and I bet Owen was well aware of it as well.

'I was only with him yesterday,' Dina says, as she releases my hand.

'Does anyone know what happened?'

A shake of the head. 'Someone said carbon monoxide but I think they were guessing.'

We watch as a uniformed police officer tries to shoo away a young woman who's either taking photographs, or filming. There's a stand-off as he tries to block her view while she argues that she pays his wages. I'm consumed by my own selfishness – because Owen has my tape. I have some of it as a voice note on my phone but nowhere near all of it. I wonder if it's in his flat, or his work bag. His car, maybe his work locker? How can I find out? How can I get it back?

None of which I can ask, of course, because a young man we know has died.

'I wonder if his mum knows,' Dina says, largely talking to herself. 'Would they have told her yet?'

The officer who recently entered the flat re-emerges and removes the booties. He checks something on his phone and then talks to the man who'd previously been arguing with the young woman. She's gone but the man turns in a semicircle, before pointing toward Dina. We both stand as the first officer approaches, a slim, grim smile on his face.

'Are you Dina?' he asks, talking to me.

'That's me,' Dina says and he shifts his gaze towards her.

'Are you the one who worked with him?'

'We were supposed to be on a job together today. That's our van.' Dina nods along the street towards the vehicle. The officer clocks it with a nod. He's in a suit, so a detective.

'When did you last see him?' he asks.

'Yesterday. We work together most days and we had a pair of jobs out near Gatacre.'

The officer has a pad out now and writes something with another nod. 'Can you come and talk to my sarge?' he asks. 'It's this way.'

He doesn't wait for a reply, stepping away from the kerb and back towards the flat. 'Can she come?' Dina asks, pointing to me. 'Eve worked with him too. I don't think I want to do this alone.'

The detective scans me up and down and then says it's fine, before taking us over the road, underneath the police tape and down a set of steps to the front of Owen's flat.

I'm struggling with the bemusement of it all – which isn't helped as it turns out the 'sarge' is someone I know only too well. It was around twenty-four hours ago that I was sitting with Detective Sergeant Cox in the canteen of the police station. She's as surprised as I am, rocking away a fraction and letting out a confused 'Eve…?' when she sees me. With Dina and the other detective, four of us are huddled on the doorstep – but the first officer soon steps away, leaving only us three.

'What are you doing here?' Cox asks.

'Owen was my workmate,' I say. 'Dina works with him directly and she called me.'

Sergeant Cox turns her attention to Dina, asking the same

questions her colleague had before. Owen had been at work the day before, he'd not shown up in the morning, and hadn't replied to any messages or calls. Cox makes her own notes but it's impossible to miss the sideways glimpses in my direction. How am I tied up in all this, after already arousing her suspicions yesterday?

'Do you know if Owen was having any problems?' Cox asks, talking to Dina.

'I don't think so. I was with him all day yesterday in the van. I think he said he was playing five-a-side in the evening.'

That gets a nod, as if Cox already knows this. 'There's a post on his Instagram about the football,' she says. 'We're trying to track down anyone he might've played with.'

'I don't think I know anyone on his team.'

Cox writes something on the pad.

'What happened?' Dina asks. 'Someone said carbon monoxide...?'

The sergeant lowers the pad and glances past us, up the stairs. There's nobody there. 'This isn't official yet,' she says. 'There'll be an autopsy, plus we're still tracking down family members. We've got a phone number for his mother but nobody's answering, so we've sent someone to the house...' She tails off, then checks over her shoulder towards the flat, before apparently making a decision.

'I need your discretion here,' she says, looking between the pair of us.

'I'm not going to tell anyone,' Dina says. 'I've already told the office I'm taking the day off.'

I immediately wonder who she spoke to, given I'm not at the office. Somehow I keep making things about me, which is when I realise Sergeant Cox is looking in my direction. 'I won't either.'

Cox thinks for a second more and then: 'It looks very much as if Owen hanged himself.'

'No, he didn't,' Dina replies immediately.

'I'm sorry,' the officer replies. 'Like I said, there will be an autopsy but that's what it looks like.'

'I, just...' Dina's struggling, looking to me for an answer I don't have. 'I was with him yesterday,' she says. 'We were talking about the jobs we had today.'

'His landlord has a cleaner who visits every two weeks,' Cox says. 'She found him hanging from a light fitting.'

It's brutally direct but perhaps that's Cox's way. Dina's staring towards the door and there's a moment I think she might burst past the officer to see for herself.

'He wouldn't hang himself,' she says.

Cox doesn't reply, though it's hard to know what she could say.

'Are you sure?' Dina adds.

'I am really sorry to have to tell you. We are still investigating and there will be an autopsy. We've got his phone, so perhaps there'll be clues to his state of mind on there. We'll be speaking to his mum shortly, so we might get answers then. For now, we're still trying to track down who he was with last night.'

Dina waits a moment and then clicks into action. She pulls out her phone and taps the screen, before squinting at it. 'I think that's...' she says, before handing me the device.

There's a photo of a group of footballers, some kneeling at the front, others standing behind. They're sweaty and a couple look as if they're on their last legs.

'Do either of you know anyone?' Cox asks.

And I do. Because one of Owen's teammates is a *really* familiar face.

NINETEEN

Faith emerges from the theatre, a folder under her arm, bag over her back, phone in her hand. She's chatting to a guy I don't recognise – but, as soon as she sees the car, she momentarily stops with surprise. My daughter says something to the boy and, as he heads in one direction, she strides towards me.

'Is everything all right?' she asks, as she slots onto the passenger seat. 'Why aren't you at work?'

I can't tell her that I'm worried, because it's hard to say why. Death suddenly feels close. Too close. My father could've been expected – but Owen wasn't that much older than Faith. One evening, he was playing football with friends; the next he's gone. When I left his flat, I had a look through his Instagram – and it's full of photos from football, or with his friends. There are drinks with his mates, plus the pride at the gardens he worked on. A trip home to his mum for a Sunday roast the other week. Sitting on his brother's sofa, watching a Wednesday night football match on TV. A normal young guy making his way through life.

And it's hard to explain all that to Faith, because she's so young.

'It's been a long day,' I say instead. But she isn't quite a child – I can tell her what happened. 'A colleague at work killed himself.'

She'd been looking to her phone but Faith lowers it. 'Oh. Why?'

'I don't know. I just figured I'd pick you up.'

Faith doesn't question this and perhaps she has a better understanding of how I feel than I give her credit for. When we get home, she lets me cook for her, even though she usually likes making her own meals. We have a constant back and forth over whether she's eating enough – but not tonight. She lets me be her mum and we eat from our laps, half watching the early evening quiz shows but not really. Instead, she tells me about her course and her friends; the prep for her overseas trip, and how everyone's looking forward to it. The students on her course are going to visit the opera, plus they have group tickets for a play. They're going to meet with a group of youngsters doing a similar course to collaborate on a joint drama piece.

I don't have a lot to say – but perhaps that's what I need. It's Dad's funeral tomorrow, which would be an issue even if it wasn't for everything else going on. It's good to hear somebody else talk excitedly and passionately about the things going on in their life.

We finish eating and Faith helps me unload and then reload the dishwasher. She asks if she can go to her room and I tell her of course.

That leaves me in the living room by myself, listening to the quiet, wondering how many of Owen's football team have been spoken to.

Did Owen *really* kill himself? I know depression is a chemical imbalance, that it's unpredictable and can be hidden, yet wouldn't there be a sign somewhere?

This is the real reason I picked up Faith, even if I've not been able to say it out loud.

What if Owen was killed *for* the tape?

It's hard to know who could've done it – but Mark overheard when I gave Owen the cassette yesterday. I also told Kieron about it, and he said he was going to talk to some of his old colleagues. Owen could've told anyone himself, plus I think I told my brother about it. That's potentially a lot of people who knew.

It's paranoia.

But what if it isn't?

'If they say I'm missing, I'm not. I've been killed – and I need you to know that I love you.'

I listen to my voice note recording of Mum's tape but there's a hiss and a scratchiness that makes it even harder to make out than the original.

I've still not even started to process Dad walking out at the exact same time as that first Earring Killer murder. Even Harriet said he'd disappeared for nights at a time. A few more hours and he'll be ashes.

He was a long way from perfect but it was always reassuring to know he was on the other side of town. I could pop in, make him a cup of tea, listen to him talk about the day's crossword clues. Hearing him complain about the nonsense he'd seen on Facebook was annoying a month ago but I'd crave it now.

What is the connection from my parents to the Earring Killer?

I'm so certain there's something and find myself skimming through old articles. There's not as much as I'd expect, though perhaps that's because the most recent killing was thirteen years ago. I sometimes have to remind myself that not everything ended up online in the late-nineties and noughties.

There's a book by someone named Vivian Mallory that I

don't own and have never read. It was out ten years ago and I remember a debate online about whether it was in bad taste. There's an article from her in *The Guardian*, with an extract of the book. She explains how the first victim was someone named Carly. She worked at Prince Industries and left to walk home, and then—

I stop because I recognise that business name.

Did Dad work there for a while? He did a few jobs, usually around driving, but I don't really remember him being in a factory. I don't think my brother ever had a manual job either – but if not them...

Then I remember.

I've read the name of the factory hundreds of times – because every time my boss annoyed me, I visit the company website to remind myself of the bio he wrote for himself.

Mark Dixon is one of life's success stories. Self-made and self-effacing, Mark is a dreamer, who started his burgeoning career on a production line at Prince Industries.

CARLY

Extract from *The Earring Killer* by Vivian Mallory, © 2015.

The Prince Estate is a modern-day maze. Boxy red-brick houses have been built on top of one another, each with a postage-stamp back garden, plus a single parking spot at the front. The surrounding roads are dotted with vehicles parked in front of signs saying no ball games are permitted. Each cramped block of houses is linked to another by a complex web of cut-throughs and alleys that all look the same.

Or perhaps it's just me. An outsider's take.

I pass a small green scarred by motorbike wheel marks, then check my phone to make sure I'm on the right street.

Lorna Smilie opens her front door with a quick glimpse to her watch to make the point that I'm five minutes late – although she's too polite to say so. She's in jeans and a green-grey top, a woman of leisure since retiring a few years back. She does the pocket pat – keys, wallet, phone – then closes her front door and leads me back to the green.

'This is where the factory entrance was,' she tells me, indicating the nearest block of houses. 'I worked there thirty years.

When they closed the factory, I ended up buying one of the houses. My wife says I couldn't quite leave the place – and I guess she was right.'

Lorna was the only female foreman at Prince Industries though lost her job when the site was closed in the early 2000s. The factory produced shoes on this very spot. It's the sort of manufacturing that rarely exists in modern times: certainly not so close to a town centre. Prince Industries still survives to a degree – but the shoemaking has been outsourced, with the product now imported back into towns like Sedingham.

More than a hundred jobs disappeared when Prince Industries closed – Lorna's among them. She was in her early fifties, with decades of manufacturing experience. But nowhere wanted those skills. Even if there was a demand for them, there would be a new generation of workers with GNVQs and apprenticeships, who would work for less. There wasn't a large demand for a skilled woman already in her fifth decade.

Lorna and her then girlfriend downsized, to this house, while topping up her income with shifts behind the bar in the local social club. Takings were low, profit margins small, but there was just enough to get her through to retirement.

It wasn't the finish to her working life that Lorna envisioned – and now, barely across the road from her front window, is a constant reminder of a life that once was.

But at least she still has hers.

One of the biggest problems with catching the Earring Killer is that police always struggled to link the victims. For a while, they were unsure which victim came first; whether a missing earring was something to do with the killer, or an accidental connection. What is not now in question is that Carly Nicholson was a victim of the Earring Killer – and likely the first.

A criminologist told me that killers, including serial killers, rarely start with a random victim. They might graduate to that – but the first victim is usually connected in some way.

Carly worked on the production line at Prince Industries, with Lorna as her direct line manager.

'It was a normal Thursday,' Lorna says. 'People would be talking about what they were going to do at the weekend, maybe even organising a night out immediately after shift the next day. Carly was meticulous about the time and never late. It's one of the reasons I liked her – she was so reliable. She was really quick to learn as well. If you showed her something once, you wouldn't need to again. I thought she was going to go a really long way, regardless of what she wanted to do.' She waits a beat. 'If I'm honest, I liked her because she was a woman, too. I reckon ninety per cent of the people on the floor were men. We had to look out for each other.'

Lorna tugs at her top, looks up to where the factory would have once been and I have the sense she does this most days. Not many people spend so much of their lives within a single one hundred metre radius.

'I was a bit jealous of her, if I'm honest,' Lorna says. 'She liked tattoos at a time when women were looked down on for such a thing. She had them on her arms and once showed me her back. They were beautiful and she had such an eye for what suited her.'

From nowhere, Lorna rolls up her sleeve to reveal a four-leaf clover on her upper arm. 'I got this because of her. I told her I really liked the way she had her own style and look. That she didn't care what people thought. She said I should just go for it, get a tattoo as well. I was older than her but always remember that talk because it was like she was the wise one. It's supposed to be us old farts telling the kids to follow their dreams and not be scared – but it was the other way around. I got this done a few months after she, well... you know.'

I do know.

Carly Nicholson was walking somewhere near the canal when she disappeared. Her story is so similar to the other victims that it's sometimes hard to distinguish between the whos, whats, wheres, and especially the whys.

She said goodbye to her workmates, then set off to walk back to her flat. The last time anyone saw her was a bus driver, who says he watched her use the zebra crossing while he waited. Carly waved in gratitude and then headed into an alley. She lived by herself but never turned up for work on the Friday.

'I knew right away there was something wrong,' Lorna says. 'She was never late. Never. Even on the odd days she was ill, she'd call the office and leave a message. It was all landlines then, so I called her flat but nobody picked up. I almost went over…'

Lorna lets the sentence slip away – but it would have already been too late.

'Her parents were on holiday,' Lorna adds. 'She didn't have a boyfriend. I suppose I've always thought about that since – because anyone who knew her would've known that. There wouldn't have been a better time.'

The police definitely considered that.

Carly was an optimal target killed at the optimal moment. The next time anyone saw her was in a shallow grave in the remote hills outside town. It was the middle of the following week and a couple walking their dog stumbled across the grim sight.

Police treated it as a murder immediately. The fact Carly was wearing just one earring was noted in the autopsy, though not a particular focus until the body of Janine Bailey was discovered four months later. By the time a third victim was killed almost exactly a year later, the words 'serial killer' were being spoken about seriously.

Lorna knew none of that at the time of Carly's disappearance, of course. 'I just couldn't get over what a waste it all was,' Lorna says. 'I assumed the police would find someone but they never did. Then there was another victim, then another. Suddenly we were all making sure everyone had a safe way home. Women would go out of their way to ask other women what their plans were, things like that. Maybe that was a positive – but nothing made up for Carly.'

We're back in Lorna's house now. It's shoes off at the door, rows of family photographs on the walls and up the stairs. A pair of comfy sofas face the television, with the window above – and the ghosts of a factory long since gone.

'I went to the funeral,' Lorna says. 'Carly doesn't come from round here. She'd moved for a boyfriend and when they broke up, she stayed around. I went to her hometown and met her mum and dad, plus loads of her old school friends. Nobody had a bad word to say about her. Her friends said she was smart and fun. They all assumed she'd end up running something, or creating something. Just one of those people who got on with everyone.'

Lorna stops, stares through the window into the invisible abyss. 'It's such a waste,' she says. 'Even now, years later, it's such a waste.'

TWENTY

It would be easier if I stayed in for the evening – but I find myself back at Dad's house. Faith and I finally made some real progress in clearing the garage the day before but there's still so much to do. It doesn't help that my brother is keen for us to sell but has no interest in doing the work that will make that happen. He knows I need the money more than he does. He can wait – I can't, especially now I quit my job.

It's just about still light outside as I continue filling bags with rubbish. It feels as if my mind works clearer in Dad's house.

Poor Carly Nicholson was the first victim of the Earring Killer, back when I was nine years old. She worked in the same place as Mark at the time, when he'd have been in his early twenties. It's a weak connection – but I discovered that just hours after seeing him in that football photograph, standing behind Owen.

Two people, both dead, decades apart, but there's a chance Mark could've been the last person to see the pair of them.

That's more of a link than any of the victims have to my

father. Because one thing is for certain. Despite my curiosity over when he left home, and what he was doing on those nights he told Harriet he was out walking, he couldn't have had anything to do with whatever happened to Owen.

I clear more of Dad's things, wondering if there's a link from Mark to any of the other victims. He overheard me talking to Owen about the tape, and I can't remember whether I mentioned 'Earring Killer'.

Did I get Owen killed?

It's hard to ignore the thought that if I'd kept the cassette to myself, he'd still be around. The guilt and grief overwhelm for a moment. A lump in the throat, itching behind the eyes, so many blinks to try to control myself. Nothing is certain and I need to push on.

I'm on a roll: eight bags filled and it's close to the point where the only things left in the garage are items that might actually be worth something. It feels symbolic with Dad's funeral only hours away. My phone pings and I assume it's Faith, asking either when I'm going to be home – or if I can pick up something for her on the way back.

I almost jump because the name on the screen is the person I've spent the last hour obsessing over. It's as if he's been reading my mind from afar.

Drop in ur keys 2moz

It takes a second read for me to realise I still have a set of keys for the gates of both of Mark's businesses. On the rare occasion he's off, it's me who opens up the landscaping yard, plus the storage office next door. I rarely have to use them and they're in the bottom of my bag.

The last thing I want, especially now, is some sort of confrontation with my former boss. For one, it's Dad's funeral tomorrow – but, second, I'm in such a frame of mind that I can see myself either accusing him of murdering Owen, or falling to my knees and begging for my job back. I'm not sure whether I can trust myself at the moment. I try a couple of possible replies, but nothing comes out right. Then I figure I can drive to the office, put the keys through the mailbox and leave it at that.

I finish filling another bag and then drag everything to the front of the garage, ready to take to the tip. That done, I cross through the front of the house and lock the front door. I'm about to get into my car when the hairs on the back of my neck rise. I stop, standing straighter and turning to take in the street. The sky is a bluey purple, and neighbours are starting to close their curtains. There's someone in an upstairs window across the street, though they aren't paying me any attention.

Then I spot the small silver car.

It's parked half-a-dozen vehicles along the road, slotted underneath a different streetlight. The same car I saw here yesterday; likely the same one Faith said was following her near the college.

The one she speculated could be being driven by her grandmother.

I move across to the pavement, half slotted in behind a bush as I peer along the street properly, trying not to make it obvious. As far as I can tell, there's nobody inside the vehicle, nor anyone on the road. I move around a parked car and cross the deserted road, then start walking towards the silver vehicle.

I'm a couple of car lengths away when a woman strides purposefully from the nearest alley. She's holding a phone, the screen lit, as she plops her bag on the car bonnet and starts to hunt for something.

She hasn't noticed me but Faith was right about her appearance. She's likely mid-sixties, with whitish-silvery hair in a bun. There's a similarity that's hard to define yet difficult to dismiss. I'm a few paces away when the woman finds her car keys with a satisfied sigh. She blips the fob to open the car and then turns to see me standing in the shadows.

The word is out of my mouth before I know what I'm saying.

'Mum?'

TWENTY-ONE

The woman is resting on her car door but angles towards me. 'Pardon?'

I step nearer, holding my palms out at my side, no threat to anyone.

'Sorry,' I say. 'I thought I might know you...'

It's not my mother – but there is a similarity – even down to the way the other woman dumped her bag on the bonnet to go through it. Mum used to do the same on the kitchen table all the time.

'Are you the owner of number twenty-seven?' she asks, managing to neatly sidestep the fact I called this stranger 'Mum'.

I reply with an instinctive 'no', before I realise that I kind of am. 'Jointly,' I add quickly. 'My brother and I are waiting for the probate to go through.'

The woman closes her car door and starts hunting through her bag again. She finds a business card that she passes across. 'Lovely to meet you. I'm Mary,' she says.

I have to squint to make out the card in the gloom – but

'Mary Edgars, Estate Agent' is printed in neat type across the centre.

'You're an estate agent?' I say, somewhat needlessly.

'Yes, and I'm sure I can help you out. I hope you don't mind, but a friend on the street told me that number twenty-seven was going to be empty and might go to market. I've got good news: there's loads of demand around here at the moment. The primary school at the end of the road got a good Ofsted report. I've got at least four families who'd love to offer if number twenty-seven's going to be available.' She smiles brightly.

I look to the woman, then the card, trying to put the pieces together. The familiarity with my mother ended the moment this other person started to speak. Mum could be rambling and hesitant but Mary is brusque and confident.

'Were you at the college yesterday?' I ask.

Crinkles appear in her forehead. 'How'd you know that?'

'I thought I saw this car...'

There's a sort of truth there – and Mary follows my gaze to her vehicle, before looking back to me. 'It might've been me. I was taking photographs for one of my clients. I'd come back here this evening to see if there was anyone home. I did put a card through the door.'

I had left off the lights in the main house, only using one in the garage – so this sounds possible. I'm not sure how I missed the card, though.

Mary waits a moment and then: 'So you and your brother will be joint owners...?'

My first instinct is to tell her to get lost. My father hasn't even had his funeral yet and this ambulance chaser is busy trying to sell his house from under him.

And yet... this *would* be a great family home, not least for the school at the end of the street. There's a park barely five minutes away, plus a decent garden at the back. My brother wants rid so he can get his share of the money and I probably want that too. It's another moment in which it feels as if I should be angry and yet I just can't bring myself to be so.

'The funeral's tomorrow,' I say.

Mary touches her chest. 'My God, I'm so sorry to hear that. I don't want to impose, or push you into anything. I would never have said anything if I'd known.'

She motions to reopen her car door but I tell her it's OK.

'The house is a bit rundown on the inside,' I say. 'I've been trying to clear it but Dad kept a lot of things. There's so much.'

'I can help if you want...?'

Mary tells me this is common and she knows someone who specialises in house clearances. They'll come and collect all the bin bags, plus drag off anything else I don't want, including the furniture. No fee, apparently, although I'm sure Mary's thinking further down the line. I'm not naïve – but that doesn't mean we can't both get what we want.

We chat for a few minutes more as the sky darkens around us. It's almost heartening to talk about the house and its problems in a way that doesn't involve discussing the memories that come with it. It's bricks and paint; plaster and wallpaper. Mary says she could have the whole place emptied and redecorated within a week of me giving her the say-so. As we walk, it's impossible not to see there *is* a hint of my mum about her. It's surface in that they look somewhat alike. Or, more to the point, if Mum was still around, I can see how she might have morphed into this person.

I say none of that but listen and there's a sense of satisfaction of having a grown-up in the room. At least somebody knows what they're doing. We leave things with a promise that I'll call as Mary gets into her car and drives off. I head back to my own vehicle, where I sit and stare at Dad's house.

One week.

I can give Mary the say-so, while we wait for the probate,

and that will be the end. No more house, no more ignored texts to my brother about who's responsible for what. Mary doesn't seem the sort to over promise.

One week, and this part of my life could be over.

It feels as if a weight has lifted, even though I'm not there yet. It's only now I realise how badly I want rid of the house. There is no particular fondness as I didn't grow up here. A part of me resents the direct link my brother and I share.

One week.

I try to remember where I put my car keys, then realise they're still in my bag – along with the ones I was going to return to the landscaping firm. The suspicions I have around Mark had momentarily gone, though the cloud returns as I remove the fob with four keys from my bag. It's not only him, of course. I'm suspicious of everyone. Mum's cassette has made me paranoid.

Except Owen is dead.

It's not entirely in my head. He had that cassette and perhaps I got him killed.

The landscaping yard isn't quite on the way home, though it's not far off. The streets are quiet as night slips across Sedingham. As I arrive on the industrial estate, a single vehicle is parked further along the road, though nobody's in sight around the yard itself. It's dark, aside from a spotlight high on a pole close to the fence.

It feels wrong to stop directly outside the yard, so I leave the car on the opposite side of the street and then cross back to the secure mailbox that sits next to the main gates of Mark's landscaping firm. I'm holding the fob and keys, and reach them into the slot... except I don't let go.

Owen is dead and, despite everything DS Cox said about him killing himself, I can't get past the thought that it's my fault.

It's a bad idea, I know, yet I unlock the side gate, wincing as a rusty creak burns through the silence. It's a sign I should turn and walk away, yet the thought is with me now. It's only as I enter the yard and pull the gate closed that it occurs that this is what my mother was describing on the tape. Do I have impulse control issues? I could have left the keys but the moment I had the idea to explore Mark's office, I knew I was going to do it.

Such a bad idea.

I cross the yard, sticking to the shadows and trying to remember if the cameras actually work. There's definitely a dummy one at the front, because Mark fell out with the security company over their prices. He said the imitation would do the trick. Hopefully he was too cheap to pay for any at all.

I unlock the door of the office block and head into the gloom. The only light is a glimmer from the large spotlight outside which leaves silhouettes stretching across the office.

My old desk is as I left it and there's a momentary disappointment that, somehow, the world has continued without me. It's the same as when I have a week off: a disbelief that, somehow, my workplace hasn't crashed and burned because I've been away.

I shouldn't be here.

Except Owen is dead. Carly Nicholson is dead. Mark was possibly the last person to see them both. There has to be something here because, if not, I'm back to being suspicious of my own parents.

The door to Mark's office is slightly ajar and I push my way inside. He has a large leather office lounger, facing the wide window that offers a view of the yard. With my desk a few metres away, if the door is open, I'll often hear him in here, mumbling and criticising the people he can see. Someone's not loading a van quickly enough; a different person has spent a couple of minutes talking, instead of working. His business, his rules.

Mark's desk is a mass of receipts. There's one for KFC on top and another directly underneath for Burger King. Beneath those are pages of A4 for various personal expenses. There are two massages from this week alone; two more for petrol. I leave those, not sure what I'm looking for. As I move my arm, I nudge the mouse, and the monitor immediately glares bluey-white, asking for a password. The light illuminates Mark's bikini babe of the day desk calendar – which has already been turned to tomorrow.

I consider trying to guess his password, though quickly realise I have no idea what it could be. There are Post-it notes pinned to the monitor, though nothing with what could be a password. An earthy, slightly sweet stench comes from the ashtray, in which an extinguished cigar has been mashed.

It's all a bit 1980s blokey bloke. Almost a parody, except I've worked in the next room for years and know it's all too real.

The monitor is now lighting up more of the room, as I spot the safe tucked into the corner. There's a push-pad on the front, though I have no idea of the code. Mark's wall calendar is labelled as 'arctic foxes', though that apparently means scantily clad women wearing not very much in snowy conditions.

It's only as the monitor blinks off, leaving me in near darkness, that I realise the door of the safe isn't closed. A sliver of yellow light beams through the gap, creating a small triangle on the floor. When I pull the door open, the lock bars are engaged, as if someone's not quite pushed it fully closed before entering the code. Someone in a hurry.

I crouch, probably expecting cash, because Mark seems the type – but there's no money in the safe. At first I think there's nothing at all – but then I see a small black rectangle pushed to the side, almost hidden by the shadow.

The door creaks further open as I remove the battered canvas wallet. It's not the sort of thing a fifty-year-old cigar-chomping company owner with a two thousand word biography on his website would own.

The Velcro pulls apart with a crinkle and then I see a

driving licence slotted into the front compartment. Nobody takes a good official photo – and this isn't an exception. A pair of unblinking wide eyes stare out at me, the skin white and pale.

The eyes of a dead man.

Owen's.

TWENTY-TWO

Owen looks so young. I'd guess the photograph was taken when he was sixteen or seventeen. As I look into his eyes, I know it'll never be renewed.

A debit and credit card are slotted into the other sections of the wallet, each with Owen's name. There's no cash, though maybe he never carried it anyway.

I sit in Mark's big chair, checking each of the wallet pockets. There's a scrap of paper with Owen's address, and another with his mum's phone number – saying to call in an emergency. As well as his bank cards and driving licence, there's a crumpled photo of a shaggy brown dog sitting on the lap of a young boy I quickly realise is a twelve- or thirteen-year-old Owen.

Why has Mark got Owen's wallet?

I sit, staring at the poor man's driving licence photo, when I realise there could be an obvious answer. I saw the Instagram photo of Owen playing football the night before, with Mark on the same team. Perhaps he left his wallet behind by accident, and Mark took it for him? They don't necessarily have to be friends to play on the same team – but maybe they were outside of work, and I never knew? After Dina and I identified Mark to Detective Sergeant Cox, she said she would contact him to ask about football from the night before. Had Owen told anyone he was having problems? Did he seem down?

I wonder whether Mark told them he had Owen's wallet. Whether they have any idea he worked at the same place as the first Earring Killer victim so many years ago. If any of it matters.

It probably would have helped if I'd told Detective Sergeant Cox that Owen had my mother's cassette.

I'm not sure what to do, though sitting in an office I shouldn't be in isn't going to help. I move back to the safe, return the wallet, and push the door closed, which is when I notice something poking out from the slim gap behind. I start to pull and it takes a moment to realise it's a curled loop of twine. Not quite thick enough to be rope but stronger and heavier than it looks. I've already dropped it back into place and started towards the door when I realise what I was holding.

Cox said that Owen hanged himself.

I have no way of knowing what he used – and something like twine is always useful to have around a landscaping yard. And yet…

I don't know what to do. I could call an anonymous tip into the police but how do people realistically do that? I couldn't use my own mobile, and phone boxes haven't been a thing in a long time. Even then, I now realise my fingerprints are on Owen's wallet and his bank cards. If I somehow *did* manage to get the police out here, I could implicate myself.

I return to the safe and retrieve Owen's wallet, then drop it into my bag. I'm going to have to come up with a better idea – but that's for another time. Instead, I hurry to the door, let myself out and then re-lock it. I can still leave the keys in the mailbox, then text Mark to say I've done so. No need to let on I was in his office.

All of which would be fine – except the yard gates are somehow open. They were closed minutes before, which means someone else is here.

I get the answer a second later. There's a flash of Mark's shiny black BMW, and then his headlights glide across me.

TWENTY-THREE

I'm frozen, unsure whether to dart for the gate, hide in the shadows, or stand still. The headlights were on me for a second, maybe less, arcing wide as Mark swung the car around before pulling into his parking spot.

I daren't breathe. The car is barely five metres away, idling quietly. Mark is going to open the driver's door and ask what I'm doing here.

Except he doesn't. He's sitting in the car, phone lighting up his face as he talks to someone on speakerphone as if he's about to get booted off *The Apprentice*. His voice is muffled but the anger apparent.

I assume he was on the phone while driving, which is why he didn't spot me as the headlights silhouetted me against the office. Carefully, so carefully, I take a step backwards, edging into the shadow. One step, two – and then I'm at the side of the office, peeping around the corner towards Mark in his car. He jabs angrily at his phone, then punches the steering wheel before swearing loudly at himself.

A few seconds pass and then he opens the car door and clambers out, before slamming it with an echoing clang. Mark crunches towards the office but, just as I think he's about to head inside, he stops at the door and pulls out a vape device. He leans against the front of the building and sends a sweet, chocolatey plume of mist into the air as he pokes his phone again. It looks like he's starting another phone call and, as soon as it connects, there's no hint of a 'hello'.

'I didn't hang up, you must've done,' he says. There's a second of silence and then a furious: 'Well maybe it cut out then? I don't know.'

A pause.

'Why would you say that?' — 'Oh come off it' — 'That's 'cos you listen to your mum all the time' — 'She acts like a psycho, I told you that' — 'I didn't call your mum a psycho, I said she *acts* like one' — 'It's not the same thing. If you're a psycho then you're *always* a psycho. If you're *acting* like one, then you're temporarily one' — 'Maybe try listening, then. I didn't call you *or* your mum a psycho!'

Mark goes quiet but he's pacing outside the front door, not quite reaching the corner where I'm hiding, though not far off. There's a force to his movement, as if he's trying to stomp a hole through the ground.

When he next speaks, he's slightly calmer, though perhaps it's exasperation. 'Fine. All I'm saying is that they can't prove anything.' A pause. 'Exactly. Just tell them I was with you. We were watching TV. What's the problem?'

I strain, desperate to hear the other half of the conversation but there's nothing. Mark's stopped pacing now and is standing somewhere near the door. He sighs, almost theatrically, as if he knows he's being watched. 'We'll talk about this when I get home,' he says. 'I'm at the yard but I've got to go.'

Mark has another puff on his vape, then slips it into a pocket, before fumbling in another for keys. A few seconds later, he swears under his breath, then heads back to the unlocked car, where he scrambles inside before returning with a set of keys. As he walks, he tosses them from one hand to the other, muttering something incomprehensible under his breath as he nears the office. I'm waiting for him to go inside, so I can dash away.

Only a few seconds now. So near.

Except something cramps in my leg. It happens so fast that I have no time to think, instead acting instinctively as I shift weight from one foot to the other. A crunch of gravel booms through the silent night, just as Mark reaches the door. He stops, looks down to his feet, and then along the line of the office to where I'm huddled behind the corner.

Time slows. Time stops. And then: 'What do we have here?'

FRIDAY

TWENTY-FOUR

I roll over in bed and reach for Mum's cassette player. The cord is too short to extend from the plug socket to my dresser, so the device sits wedged half under my mattress.

Mum's voice sent me to sleep once more, and I wonder if this will ever grow old. It was a different tape, one with a month and year on the sleeve. Something I'd not tried before. Mum was talking about doing the Three Peaks Challenge, back in a time before everyone had a GoFundMe set up to do one. Outside of winter, it was somewhat common for Mum to disappear for a day by herself. She would return late in the evening, caked with dried mud, then sit in the bath. It was another interest she and Dad didn't share. Except, now I wonder whether she was doing that at all. She was a liar, after all.

I push myself out of bed and rewind the cassette, listening for the once-familiar scrapes and squeaks until it clicks off. I return the tape to its case, and then the box. There are so many more I've not started and it's impossible to ignore the exhilaration that there are so many more memories to listen through.

Even though Owen had the one I really want. Now, he's dead.

Memories swirl of the cramp in my leg and being frozen at the corner of the office block as Mark looked directly at me. Except he seemingly didn't spot me in the dark. He crouched and picked up something metal, perhaps a tool. I couldn't quite make it out given I was trying not to move. He complained to himself about his staff wasting his money – and then unlocked the office before stumbling inside. I hurried through the shadows, dumped the keys in the mailbox, and then crossed the road and drove home. It felt as if I barely breathed the entire time – which is why I put on another of Mum's tapes to send me to sleep. When she's talking about her life, there's something soothing and calm that means I can barely keep my eyes open.

I think through all that before I remember it's Dad's funeral today. Somehow, with everything that's been going on, it wasn't my first thought.

'...I need you to know that I love you.'

Mum haunts me from the voice note. I've clipped the final part to be as succinct as possible, and I play it three times in a row.

For a moment, just a moment, I *really* thought she was next to that silver car. Something about the way Mary moved; how she had her hair.

Somehow, my real mother's fingerprints were found on a gun. It's impossible not to imagine her being out there somewhere.

'...I need you to know that I love you.'

I listen to the clip a few more times and then haul myself out of bed. There's movement downstairs, and I head down to find Faith sitting in the living room, legs curled underneath herself, eating a yoghurt. She hops up as I yawn my way into the room.

'You look tired,' she says.

'Thanks for the pep talk.'

She laughs kindly but there's a moment in which I wonder whether she's going to mention how late I got in. I don't know whether she was still awake and keeping track. Either way, she's quiet on that, instead nodding towards the kitchen.

'Can I make you breakfast?'

I rub my eyes, wondering how long I was asleep. 'Is this AI or something? Where's my *actual* daughter?'

She humours me with only a gentle roll of her eyes. 'I boiled the kettle for you,' she replies. 'I was going to poach some eggs. I'm getting good at it now.'

I'm not hungry but tell her poached eggs on toast, with a cup of tea, would be perfect. Faith is delighted at this, having clearly thought this through. She pauses in the doorway. 'You were out late…?' she says.

'I was at Dad's house,' I reply – which is partially true.

Faith waits a moment, likely suspecting this isn't the entire truth. 'Are you going to be all right today?' she asks.

'I think so. You?'

'I think so.'

We stay still for a moment and then she turns and heads into the kitchen. Motherly instinct tells me to watch over her and make sure she isn't going to set fire to anything – except I remember the first time I tried to make a cup of tea for Dad. I was probably eight or nine and he stood in the kitchen doorframe, telling me I'd put too much water in the kettle, too much milk in the mugs, not left the teabag in for long enough. It still sticks, even now. She poaches herself eggs most days anyway.

I leave my daughter to it, listening as she hums and then softly sings to herself.

I don't want to be either of my parents.

Time passes and then Faith returns to the living room, with a pair of plates, then my mug of tea. She's off carbs, so no toast for her – but a pair of poached eggs sit neatly on her plate. We eat together with a melancholic silence between us. Dad's death feels so much more real now the funeral is on us.

When we're done, Faith takes everything into the kitchen and stacks the dishwasher. This is a week's worth of house chores. After, she's back in the doorway. 'Do you have anything that needs ironing?' she asks – and it's so out of character that I can't stop myself from laughing. She shows faux outrage but it only lasts a moment before she joins in.

'I'm trying to help,' she says.

I cross the room and hug her. For once, she doesn't pull away, instead cradling her head on my shoulder.

'Are you sure you're OK?' she asks.

'I should be asking you that.'

'But I'm asking you.'

I tell her I'm fine, though I'm not sure that's true. There's an ache that I don't think I ever quite had this relationship with my mother. Was it me, or her? She was obviously the adult but I don't think there was ever a time when I stopped to ask if she was OK.

When we separate, Faith pulls the hair from her face and says she's going upstairs to iron her top. I listen to her head upstairs and it's impossible not to wonder whether I should try to forget all this. Mum was an unquestionable fantasist and, though some of the things from her tapes definitely happened, there are others that didn't. Chasing what could be a lie might have got one person killed and I need my daughter to be safe.

I'm thinking of her but I'm also thinking of Owen when the doorbell makes me jump. I call up to tell Faith that I'll get it – and it's a good job I did. Detective Sergeant Cox is on the doorstep, wearing the bleakest of looks. I picture Owen's wallet, sitting in my dresser upstairs, and wonder if the officer somehow knows.

'Have you got a minute?' she asks.

'It's my dad's funeral in about four hours.'

Cox blinks at me with surprise. 'Oh. I'm sorry. I didn't know. I can come back.'

'Is it important?' I ask.

I see the conflict in the other woman. She shuffles from one foot to the other. 'Maybe.'

'Tell me.'

'We got some results back from the gun late last night,' she says.

'About Mum's fingerprints?'

'Do you remember I told you we were checking to see if it had ever been fired? Truth is, I didn't think anything would come of it. Except the gun has definitely been shot at least once.'

'When?'

The officer rocks on her heels and looks from side to side as if to make sure there's nobody else around. 'Do you remember a few years ago, there was someone shot outside a cinema? There was confusion over what happened? This was the gun that was used.'

I open my mouth to reply but just about stop myself. Because I do remember that gunshot and the confusion. I remember it so clearly because, at the time somebody was being shot *outside* the cinema, Faith and I were sitting together inside.

TWENTY-FIVE

Weddings are usually split, with different sides of the ceremony for guests of the bride and groom. I don't think funerals are supposed to be like that but, somehow, Dad's is.

My brother has monopolised one side of the hall, along with people who knew our dad when he was married the first time. The divide is unquestionably slightly older but there's also something less subtle. The suits are better tailored, the dresses nicer. Other than the front row, there's no set seating, yet that's how people have placed themselves anyway. It's not a huge crowd but there are around forty people across the two sides of the crematorium's main room. Most are people I directly invited, though a handful likely saw the notice in the paper or on Facebook.

I tug at my dress, which is uncomfortable across the shoulders. I can't remember buying it and am not sure why I picked it. Despite the funeral plans, I'd somehow forgotten myself when it came to the actual event.

'Are you all right?' Faith asks. She's demure and beautiful; and it's impossible not to sense a role reversal as she continually checks in on me. I tell her I am and she asks if it's all right to go and talk to Shannon. It is, of course, so she drifts to the side where she instantly huddles with her friend.

I'm left near the back of the hall welcoming the latecomers, listening to the drab, flat background music that Dad would have hated. He was never one for these mawkish moments. It's not that he'd hunt out happier alternatives, simply that he'd pretend such gloom wasn't happening. The room is everything he wasn't: inoffensively offensive with its bland beige.

A woman comes in who seems to know me. She says all the right things: sorry to hear what happened, hopes I'm all right, love to Faith… all that. I have no idea who she is as she trots across to Peter's side of the room and says hello to someone there. Dad once told me he'd reached the age where he only ever got invited to two things: funerals or prostate exams. 'Dunno which one I prefer,' he added.

I think of that now until I realise someone's at my side. I've not seen Nicola since the lunch with her mother. After that, she told her father she was worried about me, although I sort of expected it.

Her mum is at her side, wearing a slinky black dress as if she's off to a Halloween ball. 'Such a shame you had to rush away from lunch the other day,' she says, making it sound an awful lot like it wasn't a shame.

'How was the wine?' I ask, almost laughing as she reels slightly. She quickly slips into a smile. 'Lovely, of course. We'll have to do something again soon: the girls all together.' It's all fake, all surface. 'While I'm here, I thought I should apologise for if I came across as rude the other day,' she adds.

The classic non-apology apology. Sorry if you were offended and all that.

'It's no problem,' I reply, even though it *was*.

'Lovely,' she replies, before turning to Nicola and widening her eyes, making it very clear for whom the apology was given.

'I suppose I'll take my seat,' she adds – before trotting off to join her husband.

Nicola waits for her mum to go and then turns to me, where we share a second of acknowledgement. We both know what's just happened. 'How are you holding up?' she asks.

I nod to the woman that recently entered, who is now slotting herself onto a chair three rows from the front.

'Do you know who that is?' I ask.

Nicola angles forward and then back. 'I don't think so.'

'Me either. She knew me though.'

Nicola leans towards me a fraction. 'Might be a gatecrasher here for the free food. I can get Dad to kick her out.'

I laugh as Nicola touches my side. 'You sure you're all right?'

'I think so.'

'You said you'd been thinking about your mum...?'

I sigh, not sure I want to talk about this now. 'Maybe I'm just that age,' I say. 'You get to forty-odd and people start dying.'

There's a moment when it feels like Nicola might be about to make a joke, though she stops herself. I almost tell her to go for it. I'd prefer that to the pitied looks coming from others.

It's not the time and definitely not the place, though I don't know whether Nicola will be hanging around after the ceremony. 'Do you remember when we were at the cinema a couple of years ago?' I ask.

It's out of the blue, so Nicola's 'Huh?' is understandable.

'You, me, Shannon and Faith were there,' I say, thinking it was probably the last time we did something with all four of us together. 'When there was that shooting.'

Her eyes widen in recognition but she's still baffled as to why I'm asking about this now. 'Course I do.'

'Did you actually see the person get shot?' I ask.

She looks surprised. 'I was with you.'

I try to remember. The gunshot was before the movie

started and Nicola had definitely nicked outside for a smoke at some point. I don't know whether she was in or out when it happened.

'Are you sure you're all right?' Nicola asks, as she touches my arm.

'There's something weird about that day,' I add. 'I looked it up before I came here. Somebody was stabbed outside the cinema. The guy who did it was about to come inside – but he was shot in the arse as he was going through the doors. The bang meant everyone's eyes were on him, and everyone realised he was carrying a knife. Someone got him on the floor and someone else called 999. So whoever shot him, it worked – it stopped him. The guy with the knife has been in a secure unit ever since – but nobody ever found out who shot him.'

Nicola frowns. Maybe she knows this, maybe not. When we left the cinema two-and-a-bit hours later, there was police tape and blood on the ground. We'd missed the lot because they hadn't stopped any of the movies. It was one of those moments we weren't a part of, and yet it always felt as if we were. What would have happened had the knifeman made it further into the cinema? What if Faith had left the auditorium to go for a wee and the man with the knife had been right there? Who shot him?

'The pistol the girls found at the back of yours is *that* gun,' I say.

Nicola was seemingly about to say something else, though stops herself. 'What do you mean?'

'The guy with the knife at the cinema was shot by someone. Nobody knew who – and they still don't – but the gun used was the one Faith and Shannon found the other day.'

Nicola is open-mouthed. 'How do you know?'

'The police came round this morning.'

Nicola's 'What...?' is an understatement. She's quiet because a new couple hurry up the stairs and stop to say hello to me. I vaguely recognise them as neighbours who live a couple of doors down from the house I'm in the process of selling. We go through the usual hellos and sorries, before they take a seat on what's turned into my side.

'I don't think I understand,' Nicola says. 'The shooting was two years ago. More. How did it get to the back of my house?'

She has a point – but, unless her dad told her, she doesn't know all of it. Mum's fingerprints are on that gun and, by the time it was shot, she had been disappeared for a little over a decade. Did she *really* pull the trigger that day? Was she somehow a guardian angel, watching over Faith and me?

It feels impossible and yet.

I turn from Nicola and scan the room, wondering if Mum has somehow snuck in. Perhaps she's one of those I don't recognise. Not someone like Mary the estate agent, but a person who's reinvented herself over the last thirteen years. Weight lost or gained, different hair.

Or maybe the Earring Killer is in the room. Mum claims to have known who it was, so perhaps they're living in plain sight.

Everything feels possible and I find myself suspecting everyone.

Harriet is in the corner on my brother's side of the room, head bowed underneath a large hat. She catches my eye, then turns away. I invited my father's mistress, but no need for any of us to celebrate it. Allie Rowett is sitting on the opposite side, in the back row, a dark veil covering her face. She kept quiet when her husband assaulted me and the apology feels a little late now. Nicola's parents are sitting directly in front of her but I can't make eye contact with Kieron. I wonder whether he mentioned Mum's cassette to any of his former colleagues, or if he truly believes it's my attention-seeking voice on those tapes.

From nowhere, a man in a suit appears at our side. Nicola's husband, Ethan, looks nervously between us. 'How are you holding up?' he asks, talking to me. It's the same question on a loop.

'As well as can be expected. Thank you for coming.'

'It's not a problem. Did Nic tell you I can't hang around for the wake? I'm really sorry but I've got some appointments I couldn't cancel.'

I tell him it's fine and I appreciate the effort anyway. He smiles between us and then heads off to sit next to Nicola's father.

Nicola watches him go. It feels as if she wants to complain about his job again, though it's not that. 'How can it be the same gun?' she whispers. My friend is closer now and I can hear the uncertainty in her voice. Just like her father, she thinks I'm losing it.

'I don't know,' I say. 'The police told me.'

'Why'd they tell you? The gun was at mine.'

I realise she doesn't know about Mum's fingerprints. I haven't told her and I suppose neither the police nor her father have. I could tell her.

I shouldn't have started this conversation.

'I suppose they put my name on the file,' I say. 'Or Faith's. She called it in but she's underage.'

I don't know why I don't tell her. It doesn't feel right, somehow.

Nicola starts to say something then stops herself. 'There are sometimes hikers in the trees,' she says, although it doesn't sound convincing. She quickly adds: 'Isn't it weird the police spoke to you, not me?'

I can't answer that, not without saying Mum's fingerprints were on the gun. The more I've said over the past few days, the more trouble I've caused.

Except it's awkward. I'm still scanning the crowd, looking for my mother. She shot that gun two years ago, more than a decade after she disappeared. She knows who the Earring Killer is and has been hiding all this time.

'Eve...'

Nicola touches my shoulder again and, when I turn to her, I feel the dribble from my nose. She finds a tissue and slips it to me as I dab the red. It's been a long time since I had a nosebleed and Nicola's attentive stare is filled with worry.

'You should sit,' she says.

I don't argue and at least I'm out of the conversation I started. It's becoming increasingly harder to maintain the veneer of being in control. I turn my back, trying to clean myself up, though when I look back to the front, I realise Nicola's father has been watching. He already thinks I faked that tape, suspects I might be drinking again, now this.

Luckily, things are starting to move. The director emerges from a side room and gives a wave. I follow him to the front taking Faith with me, and then it's real.

Peter reads a poem that our father would have hated, and then Faith has a Bible reading that was suggested by the funeral director. It doesn't feel like Dad but then it was hard to come up with things he'd have actually liked for his send-off. There are two hymns he would've probably recognised, and then a final address from the director who says something about the dead living on in how we choose to remember them.

It isn't a great funeral, certainly nothing memorable, although I know that's all on me. Peter said he'd agree with whatever I wanted – and I more or less let the funeral director choose everything. Neither Peter nor I wanted to make these decisions, so perhaps we're more alike than we admit.

I made my peace the first time I saw him with that waxy skin after the embalmer was done. Music plays and people stand as my father's body passes behind the sheet at the back. Faith leans in to ask what happens next and I can't answer. I think she knows anyway. He'll be burned and then we'll get the ashes in a box.

That's it.

One parent dead; the other who knows where.

The sheet closes and the gentle murmurs start as people head for the exit. I remain in my seat, clutching my daughter's hand, sensing the wash of loneliness that I'm not sure will ever be fixed.

TWENTY-SIX

There are posters in the entrance of the local Labour Club, advertising Rob Stewart for this weekend, then Stung for the Saturday after. Cheap tribute acts and cheaper bitter is more Dad's scene. He'd have particularly enjoyed Marvin Gray's Motown night next month.

It's lunchtime and the bar is lined by half a dozen men who look as if they've been sitting in the same spot since Reagan was elected. There's a pool table with ripped felt, a small TV on the wall showing Sky News, then a dartboard with pinprick holes dotted across the wall behind.

The guy behind the bar has a towel over his shoulder and points towards a door on the far side. 'In there, love,' he calls, and I follow the direction into the function room. This really *is* Dad's scene.

There's tinsel in the corner from a Christmas that I doubt was last year's, plus the sort of bobbled, patterned beige wallpaper more fashionable during the three-day week. It's so outdated that I'm almost certain I threw out a roll of it from Dad's garage.

I have a clarity now I'm away from the crematorium. Of

course Mum wasn't hiding there. Of course she isn't about to reveal herself.

Faith held my hand for the walk to the car, then asked if it was OK for her and Shannon to disappear off. I told her it was, knowing this sort of social club is barely for people my age, let alone hers.

Most from the funeral have made it to the wake. They head in with bowed heads, buoyed by the chance of free ham and pickle sandwiches, plus Fosters at happy hour prices.

Fosters.

I don't even like lager and yet it would be so easy to get a drink. Cheap. The barman wouldn't even think twice. I booked this place because Dad would end up here once or twice a week. This is where his old-time crew hang around. There's a bookies' next door, which helps. I could've picked somewhere that didn't serve alcohol but it's not about me.

I won't drink but that doesn't mean I consider it.

It's only as I say hello to one of Dad's old workmates from his time at the quarry that I realise, properly, both Nicola and Faith have gone. Nicola had to head off to work and there's nobody here I particularly want to talk to, nor anybody coming. I say a lot of hellos, over a bunch of waves and nods. Harriet has gone, which is probably for the best. When it comes to people asking how she knew the deceased, it's not easy to pipe up and say she was his mistress.

Allie Rowett's here. She says a sheepish hello, but we said all had to on Wednesday. Her husband assaulted me and she kept quiet about it until after he'd died. None of that stops her tucking into a glass of house red, an egg sandwich, and one of the yellow French Fancies.

I do the rounds. *Hello. Goodbye. Thanks for coming. Yes, it's a great spread. Yes, it was a lovely service. Yes, it's a shame. Yes, we'll have to catch up soon. No, I don't have your number.*

The same conversations with the same kinds of people.

Everyone means well, nobody manages to see that I don't want to be here and I wish they'd all go away.

It's probably not a surprise but I had no real conversation with my brother at the funeral. I find myself standing next to the tea urn, filling my third cup because it's better than alcohol. My brother's wife, Bridget, my sister-in-law, picks up one of the empty cups, smiles politely, then realises it's me.

'Eve,' she says. 'I was hoping to catch up to you. You look lovely.'

I know I don't – and the damned sleeves still won't sit in place – but I thank her anyway and return the favour. Yes, the service was lovely. It really was a perfect send-off. Yes, this was his favourite place. No, I don't come here often. No, I don't know why there's a poster for the 1984 Milk Cup final on the wall, nor do I know what that is.

'Thank you so much for organising,' she adds. 'And for doing everything at the house. I know Peter can be a bit, um... hands off.'

That's an understatement – but at least it isn't only me who thinks it. Bridget and I are standing close to the abandoned tinsel, each sipping our tea. She's so far out of my brother's league that it's baffling how they're together. Not only is she a nice, considerate person, but she has that sort of prettiness that's borderline sickening.

'He said you both had a chat at the house the other night,' Bridget says.

I'd almost forgotten about Peter dashing upstairs, spending time in Dad's room, flushing the toilet and then returning downstairs with something stuffed in his pocket.

'I offered him one of Dad's watches,' I say. 'He took it but didn't seem too keen. I did say he could look around the house and take anything he wanted. I presume he brought home a few things?'

I'm such a good liar when I'm thinking about not drinking.

Bridget thinks. 'There was something...'

She tails off because a small boy with a bowl cut trots across. He has a French Fancy, Bakewell, Viennese whirl and Battenberg all on the same plate. A perfect Mr Kipling tapas.

'You can't eat all those,' Bridget says.

He looks up with dinnerplate eyes, reinforcing the fact that my brother and Bridget have fantastic genes. Even I want to tell him it's fine.

'Pick two,' Bridget says.

'Four?'

'Two. You pick, or I'll pick for you.'

The boy fingers the Bakewell, which feels like a good number one pick. His mum catches my eye with a gentle upturn of the lips. 'Timothy,' she says, answering my unasked question.

Their twins are called Timothy and Thomas, but I once joked to Faith they were Timothy and Tomothy – and now I can't think of them in any other way. I certainly can't tell them apart.

'Where's Thomas?' I ask, just about getting the name right.

'He had a bit of tummy trouble, so Peter's gone to drop him at my mum's.' Bridget checks her phone then frowns. 'I thought he'd be back by now.'

Timothy takes a nervous bite of the French Fancy but we all know he's not giving up the other two cakes without a fight. Bridget catches his eye but is immune to his charms. She snatches the Battenberg and Viennese whirl from the plate and holds them in her hand.

'We're putting these back,' she says.

'I've licked them.'

'Fine. I'll eat them.'

Bridget gives me a *what-can-you-do* look as my nephew grins at the pair of us. Before I can ask what my brother brought home from Dad's house, someone else Bridget knows steps between us. They do an air kiss.

'Tell Faith I thought her reading was brilliant,' Bridget adds, before saying her goodbyes, and moving to a different corner. Timothy waits until his mum is out of sight, then makes a beeline for the cakes. He snatches a mini roll, scoffs it in one, then gets down a pair of Jaffa Cakes in record time.

He flashes me a grin and then trots back to his mother.

I do the rounds again.

Oh, are you leaving? Great to see you. Yes, I do remember the time I played Lego on the floor of your living room when I was about five. No, I don't know someone named Alan. Yes, it's a great spread. Yes, it was a lovely service. Yes, it's a shame. Yes, we'll have to catch up soon. No, I don't have your number.

And on.

As the food diminishes, people finally begin to drift away. The room thins and it's only really the egg sandwiches that are left. Anything with meat or cheese has long since gone, not to mention the cakes. Dad would be proud of his friends: the greedy sods.

I'm back at the tea urn, cup number six, when I realise a woman is sitting in one of the uncomfortable school-style chairs watching me. I expect her to look away as we make eye contact but, instead: 'You don't remember me, do you?'

She's probably late-fifties, though it's difficult to know. Anyone older than me is decrepit, anyone younger should be banned.

'Lorna,' she says, standing and moving across to me. Her breath is cheap Fosters. We shake hands, though I have no idea who she is. Lorna knows it.

'I used to know your dad in the old days,' she says. 'Think I might've babysat you a couple of times, actually.'

Clouds swirl. 'You had a girlfriend,' I say – and she laughs.

'She's my wife now – but yes.'

'I didn't mean it like that.'

The grin widens. 'I get it, hun. Not many out lesbians back then.'

It's odd that this is why I know her. I remember her babysitting when I was six or seven, and Mum explaining that she had a girlfriend. Anything other than a man and woman baffled my young mind, even as Mum explained that sometimes women loved women and so on.

Different times.

'I really am sorry,' I say – but Lorna waves it away, holding up her hands to indicate the club. 'Believe it or not, this was a safe space for me and my partner. I'd come after work most days – which is where I met your dad. I ended up doing shifts behind the bar.' She pauses a moment, then shrugs. 'I guess it gets us all in the end.'

I assume she's talking about death, though she seems a bit young for that. We're already at the dying stage of small-talk and there's a second of awkward silence before she asks what I do. Before I can answer, she quickly adds: 'Don't you work for Mark Dixon?'

'How'd you know that?'

'Your dad. I'm not here anywhere near as often as I used to be – and neither was he – but we ran into each other now and then. He'd always talk about you.'

'Would he?'

This gets a confused response. 'Of course. He'd tell me how his granddaughter was doing great with her exams and school; that you had a terrific job and were excelling. To be honest, I was a bit surprised, considering your boss.'

I'm so struck by the idea that Dad talked proudly of me that I almost miss the rest. 'What about my boss?'

Lorna shrugs a little. 'I mean, Mum always told me that if you don't have anything nice to say...'

She grins in a way I know is asking for permission.

'I quit yesterday,' I say.

'Sick of him then?'

'Something like that.'

Lorna nods towards the bar in the other room. 'Can I get you a drink...?'

I hold up my teacup. 'I'm an alcoholic,' I say – largely because there's a part of me desperate to find a corner and spend the rest of the day getting pissed with Lorna. It's often better to be honest – because then the other person does the work for you.

'My God, I'm so sorry,' she replies, touching a hand to her chest.

'We're both sorry then.'

She smiles kindly – then nods me across to the squishy seats near the fire exit. It's quieter there and that part of me so wishes we were sharing a real drink.

'I used to know Mark Dixon way back,' she says, once we've settled. 'This was before he had vans everywhere with his name on. Have you read his website?'

I have, of course – and laugh until my stomach hurts because Lorna knows it off by heart. 'Self-made and self-effacing,' she says – which is more than enough to set me off, before she adds: '...he soon realised he had the ambition, work ethic, and intelligence to start his own business.'

I have to ask her to stop after the fifth quote, because people are starting to notice that I'm howling at my own father's wake. She waits until I've composed myself and then adds: 'Mark Dixon knows when to hold 'em, when to fold 'em and when to walk away.'

It's my favourite line of his biography and there's a moment in which I almost have to step outside to compose myself.

'You have to stop,' I say – and, mercifully, Lorna does.

'How do you know him?' I ask.

'I was his line manager,' she says.

'When?'

'Prince Industries. You'd have been young then. I don't know if you remember the factory.'

I tell her I do.

'It's all houses now,' she adds. 'I live in one almost right by the old doors. That's where I met Mark. He came to us straight out of school.'

I picture him pacing up and down the night before. *They can't prove anything... just tell them I was with you.*

I could've recited that back to Detective Sergeant Cox this morning when she called round. But then I would've had to tell her why I was hiding around a corner late at night, how I'd broken into the office, that I had Owen's wallet. It would be a lot to explain, even if she believed me.

Cox knows my history, about the alcoholism and the attack on Jake Rowett, and already made it clear she was suspicious. Mark could've easily denied the phone call, then said he'd never seen Owen's wallet – that I'd planted it there. It would have looked very bad for me.

The thought of all that clears the hilarity of minutes before. Because Mark Dixon worked at Prince Industries when the first Earring Killer murder happened. And he knew Owen had my tape.

I don't let on about any of that, instead prodding Lorna into telling the story she's clearly desperate to.

'What was he like?' I ask.

'A whiny little twerp. He used to think he knew everything, even though he failed all his exams. His dad knew someone, who knew someone – which is why he got hired. It definitely wasn't talent. He'd barely been there a week when he was telling people how they should be doing jobs they'd been doing for twenty years. There were all sorts of divisions in that factory – old versus young, union versus non, men versus women.' She pauses. 'Everyone came together as one to declare that Mark Dixon was a complete clown.'

She laughs but I find it harder to join in now.

'The thing with that silly biography on the website is that even the bits that could be true aren't. He didn't leave Prince for a greater calling. He didn't leave because of ambition or intelligence — and it definitely wasn't work ethic. He left because nobody could stand him. This one time, he gave a line manager a bit of lip. Something like "You're too old to know what you're doing", that sort of thing. Anyway, the manager went into the changing rooms, broke into Mark's locker, grabbed all his clothes, then threw them in the toilet. All the blokes took their turn to, well… you can figure out the rest. I'm not saying it was right — Mark was only young himself, but he'd been pushing his luck since his first day. He never came back to the factory after that.'

I consider that for a moment. It all sounds very 1990s bantery — and unquestionably grim. Possibly deserved. I find a part of myself feeling sorry for Mark, then remember all the times I've seen him talk to people in a similar way.

'I thought Mark was a manager?' I say.

Lorna laughs. 'He couldn't manage tying his own shoes. He was terrible at his job, rude to everyone, never listened, constantly made mistakes, and had no interest in learning. He lasted about a month.'

'Is that all?'

'I know. He makes it sound like he walked in and started running the place — but I've had gall stones that lasted longer than he did.'

She flashes me a smile.

'Do you remember exactly when he left?' I ask.

'I know it was the week before Christmas because we had a pool going on whether he'd turn up for the party. I had three quid on him showing.'

'Did you win?'

'I don't think even he was that shameless.'

I take a moment, re-considering the timing.

Lorna asks if I smoke, then, when I say no, says that she doesn't either. Her grin is infectious as she adds: 'Don't tell my wife that I asked if you wanted one.'

I find myself yawning, not because of her. It's been a long day and the night before was long too. My teacup is empty and I'm not sure I can force down any more. There's less than a dozen people in the room and, as I look towards the main doors, my cavalry has finally arrived.

Liam starts walking across the floor, hands in his pockets. 'You OK?' he asks, as he stands over me.

'What took you so long?' I ask.

'Stuck at work.'

I check the time, realising Lorna and I have somehow been talking for an hour and a half.

'Husband?' Lorna asks.

'AA sponsor.'

We both stand and Lorna shakes hands with Liam. 'One of Dad's friends,' I tell him. He eyes her with curiosity, though that might be because there's alcohol on her breath, then he looks back to me.

'Let's go have that drink,' he says.

We explain to Lorna that 'let's have that drink' is our stupid, inside way of asking the other if we fancy a cup of tea or coffee.

But my mind is still on Mark and Lorna. If Mark left Prince Industries the week before Christmas, he wasn't there when the first killing happened. It's only his invented biography that makes it sound like he was. Does that change things?

I still overheard him on the phone saying he was lying about where he'd been. Owen's wallet was still in his safe. And so was the twine.

But maybe this means the Earring Killer is someone else entirely.

TWENTY-SEVEN

Liam was supposed to save me an hour ago. We head back through the social club to my car and then set off for his house.

'I heard from your police friend,' he says as I pull away.

'Kieron?'

'He asked how you were doing...?'

I'm quiet for a moment. After our talk in the beer garden, I'd sort of expected Nicola's father to check in and make sure I wasn't drinking again. It still feels like something of an invasion.

'What did you say?' I ask.

'That you were doing great.'

I can't think of anything to reply. Liam and I do this sometimes, when each of us have a long day. He's married but our relationship isn't like that. I'll sit in his living room, or he'll sit in mine. We'll drink tea and watch bad television. Sometimes we'll talk but often we won't. It's the company that counts.

For now, he asks about the funeral and I tell him it went as well as expected. It feels as if I've had that conversation a lot recently. Liam sits quietly in the passenger seat, giving me space to say more, though not forcing it.

It's almost accidental but his house is a short distance past my dad's. I've visited so many times in the last week or so that I slow instinctively as I drive past, almost flicking on the indicator to head onto the drive when I remember this isn't where I'm going.

But then I do stop. I'm blocking the road, though there's nobody behind.

'What's up?' Liam asks.

I strain against the seat belt, and then pull to the side of the road, wondering if I've seen what I thought I have.

Once I'm out the car, Liam joins me on the pavement. 'Eve...?'

I'm not sure what to say but he follows me onto Dad's driveway, then to the side. The door is hanging open, one of the hinges busted, the other hanging on by a couple of screws.

'This is Dad's house,' I say.

Liam's at my side as we stare at the smashed door. 'It's been crowbarred open,' he says.

TWENTY-EIGHT

There's no broken glass but the door is a mess. I wouldn't have guessed a crowbar, but Liam's probably correct. The wood has splintered near the hinge and there's a large gouge in the frame.

Inside, and three of the kitchen cupboard doors are open. They were more or less empty anyway. Into the living room and it's not an obvious burglary. The television is there, as well as Dad's record player. Some of the drawers of his bureau are fractionally open, even though I'm certain they were closed. I check and his pile of bills and bank statements remain in place.

Liam is behind me, pointing to a small cabinet with its doors open. I try to remember what was inside but doubt it was valuable.

'People would've known the house was empty and that you were going to be out all day,' Liam says – and he's right. Dad's funeral had been publicised. It would be known that he lived alone and people knew the times I'd be at the crematorium and then the social club.

Liam looks towards the TV and I suspect we're both thinking the same. 'What was the point of breaking in?' he asks.

I look to him blankly, wondering whether people still nick

televisions nowadays. It feels like a throwback to a time when they were more expensive and not everyone had a smaller version in their pocket.

'I'll check upstairs,' I say, then leave Liam in the living room as I head up. Dad's clothes are still in his room, though a burglar taking those really would have left some serious questions. The drawers on his chest are half open, half closed – and it looks as if a couple of rings could've been taken. I hadn't catalogued everything, and doubt they were valuable anyway.

The other rooms seem broadly untouched, though Dad had only been using them for storage anyway. Much had already been carted off to the tip.

Back downstairs, Liam is waiting in the kitchen. 'Has much been taken?' he asks.

'I don't think so.'

He raises a confused eyebrow, then looks to the back door.

'I was always getting on to Dad about having better doors and windows,' I say. 'They were old and wooden and he'd complain about his electric bill. I said he could probably get a grant for better windows, which would make his heating bill lower. He said it sounded like a lot more trouble than it was worth...'

I tail off, partly because I'm boring myself but mainly because it feels so inconsequential now. Nobody gets to the end of their life and wishes they'd had more conversations about windows.

'Maybe whoever broke in didn't know you'd already cleared so much,' Liam says. 'They were trying it on to see if there was anything valuable...?'

It's possible, perhaps likely, but I wonder whether this is a one-off. If there was a person out there breaking into houses based on the times of funerals, wouldn't someone have noticed by now?

'You should probably call the police,' he says.

'I don't know if anything's been taken.'

'It's still vandalism.'

Liam looks to the door again but I'm thinking of Detective Sergeant Cox and how I keep appearing in her investigations. It likely wouldn't be her who came here – but she'd notice. I can imagine the conversation with an officer, trying to explain that I don't know if anything was taken. Do officers still attend for this sort of thing anyway? Don't you just get a crime number over the phone?

'I need to call a locksmith,' I reply.

'I can wait with you.'

'It's OK. I messaged when I thought I was going to spend the whole day stuck saying hello to people with the bar right there. I thought I'd need a bit of help – but I ended up meeting Lorna and it wasn't as bad as it could have been...'

Liam bites his bottom lip, considering what to say. He only lives a few minutes away and has taken the trouble to rescue me, only to be told he isn't needed.

'Are you sure?' he replies. 'I've got all evening. I can wait, and we can do something after?'

'I think maybe I need a bit of time to myself. I've been with people all day.'

I can see the uncertainty in Liam. We've known each other a long while now but we don't talk about the important things, or even really the unimportant ones. We're often just there – and it's enough.

'If you're absolutely sure,' he says, holding up his phone. 'I can come back, or we can still do something later. I want you to promise you'll call or text if you need something.'

'I will.'

He steps towards the door and picks up a few large splinters of wood that he puts on the counter. I know he'd rather stay. There's a final look over his shoulder and then he moves decisively out of the house and around the side back to the front.

I'm alone again and maybe this is what I want for now. I search for locksmiths and call the first one on the list. I explain that the door is partially off the hinges, though she says they can help with that, or fix a new door entirely. I can't be bothered calling around, so tell her that's fine. She says it'll be around ninety minutes, and so I pull the door as closed as it gets and then head into Dad's living room to wait.

I probably should call the police, if only to get that crime reference number – but I've also had so many dealings with them in the past days that I don't think I can take more bureaucracy. It would be different if I could specifically tell them something that had been taken.

Did someone *really* see the funeral notice and take a chance? It would have to be someone who knew where Dad lived.

I text Peter, to say someone broke into Dad's house during the funeral, but that it doesn't look as if anything was taken. It's half his house, after all – and maybe he'll insist on calling the police. Perhaps my brother will even come here and do it himself.

Then it occurs to me that somebody could have been specifically searching for the engraved jewellery box. The reason I haven't noticed anything missing is that I didn't know where it was to begin with.

Now the thought is there, I can't escape the idea that the Earring Killer was here while I was either at the funeral, or wake.

Peter himself didn't get to the wake. His wife said he'd taken one of their ill twins but that he was taking longer to get back than she thought. Except my brother has his own key for the house and could have come by to search at any time. Plus he'd likely removed something when we met here a few days back. Why wait?

There is an obvious answer to that. There's no better way to get away with stealing a small thing than by hiding it among lots of other items. Somebody else could easily assume I actually did have a manifest of everything in Dad's house, meaning I'd notice a single thing taken. But if that one thing disappeared along with a couple dozen others, it wouldn't have such significance.

It would be much smarter to make something *look* like a burglary.

Or... maybe I've completely lost it. I've spent the past few days suspecting everyone from my father, to my boss, to my brother, and who knows who else. They're all the Earring Killer; the person Mum said was going to murder her.

I've been poisoned by Mum's tapes. Despite the clear lies of stealing the neighbour's car, or robbing a bank, I can't stop believing that the other stuff is true.

I sit and wait. I might even nod off for five minutes because, when I next check my phone, Peter has replied to my text about the break-in.

OK

I swipe out and back, wondering if there's more – but that's it. My brother co-owns this house and doesn't seem too bothered that someone broke in while we were at our father's funeral. I should be surprised but he told me to my face he was sick of the drama caused by the women in this family. He likely thinks this is more of that. Nicola's father said something similar in that beer garden, when he questioned whether it was my voice on the recording, not my mother's.

Is that how people see me? An attention seeker?

I check the window but there's no sign of a locksmith, so I do a bit of cleaning up in the kitchen, while listening to my voice note recording of Mum's tape.

'This is my second go at this. My name is Angela and I've been murdered...

...
...
Well, I think I'm going to be murdered.
...
...
I don't know. It's just... I don't think I'm a good person. I did something. I've done lots of things...'

I recorded the first part of the tape to voice notes but rarely listen to it, instead skipping for the part to which I'm addicted.

'... if this is Eve listening, I just want you to know I'm sorry. If they say I'm missing, I'm not. I've been killed – and I need you to know that I love you.'

I drop a pan of dust and splinters into the bin – and finally realise why I need this to be true. It's because it's all part of the same sentence. If Mum's lying about being killed, then she's lying about loving me. It's why I can't let it go, why I'm so desperate to prove this. I can ignore the obvious lies later on the tape but it's this line that must be real.

And that's when I really listen to the start and realise the obvious thing I've missed this entire time.

'This is my second go at this...'

If this broken, incomplete cassette is Mum's *second go*, then where's the first?

KIRSTY AND SARAH

Extract from *The Earring Killer* by Vivian Mallory, © 2015.

The man in the silk waistcoat looks up at the concrete block to our side. There's pebble-dashing across the top, then an exposed set of stairs with a metal railing at the side. Bomb shelter chic.

'I doubt we'll last the year,' the man tells me. 'It used to be full of students but they were different times. We'd offer membership discounts and some kids would spend entire afternoons in here. Two quid a pint, unlimited snooker or pool, but now they have other things.'

'Like what?' I ask.

Marlon has been the manager of Green's Snooker and Pool for the past twenty-one years. It sits on the top floor of the bomb shelter building and has been resident for more than three decades. He smooths the front of his waistcoat and shakes his head. 'Phones, I guess. No point in playing snooker for real if you can do it on your phone.'

He has a point, if not about phones then the changing times. He takes me up the stairs, which doesn't help the appeal of the place. He says the lift stopped working more than a year ago but that the landlord won't pay to fix it. I'm out of breath as we reach the top step, but the inside of the snooker hall is warm and welcoming.

'We did everything up about eighteen months ago,' Marlon says. 'Didn't make a difference.'

The bar area is a wash of soft reds and blacks. Each corner has a television showing a different sport, while the bar is stocked with the usual array of drinks. A blackboard is advertising happy hour chips and gravy for £1.50.

Marlon and I sit at the bar and he picks up a beer mat that he twirls on the end of his finger.

'I knew Kirsty fairly well,' he says. 'If I'm honest, it probably wasn't a great time to be a woman here in the 2000s. Something like ninety-five per cent of our membership was men and some of them were a bit, well... laddish.'

I point out this might have been down to the two quid pints, which Marlon concedes is likely.

'Kirsty didn't seem bothered by any of that,' he adds. 'I remember asking her once why she worked here and she was baffled by the question. Her dad was a publican, so she found the work familiar and easy – except she'd seen what it was like in a pub. She said there was none of the late-night nastiness here. It was just a few clumsy advances from students. She thought it was hilarious that she was old enough to be their mum.'

It had been four years since Ophelia Baron was killed when her car broke down on the way home from hockey practice. Before that, there had been a three-year gap since Laura March disappeared on that canal bank.

Those now familiar rumblings that perhaps the police were mistaken had returned. There had been four killings in three years, then only one in the following three. Four deaths in three years felt like a serial killer; five in six was more like the police were reaching. During that period, the HAVE FUN messaging had broken through – but women had started to come up with their own ways of seeking safety.

A movement had taken off to simply not wear jewellery, especially earrings.

Maybe that worked? Maybe that explained the single killing in seven years?

Maybe.

'I think people forgot,' Marlon says. 'But maybe that's me looking back with modern eyes. People shouldn't have to adapt their behaviour and it is victim blaming, really. If someone wants to wear earrings, why should they stop? But there was this thinking from some people that if you did that, you were asking for trouble. That you'd deserve anything that happened. Maybe that's just what it was like in the 2000s, especially for women?'

Marlon pauses and puts down the beer mat with which he's been fiddling throughout our conversation. He bows his head a fraction and turns towards the bar.

'One of our regulars was in a day or two after it all happened and he said something like, "Well, she was wearing earrings, wasn't she?" – as if it was her fault. I don't think I said anything. I didn't agree with him but I didn't say he was out of line, either. I just sort of went with it – and I think about that all the time, even though it's years later. It's like I let her down.'

Kirsty McIntosh worked five days a week behind the bar of Green's Snooker and Pool. She often volunteered for Friday nights because it meant she could take off the Saturday. It was late on a Friday that she wound down for the evening, ushering out the snooker and pool players, then locking the doors to give herself half an hour to clean up. She left a note for whoever was on shift the next morning, saying that they needed to reorder some crisps, because stocks were low, then set off for her car.

It was the same short walk she made five nights a week, every week.

Except, that Friday night, Kirsty never made it.

Her boyfriend had been waiting up and ended up driving himself into town a little after two in the morning. He found her car parked in its usual spot, untouched and locked; the small plush Minnie Mouse was still dangling from the mirror. He walked across the car park, down the stairs, across the plaza and through a pair of alleys until he reached this bomb shelter of a building, where he climbed the stairs and knocked on the door.

The lights were off and nobody answered, because nobody was inside.

It was then he called the police to report his girlfriend missing. The search didn't take long. Early on the Sunday evening, not even forty-eight hours later, the body of Kirsty McIntosh was discovered in woodland a few miles outside town.

A triangular green earring was in one ear, while the other was bare.

Police were careful at first. It had been four years after all. Was the Earring Killer back, or was it some sort of copycat? Could it be a coincidence? Perhaps Kirsty had lost an earring earlier in the evening?

But while the authorities sat on that information, trying to find truth among whispered assumptions, something else happened. Something that had never occurred before among the lore of the Earring Killer. Something nobody, least of all the police, expected.

A few miles from the snooker club, and the running track at the back of Sedingham Secondary School is a sand-coloured gravel path. I walk a loop and the soles of my shoes end up covered in a chalk-like dust. There are hockey goals at either end of the grass in the middle of the track, with a shot-put and discus net in another corner.

I stick to the third lane, leaving space inside for a sinewy man in short shorts and a loose white vest to run laps. He checks his watch at regular intervals, while crouching to grab a bottle from the grass. He sips the water, then drops the bottle a few metres further on, barely breaking stride.

Just three days after the body of Kirsty McIntosh had been discovered, Sarah Graham was running laps on this track. She was training for the Great North Run and would run the mile and a half from her house to this track. Four laps is approximately a mile, and she'd run anything from twenty to forty before looping back to where she lived.

The first part is an overgrown path around the back of the school. It passes a graffiti-covered, old school bike shed before reaching the main road. A largely deserted pavement tracks the next couple of hundred metres with a steady stream of traffic lining up from a set of traffic lights. Three drivers saw Sarah as she jogged past them, her own water bottle clamped in her hand.

From there, Sarah would have passed through a series of chicane-like alleys, with varying degrees of gates and barriers to stop motorbikes cutting through. She would have emerged in a cosy cul-de-sac before heading around a bend, through two more lanes and then onto her own road.

Michael Graham is sitting on a wall close to a corner shop. His sleeves are rolled up and the top button of his shirt is undone, showing whispers of greying hair. He's stubbly, at the stage where it could be the beginnings of a beard, or perhaps he's one of those men who skips a day with a razor and ends up with what looks like a week's growth.

We shake hands and he points across to the lane from which Sarah would have emerged.

'Sarah had never really run before,' he says. 'Athletics wasn't her thing at school but she'd always been fit in the sense that she looked after herself. I think Paula Radcliffe had won *Sports Personality of the Year* before, something like that. Sarah and I watched it together and she'd decided she wanted to run the London Marathon. It was all a bit out of the blue but I wanted to support her. I bought her a pair of training shoes that Christmas.'

I point out that the running track feels a bit Iron Curtain and Michael laughs. 'Sarah used to complain about that all the time. She'd say it was slippery, especially when it had been raining. Except it's the only track in town and it meant she could just run. She didn't have to worry about crossing roads, or dodging people who were walking on pavements. That's why she liked it.'

I ask if Michael ever ran with his wife and that draws another laugh. 'Not my thing,' he says. 'I played a bit of football when I was younger but I don't think I could handle that monotony. Lap after lap, you know? You have to be a certain type of person for that.'

He thinks a second and there's a distant gaze.

'She really did want to run a marathon but she was working up to it. 5k, 10k, then a half. She had a whole training plan that she'd worked out herself. That last run was one of the longer ones. I think she might've done nine or ten miles.'

Those three drivers were the last people to ever see Sarah alive. She never completed that final mile of her run – and it was almost seventy-two hours later that her body was found near a lay-by a short distance outside town. She'd only been wearing stud earrings – but one had been removed.

This time, the police did not hesitate as they released an urgent alert regarding safety for women in the local area.

There was vicious criticism in the coming weeks, especially in regards to the murder of Sarah. If they'd only been upfront after the discovery of Kirsty, then perhaps Sarah would still be alive. Perhaps those detractors had a point, except it's easy to say after an event. In any case, Sarah's husband didn't see things that way.

'She'd have gone running anyway,' Michael says. 'She wanted to train and to run. It was her way of unwinding. You have to live your life, don't you?'

He's right, of course. If it wasn't Sarah, it would have been someone else. People want to live their lives.

But, by then, things had become very clear. After five killings in six years, then none in three, Sedingham had seen two in five days.

Seven dead women.

Seven missing earrings.

The Earring Killer was very much back.

TWENTY-NINE

The locksmith arrived after almost exactly ninety minutes. It took around an hour to fix the door and frame, then change the locks.

I wait and watch, desperate to get home to Mum's tapes that are still under my bed. Perhaps that's what the burglar had been searching for? I've told enough people about them, after all. I swap texts with Faith, who is at Shannon's house; then more with Liam who is worried about me. Meanwhile, Peter hasn't sent anything more than his straightforward 'OK'.

When I finally make it home, I realise I have a much bigger job ahead than I thought.

There are more than thirty separate cassettes in Mum's box, all of which are ninety minutes long. I start by listening to the first few seconds of each, hoping Mum will say something obvious like, 'This is my first go at this...' – which would be a real help.

Once I've established there's no obvious tape that might include her initial try at saying why she believed she was about to be killed, I start the lengthy process of trying to get through them all. I listen to a few seconds, fast forward a bit, then listen to a few more.

This is why tapes went out of fashion. The analogue world is now barely comprehensible to me – and I lived through the end part of it.

Mum talks about the walks she's taken, or the books she's read. She catalogues her arguments with Viv at book club, and how they apparently disagreed over everything and anything. The problem with trying to fast-forward through the tapes is that I find myself drawn into my mother's world, as if we're connecting in a way we never did. I knew she enjoyed reading, that she was in a book club; but I didn't know her opinions on anything. Her constant fallings-out with other people are so funny all these years later, largely because Mum refuses to believe anyone can hold an opinion that isn't hers.

The other reason it's hard to skip forward is because she talks about me a lot.

There is a sports day I don't remember, in which I apparently won a three-legged race alongside a boy named Damien. There's the time I took my piano exam and passed first time. I've not played in years but, every now and then, I think maybe I'd like to try again. Mum talks about our caravan holidays and the hours we spent pushing one- and two-pence pieces into the slider machines. There was the paddle boat lake, where Dad misjudged getting out and fell into the water. He blamed the boat, of course. Ten-year-old me had the morning off school because Mum had booked an optician appointment. Afterwards, instead of rushing me back to school, we went and got cream buns from the market.

I realise the box of cassettes is the greatest gift my mother could have left. She's been gone thirteen years and, somehow, it's only now that I realise how much I miss her. She might be a parent who didn't stand up for me when she knew what Jake

Rowett had done, she might have been a thief and a liar. A woman so far from perfect.

But she was still my mother… and maybe I'd forgotten that.

With the cassettes, I get nowhere, of course. The idea of skipping through the material seems fanciful and ridiculous. A ninety-minute cassette means listening through almost all of it, because I can't resist.

There's more talks of Mum's book club and arguments with Viv. More confessions and flights of fancy. More lies.

More darkness.

She robbed a dress from a shop but got stopped on the way out. The manager took pity on her and didn't call the police. Mum didn't need the dress but went back two days later and stole it anyway when somebody else was behind the counter.

She stole a *Children In Need* charity box from a pub but felt so guilty, she put it back the next day. Then she decided she wanted it anyway, so stole it again. She claims she robbed a security van that was picking up cash from a supermarket. I know she didn't. It would have been too big and she'd have been caught.

I struggle to know what's true and what isn't.

There's such bleakness, and it's a hard listen – yet then she'll say that she was proud of me because she went to parents' evening and all the teachers gushed about how well raised I was.

She's flawed, but everyone is. Perhaps most don't recognise it, and certainly don't record themselves admitting it. This is a diary and a confessional.

A gift.

A curse.

I wish I'd never started listening to them but part of me never wants to stop. Not really. There are so many hours.

I do stop, for now, in the end, because it's getting dark and it's been a long day. Because Faith will be home soon.

I don't think a second version of the tape is in this box.

Owen had my original, and perhaps I'll never get it back. My phone's voice recording is what's left for now.

'This is my second go at this...'

I listen to that voice note again, trying to work out why Mum would have made two recordings. Unless she means she tried to record her thoughts once and it didn't come out?

One thing that's become clear from listening through the tapes is that Mum talks about herself a lot, as well as me, but she barely mentions my father. The name 'Bruce' is clearly – and likely deliberately – absent from Mum's thoughts, no matter which year or month I choose. She was books, he was TV. She was outdoors, he was indoors. She was flights of fancy, he was practicality and the real world.

The cassette with her claims of being killed had my name specifically written on the sleeve, but there's nothing for my father. She would have never left a confessional for him, because he wouldn't have understood.

But there is one other person she was oddly close to. I never particularly understood why but it's undeniable.

And that's why I pick up my phone and scroll until I reach the number of my ex-husband.

THIRTY

The front door opens when I'm still half-a-dozen paces away. Henry's in shorts that show a chunky set of thighs, plus a long-sleeve T-shirt. There's more heft across his shoulders and upper arms than the last time I saw him.

'I always knew I had the power to open front doors with my mind,' I say.

He smiles kindly and holds it wider. He's bare-footed and his legs aren't as hairy as I remember, which has me wondering if he shaves them now. I'd never ask, of course.

'Will Tiffany mind?' I ask, waiting on the step, even though he's welcoming me in.

'She's at CrossFit and it's girls' night, so they hang around after. She wouldn't mind anyway.'

I don't let on that I find it mildly annoying that Henry's current wife would seemingly have no problems with him inviting his old one into their home. Couldn't she at least have the decency to be jealous, like everyone else? What is it with these people who are secure in their own bodies and relationships?

Henry plods through the house, his great big swimmer's

feet slapping on the bare floors as he takes me through to the deck at the back of the house. The sun is setting, but an orangey glow is in the perfect spot to bathe the table and chairs in evening warmth. Henry doesn't sit, so neither do I. Instead, we stand a couple of paces apart, the chairs between us.

'How's Libby?' I ask.

'She's great. She's in bed at the moment. She started walking around three weeks ago, so we've had to pick up everything from the floor. There are child gates all over.' He laughs and it's impossible not to remember those days.

'How are you?' he asks.

A shrug. 'Y'know…'

'How was the funeral?'

'As good as could be expected.' I wait, then: 'Faith's doing great on her course and really looking forward to the trip…'

He smiles as I realise he knows. Faith would've texted him and they probably talk anyway. She and her father have a proper grown-up relationship.

'Do you want a drink?' he asks. There's a second and then he almost jumps. 'Tea! I mean tea, or water, or Coke, or whatever. I didn't mean—'

'I can't drink any more tea today but I'll have a water.'

He eyes me for a moment, wondering whether I really did take offence – but then he heads into the house, leaving me on his annoyingly beautiful deck.

There's a covered hot tub off to the side, next to a barbecue grill. A row of towels and swimming costumes are hanging from a line that follows the fence. I sit on the impossibly comfortable bamboo sofa, with its plush cushions, wishing just one thing about the setup wasn't perfect. Even the bloody sun sets in the ideal spot.

When Henry returns, he has a jug of water, ice sloshing around, plus a pair of glasses. He places everything on the table, then sits on the second sofa which I will guarantee is equally as comfortable as the one on which I'm sitting.

'Are you sure you're all right?' he asks.

'I'm fine.'

He squints towards me, lips close, unconvinced. 'It's just it's the day of your dad's funeral and you're texting your ex-husband at eight o'clock, asking if we can have a chat...?'

'Well, when you put it that way...'

He doesn't laugh, waiting for a response I'm not sure I can give. Perhaps I have a proper reason to be here but maybe I'm a sicko who needs reminding of what I threw away. The hot tub could've been mine, the washing line with the drying swimming costumes, the deck with the perfect bloody sun.

I tell Henry everything. That I found a cassette among Dad's things, with a recording of Mum saying that she wasn't missing and had instead been killed. That she claimed to know the identity of the Earring Killer – but the recording quality is poor and perhaps she never named the person anyway.

Henry watches me for a moment and presses back in his sofa. I told Nicola's father and he asked if I recorded it myself. I wanted to tell Liam but he watched me with such a careful stare that I know he was wondering if I'd been drinking again. I talked to my brother and he said the women in our family are trouble and that he wants no part of it.

I just want someone to trust me.

'Do you believe her?' Henry asks.

A shrug and, from nowhere, I have to gulp away a lump in my throat. 'I don't know. She said she robbed a bank on the same tape.'

That gets a crinkle of the brow. 'Why'd she say that?' he asks.

'You know why.'

There's the slightest hint of a nod – because my mother loved Henry, and he knew about her fluid relationship with the truth. She would tell him rambling stories about an exciting youth involving seductions and adventures at a university she never attended. He'd listen and nod, tell her how fabulous it all sounded. They both knew the game but he was polite enough not to say anything.

'I listened to a few of the tapes,' I tell him. 'She calls herself a kleptomaniac and says she stole a book about it. She knew she had impulse control issues.'

'And she says she didn't disappear? She thought she was going to be killed?'

'Right.'

A pause. 'So... do you believe her?'

A longer silence now. The same question as before. 'I think I do.'

Henry considers this and then has a mouthful of the water. He swills it around before swallowing, as he always did. Some things never change.

There is another life in which I wasn't a bad drunk who loved drinking. Where I wasn't handed an ultimatum between alcohol and my marriage. Or one in which I was – but picked him. Henry thought he was helping and I thought I was right. Neither of us were happy, not then anyway.

'Do you believe she knows who the Earring Killer is?'

I consider that, too. It's not quite the same answer. 'I don't think she was making it up. She could've been wrong but I think she *believed* she knew who it was.'

Henry drums his fingers on the side of the chair. *Tap-tap-tap-tap* in rapid succession. He's done this for as long as I've known him.

'If she says she was going to be killed, does that mean she thought the Earring Killer would get her?'

'I don't know. Maybe.'

More drumming of the fingers. Despite everything between us, the ultimatums (his) and the broken promises (mine), our break-up was as amicable as could be. Henry could have challenged me for custody of Faith, and perhaps he'd have won. He didn't because he trusted that our daughter was better placed with me. He never had to do that for me, yet he did.

'Have you told the police?' he asks.

'Told them what, though? Mum recorded a tape thirteen years ago? In one place she says she robbed a bank, when I know she didn't – but in another she says she has been killed. Oh, and though she doesn't say it outright, maybe it was the Earring Killer who got her?' It all comes out in one breathless release, and then: 'Plus, you know about me and the police...'

He nods, because, of course, he does. Before he can reply, there's a crackle from a baby monitor I hadn't noticed. It's on a step beneath the main part of the table and Henry stretches to pick it up, tapping something on the front to silence it.

'I've got to nip upstairs,' he says.

As Henry hurries inside, I shift a fraction back into the dwindling sun. Ahead of the deck, a tidy square of lawn stretches towards a row of solid-wood vegetable boxes at the bottom of the garden. This will be Tiffany's thing. My former husband is many things, but not a gardener.

I go to have a look anyway.

Mum loved Henry to the point that I sometimes thought she preferred him to me. I was resentful at times – but, ultimately, what's not to love? He's kind and funny; patient and understanding. We didn't break up because I had a problem; we broke up because I enjoyed having it. He loves his kids and I know first-hand he's a good man. I didn't deserve him – and, unfortunately, he realised it.

At the bottom of the garden, one of the boxes has a small triangle card with carrots, while the adjacent one is potatoes. There are raspberry vines attached to the fence in the third, then cucumbers in the next. I pluck the card and read it, before slipping it back into the soil, then doing a lap of the garden.

Back on the deck, I can hear Henry upstairs singing to his daughter, trying to send her back to sleep with what sounds like a lullaby version of 'Don't Look Back in Anger'. He always wanted Faith to be far more into Oasis than she is, and I guess this is attempt number two.

I *really* messed up.

When he returns downstairs, Henry brings out a tray, this time with a teapot and a pair of cups. 'I know you didn't want one,' he says, 'but I started having a mint tea every night. I've been sleeping better.'

The sun is almost set now, leaving a sliver of purply-orange hovering over the fence. There are spotlights at the back of the house, shining a bright white across the deck.

'How can I help?' he asks.

'I don't know. I think maybe I just wanted someone to listen.' He smiles kindly as I mumble a follow-up 'Sorry...'

If Mum had left Henry a tape, he'd have said by now. Perhaps I always knew that and it's true that I simply wanted someone to listen. Someone who wouldn't accuse me of attention seeking. But maybe that smile makes it worse, because how can he be so understanding after everything?

'It's seven years and one hundred and thirty-four days,' I say.

'I'm really proud of you. Faith is, too.'

And that's it, of course. I bury my eyes in my sleeve and turn away, facing the hot tub and trying not to lose it. A minute passes, but maybe more. When I can eventually face him again, Henry is sipping his mint tea.

'I think there's another version of the tape,' I manage. 'I've been trying to think if there's someone else Mum might've given one to.'

'It wouldn't be your dad.'

I shake my head, because of course Henry knows that. He sips from his cup again, then there's a telltale glance over the shoulder. Tiffany will be home soon. She's so understanding, and they make a fantastic couple – yet I don't blame him for not wanting a conversation with her about why I've shown up on their doorstep.

'Who was that woman she knew, at her book club?' Henry asks.

And the moment he says it, I know. Perhaps I needed someone else to point it out.

'Wasn't her daughter a victim of the Earring Killer?' he adds. 'I think your mum and her went to school together.'

The memory swirls and then it's there. I spent almost two hours earlier listening to Mum talk about her arguments with Viv at book club – except it isn't only Viv *at book club*, it's Viv *her childhood friend*. How did I forget?

Henry is on his phone, though he passes it across. 'Isn't this her?'

I already know what's going to be on the screen, because I googled it the other day and somehow still didn't put the pieces together.

There's a book cover of *The Earring Killer* by Vivian Mallory. It's because of her interview with *The Guardian* that I knew about the first victim working at Prince Industries.

Vivian Mallory is Mum's old friend, Viv. Aside from them, there was no particular crossover of families, but I do remember Mum saying that Vivian's daughter was the victim of the Earring Killer who was being talked about on the news. It would have been maybe a year before Mum disappeared. I think I might have even known that Vivian was writing a book about it.

If I hadn't been so drunk all the time, I might have actually remembered some of it. There are whole chunks of my life that aren't there any longer. Sometimes it's evenings, sometimes it's weeks.

No wonder Mum talked about Viv so much on the tapes –

she wasn't simply a random woman from a book club, they were proper friends.

And Viv lost her daughter.

Henry holds up his cup. 'Do you want another?'

I'm about to tell him I should probably go when my phone buzzes. I'd usually ignore it, except Faith's name is on the screen and I never disregard her.

But then I see what she's sent.

There's a photo of Owen's wallet, open with my dead colleague's face staring out at me.

Why have you got this?

THIRTY-ONE

My daughter is waiting for me in the kitchen when I get home. Faith is on her phone but puts it down when I bluster inside, struggling with my bag, keys and phone. My bag strap catches as I try to get it over my head and I end up dropping everything on the floor, before pawing through the lot to make sure nothing's broken.

'Why have you got a dead man's wallet?' Faith asks.

She's calm but I know the tone – because, sometimes, she's her father's daughter. The disappointed, not angry voice. The *why have you let me down this time* way of phrasing a sentence.

'Why were you in my drawers?' I ask, knowing it's the wrong thing to say, even as it comes out.

'Really? That's *really* the first thing you say?'

I'm not sure how else to respond and my daughter sighs with annoyance. *Disappointed* annoyance. 'The drama trip's in six weeks,' she replies. 'They want our passport numbers. I was looking for mine, when I found this.'

Of course that's why she was in my drawer. I keep our passports and birth certificates in the same place, along with a few other documents. She knows this and I've told her she can retrieve her things anytime she needs them. But I obviously went straight to defensiveness, because that's what I do. Somebody else's fault, not mine.

Faith glances to the wallet, to Owen's face, then back to me, waiting for the answer.

'It's hard to explain,' I say.

'Are you drinking again?'

'No!'

'I know it's Granddad's funeral and—'

'I'm not drinking.' I somehow need her to believe this more than anything else. 'I'm *not* drinking,' I repeat, quieter now.

Faith waits and I'm not sure whether she believes me. She's never had to ask this before. We both look to the wallet together.

'You told me he killed himself,' she says.

'Yes. It's... very sad.' I pause. 'He was one of the landscapers,' I say. 'I'd see him more or less every day.'

It's only now I remember I've not told anyone that I walked out on my job. I was always going to be off today because of the funeral. And Faith deserves to know. Because walking out of my job is a big part of why I have Owen's wallet.

'I'll explain. But first you should know that I, uh... quit my job,' I add.

Faith's gaze shoots up from the wallet to take me in. 'You quit?'

'Yesterday.'

'Why?'

'It's sort of complicated but I had a falling out with my boss. He wasn't talking to me very kindly and I suppose I'd had enough. I probably should've tried to talk to him differently but I guess it's been a long week or two. I lost my temper.'

There's a quiver to my voice.

'I should've told you before,' I add.

Faith waits. 'And you're not…?'

'I'm perfectly capable of ruining a career without alcohol.'

I force a snigger but get nothing in response, not that I blame my daughter. This isn't a laughing matter. 'I had keys for the office but I'd accidentally left with them. My boss wanted them back but I didn't particularly want to talk to him again. I thought I'd drop them off at the office but then, when I was there, I don't know what came over me. I ended up letting myself into the office and I found that wallet in the safe.'

There's a realisation of how bad that sounds as soon as it's out. Faith is open-mouthed. 'You broke into an office, then you broke into a safe?'

'No… well… yes. But not really. I didn't *break* anything. The safe was open.'

'But even if the safe was open, why didn't you just leave the wallet? And why did you go in at all? Why didn't you just leave the keys?'

> '… I keep reading the same bit about impulse control. It says you want something, so you take it, even though you don't necessarily need it, or even want it.'

I can't stop thinking of Mum and the way she talked about herself. Is that me? I had the idea of letting myself into the office, so I did. I saw the wallet, so I took it.

Alcohol made me feel incredible, so I kept drinking it, even though I knew it was going to cost me my husband and possibly my daughter.

'I don't know,' I reply – and it's the truth.

'Oh, Mum…' The disappointment burns and I can't meet my daughter's eye.

'I suppose… I've been thinking a lot about the future and maybe the past.' I'm rambling now, but maybe Faith needs to know all this – so she can understand why I took the wallet. 'Remember when Granddad came over a few months back and put up that shelf? It's not a big thing but I guess I don't know who to go to if I have a problem now. Not just shelves but anything. Liam maybe. Your dad – but he has his own family. I guess it's just been a hard time.' I look up, making sure my daughter is looking at me. 'But I'm not drinking. I promise.'

For a few seconds, Faith doesn't move but then slowly, very slowly, she nods. She believes me.

'I still don't understand why you took the wallet...?'

I breathe. 'Maybe I don't either. But I'd had a conversation with Owen the day before he died. I told you about the tapes I found at Dad's.'

'Your mum's podcasts?'

I smile. She can't really comprehend the physical tapes – calling them a podcast is more familiar to her. 'Something like that. Owen works at the studios in town in his free time. I gave him one of Mum's tapes and he was going to see if he could clear up some of the audio for me. Then, the next day, they were saying he'd killed himself. I was really confused by it all. I suppose I saw the wallet and thought... well, I don't know what I thought.'

It's the truth, more or less. I can't explain why I took it. By the time I overheard Mark saying 'they can't prove anything – just tell them I was with you', I already had it.

Faith picks up the wallet, then puts it down.

'Do you think he killed himself?'

I can't tell the truth, because no seventeen-year-old wants to get involved with their parent's conspiracy theories.

'I don't know,' I say, which is the truth – even though there's a second truth that I don't think Owen killed himself and I'm terrified I got him killed.

'I'll give the wallet to the police,' I add. 'Or his mum, something like that. I'll make sure it gets back to who it should – but I only found it last night, then it was Dad's funeral today. It's all got away from me.'

Faith nudges the wallet across the table, seemingly accepting the explanation. All kids think their parents are nuts but Faith has more reason than most.

> *'... I keep reading the same bit about impulse control. It says you want something, so you take it, even though you don't necessarily need it, or even want it.'*

Is it hereditary? Have I cursed her? Or is this something about me that I'm choosing to blame on genetics because that's easier? I wish I knew.

'How was the wake?' she asks.

'Timothy tried to eat all the cakes and Tomothy went home with a stomach ache.'

Faith breaks immediately. 'I almost called him that when his mum was there,' she says. 'We need to stop calling him Tomothy.'

My daughter and I share a wonderful, perfect moment of synergy knowing that we absolutely *do* need to stop using the name Tomothy, while also knowing it'll be our inside joke forever.

'Bridget told me to tell you that your reading was brilliant,' I add. 'I thought so too.'

'I'm not used to reading from the Bible.'

'Nobody would've ever guessed. You were word perfect.'

Faith swells and the guilt starts to creep through me that I've changed the subject in a way that doesn't feel fair.

'We had to do a soliloquy for tutorial the other day,' she says. 'I used the Bible reading for that.'

We're at an impasse, which I'd know even if Faith didn't pick up her phone. 'Can I go upstairs?' she asks.

'You never have to ask.'

She stands and moves around me, quietly heading for the hall. 'I love you,' I say – and, in it, I hear my own mother saying the same in her crackly voice on the tape.

Faith misses half a step, though doesn't stop. 'Thank you,' she replies.

PAMELA

Extract from *The Earring Killer* by Vivian Mallory, © 2015.

It was three minutes past nine in the morning when my daughter, Pamela, said I was being over-dramatic. She was seventeen and I suppose seventeen-year-olds and their mothers are destined to argue over silly things.

We had definitely done that.

I always thought a part of that was payback because she was such a quiet child. She wasn't crying when I gave birth. Instead, there was a sniffle, a wrinkled nose, and a baffled expression at why everything was so bright and loud. By four months, she was more or less sleeping through the night – and, even before that, she was so quiet when she'd awaken in the early hours.

My mother used to tell me how it wasn't fair. *I* didn't sleep through the night until I was five years old, a fact she never let me forget. 'You owe me five years' of sleep,' she would remind me, well into my thirties.

I was the devil and my daughter was the saint.

But perhaps that's why we argued.

There was the fight about her bedtime when she was five; her refusal to wear anything that wasn't pink at six; then the refusal to wear anything that *was* pink by seven. She wouldn't wear a coat to school at eight, and kept leaving lights on when she was nine.

It's hard to know why I cared about any of those things. My dad would always tell me off for leaving on lights and, somehow, I morphed into him over the same issue. Now I know that if Pamela didn't want to wear a coat to school, the worst that would happen is she would get wet. She'd learn a lesson, and even if she didn't, all it meant was that her young mind was working out the boundaries of the world for herself.

By the age of ten, Pamela was pushing back over why her friends' parents could afford to go to Disney World but we couldn't. At eleven, she wanted to play football with the boys and was angry that the school wouldn't let her. By twelve, she didn't like her school uniform because she wanted to wear trousers but girls had to wear skirts. I agreed with her, yet we still argued because I wanted her to see that there are battles that are worth fighting, and the key is picking them wisely.

I was wrong.

If a twelve-year-old girl wants to go to war with her school over a clearly sexist uniform policy, the least she should expect is her mother to back her.

I didn't and I was wrong.

But because we argued about that, we kept on going. She had her ears pierced without asking. Two months later and it was her nose. Because she objected to the school uniform policy, she went out of her way to break it. She would be suspended, or sent home for the day – and then she would skip school entirely. It turned into a three-way battle of wills between Pamela, the school, and myself. I would lie in bed at night, thinking of my perfectly silent little baby, wondering why she couldn't just fit in.

I was wrong about that, too.

It would have meant an easier life for me – but Pamela wasn't the sort to simply 'fit in'. She saw things differently. While the vast majority of girls would wear a skirt, happily or not, Pamela was brave enough to question it.

Now, I can't remember why I was so keen for her to stop asking those questions.

I'm on the main street of Sedingham again, where a yawning man in dark trousers and a white shirt is opening the shutters of Tails. A couple of months have passed since Kelsey and Adele shared memories of the HAVE FUN education scheme with me at the bus stop. It's a part of town I have to force myself to visit, because Tails used to be known as Phoenix, which replaced Eclipse, that was once Jewel, and before that Enigma. Provincial towns and their idiosyncratic nightclub names are quite the combination.

Pamela was fifteen when she first got herself into Eclipse on a Friday night. She'd told me she was staying at a friend's house. It was a few minutes after two in the morning that the doorbell sounded. I flew out of bed, confused and half-asleep, finding my way downstairs to the front door, where a uniformed police officer with a fluorescent jacket was waiting for me. Pamela had thrown up on one of his colleagues' shoes, before being taken to the hospital to have her stomach pumped. She was fine, of course, more embarrassed than anything. On the back of that, Eclipse almost lost its licence, and ended up rebranding as Phoenix.

I walk past Tails now and then, picturing the scene of my fifteen-year-old daughter somehow getting past security. I imagine her delight at passing from the chill of outside into the sticky, humid hall beyond. Obviously, she wouldn't have been wearing a coat. Tails is not Eclipse. The ridiculous patch of sodden red carpet that used to be at the door is no longer used, nor the clippable rope across the door supposedly to signify VIP status. The dank lighting has been replaced by bright bulbs and chandeliers across the ceiling. The pound-a-drink promos switched for ten-quid cocktails, or mocktails.

It's different, yet this will always be the place at which my daughter was sick on a policeman's shoes.

Pamela and I argued about those shoes, the stomach pumping, and the sneaking into a club while severely underage. I tried to ground her but that didn't go well. I had a job and places to be – so Pamela would leave the house anyway.

But then a miracle happened less than a year later – or that's what I thought. Pamela got straight-As in her GCSEs, one of only four people in her year to get perfect results. I considered it a miracle because of what had gone before, completely disregarding everything else in front of me. The truth was, she found the level of education beneath her, because she understood it so naturally and easily. She picked fights over uniform policy because there was little else in the curriculum to push the boundaries of her intelligence. Somehow, I'd never seen that. I'd been to the parents' evening and, instead of focusing on the 'She's so clever and understands everything put in front of her' part of a teacher's comments, I'd hone in on the 'but…'

We didn't fight over my daughter's GCSE results – but it was the worst I ever let her down. She showed me her paper, with that perfect row of As and I looked at the marks, then I looked at her, then I looked at the marks again.

'This is unexpected,' I said.

They are three words that have haunted me ever since, because I should have only needed one.

'Congratulations,' is what I added afterwards, but it was too late by then. I saw it in Pamela's face, a subtle shift in the way she sucked her lips into her mouth and bit down on the bottom one. No argument, no fight, nothing thrown, no threats, just a soft bite of the lip.

I hadn't believed in my daughter, hadn't seen her for who she was, and then I'd told her that outright.

Things were different after that. We probably argued less, although a part of that was because we didn't see as much of each other. Pamela continued on to college for her A-levels and she also got her first proper boyfriend. We argued about him, of course. I didn't like his tattoos, or the short Mohican along the centre of his otherwise shaved head. I wasn't a fan of his nose ring, or the disc that expanded his earlobe.

But that was me missing the point again.

He was a good young man, who treated my daughter well. There was no longer a desire to sneak into clubs, or skip classes. In many ways, that rebellious part of her life was over – except I missed it because she now had a pair of nose piercings and another through her lip. I saw the surface, never what was underneath.

So we fought about that and about her boyfriend – and it's impossible to remember why I felt like that. Things that were big then are insignificant now. Pamela loved that boy, and, really, that was all that should have mattered. Except I remembered my father telling me how tattoos on a person meant they'd never get a real job, never contribute to society. That others would always look down on them. His opinions had somehow become mine, even though I'm not sure I ever really believed it.

And we argued.

It was about Pamela's boyfriend but, really, it was about me. I always regretted not getting the university education I wished I had, and I was so desperate for Pamela to have that. I wanted her to live my life, not hers.

And that's why, at three minutes past nine in the morning, Pamela said I was being over-dramatic. She left the house – and I never saw her again.

Back on Sedingham's main street, I head past Tails towards the corner, then follow the pavement up a slight hill, past a bus stop and a church. There's a small play park, where a boy is attempting to walk up the slide, and then a row of shops.

Pamela was last seen on the grainy CCTV outside the chip shop that has been offering the same large sausage and chips lunchtime special for as long as I can remember. She would have probably been heading for the bus stop, where she would have caught the number eight that would have taken her to the record shop where her boyfriend worked. She would hang around while he was on shift. Despite not being an employee, there were plenty of customers who later remembered her helping them find items, or who asked for her recommendations. She was known in a way I'd never realised. The owner himself joked that he had two employees for the price of one, saying she helped reorganise the entire stock, unprompted and unpaid.

Except, on that day, nobody saw her get on the bus, the driver didn't remember her, and she never made it to the record shop.

The last person she spoke to was in the mini supermarket, next to the chip shop. Pamela bought a packet of cigarettes – something else over which we argued – and she told the girl behind the counter that she liked her Metallica T-shirt. Pamela paid, then left.

The shop is a Londis now, with an A-frame sign outside advertising ice lollies, and a bin that has scorch marks across the top, plus a graffitied 'AJ' on the side.

I'm on the spot where my daughter was last seen.

Three days later, the body of Pamela Mallory was found in a gully near a sewer outlet around six miles from this spot. The next time I saw my daughter was for the official identification in the mortuary, ahead of the autopsy. There was a single jet-black plastic stud in one of her earlobes, while the other was bare.

Pamela was a victim of the Earring Killer – the first in six years since Sarah Graham; the eighth in sixteen years.

And then, precisely as Harry Bailey said, Pamela became a number. His wife, Janine, was number two; Pamela was number eight. Articles would be written in which the name 'Pamela' was barely used, yet the number 'eight' appeared multiple times. There was a clamour, a rush. Would the Earring Killer reach double figures? How long would it take?

People looked at me differently, and they talked about Pamela differently. That's how people like Harry Bailey at the cricket club, and Alan Ilverston, who lives on the canal, came into my life. Others, too.

So many others. We're all connected by a single person – the Earring Killer.

Pamela Mallory became number eight – but she wasn't the last.

SATURDAY

THIRTY-TWO

Vivian Mallory looks hardly anything like the profile photo on her author website. In that, she has flowing gingery locks, and a curt, tight, non-expression as she stares at a point a fraction off-camera. In real life, she's greyer, and older. The wrinkles are deeper and a general tiredness hangs over her, as if she hasn't had a proper night's sleep since she first started using a keyboard.

Perhaps all authors are greyer, older, wrinklier, and more tired in real life?

She's happy to see me, though.

'Eve, my word! Gosh! It's been such a long time, hasn't it?'

I wish I remembered her but Vivian is a mystery to me. She was Mum's friend, and I know the name, though there's no recognition on my end beyond the author website through which I trawled last night. I sent an email through her page and woke to find a reply inviting me to her house. I'm not sure why, but I assumed creative types lived in massive houses but Vivian's is an unassuming end of terrace that's part of a housing association block. A pizza menu is hanging half from her letterbox but she ignores it as she waves me inside.

We go through the whole 'Tea? Coffee?' thing, before we end up in her living room. A pair of battered sofas are more for comfort than appearance, which I think is the best way. I'm almost swallowed as we sit across from one another.

'It was such a delight to see your name in my email,' Vivian says. 'I saw "Falconer" and instantly thought of your mum. I thought it was a coincidence, then I realised it was you.'

I'm a little blank, because there's such familiarity from her that I can't return.

'You said you wanted to ask something about your mum...?' she prompts.

'It's a bit hard to explain,' I say. *I think my mum might have recorded a tape in which she says who the Earring Killer is, and sent it to someone, but I don't know who.*

I can't say that to this woman who lost her own child to the same killer. What if I'm wrong? What if this is another dead end?

'I think I just wanted to ask you about her. I know you and Mum were friends from book club...?'

Vivian doesn't seem to mind. 'We were friends long before that. We knew each other at school but then drifted apart, until we ended up arguing over who had the correct opinion about books. We fought over more or less everything!'

There is no malice or ill-feeling. It's more like a long-married couple bickering over who snores the loudest.

'People at book club thought we hated each other,' she adds. 'But it was all a bit of fun. You only argue hardest with the people you love the most.'

There's a gentle hint of something as she glances sideways to a photo pinned to the wall above the bricked-up fireplace. It's a picture of a teenage girl with dyed-black hair and a pair of rings through her nose.

'Mum talked about you a lot,' I say – which is true, but only because I've been listening through the tapes.

Vivian breaks into a smile, touching a hand to her chest. 'Did she? Ha! I suppose I talked about her a lot. She kept me sane, I think. I was having quite a few problems at home and I'd be going through a book trying to relax. Except I'd spend the whole time wondering how Angela would be able to read the same paragraph and have such an opposite opinion. I'd sometimes think she was doing it on purpose, just to wind me up.'

I laugh. 'Mum said the *exact* same thing about you. She thought you were coming up with opinions just to wind *her* up.'

Vivian is delighted by this. She claps her hands together and howls an infectious laugh. A few seconds later, I realise the laugh has become a sob. Vivian reaches for the box of tissues on the table and snatches a pair. She blows her nose and dabs her eyes.

'Gosh, it's been a long time,' she says, before slipping another look towards the photo of the teenage girl with the nose rings. 'You must know about Pamela. Your mother and I drifted apart again after I lost her. I stopped going to book club, because... I don't know. I suppose it didn't feel as if it mattered any more. People called, or came round, but I couldn't face them.'

She blows her nose once more, takes a big breath, then forces a smile. 'Sorry. I'm not usually like this but I saw your name, and thought of your mum and how things used to be.'

I'm stuck for anything to say, not only because of Vivian and her daughter but because I think I've been waiting for someone to tell me that my mother meant something to them.

'I think it was about a year after Pamela that I heard your mum had disappeared,' Vivian says after a while. 'I still hadn't gone back to book club, but a couple of people asked if I'd seen her, or heard from her. I was wrapped in my own life, my own grief. And it was a strange time – there were the floods.'

I nod along, because she's right. I've not read Vivian's book but I did find an article that had the timeline of the Earring

Killer's victims. Vivian's daughter was killed close to a year before Mum disappeared. Then coverage of Sedingham's floods overwhelmed any search for Mum.

Even without the floods, it had been easy for the police to assume she'd disappeared on purpose.

'Has there been any word...?' Vivian lets the question hang.

'There's been no sign of her in thirteen years,' I reply.

'Oh...'

I don't tell Vivian about the fingerprints on the gun. That's a sign of Mum, of course – the surest sign I've had. But I don't know what that really means.

Vivian and I sit in a melancholic reflective quiet for a moment, before I decide to ask the question I came to ask. 'Did Mum ever give you anything after you stopped going to book club?' I ask.

It's a question from nothing and Vivian's forehead crinkles. 'Like what?'

'A cassette. She used to record her thoughts a lot.'

I see the recognition as Vivian's eyes widen and she starts to nod. 'Gosh, that's right. She *did* record herself, didn't she? I remember now. She gave me a tape one time that was her reviewing a book we'd disagreed on. She told me I could listen to it if I ever wanted to know what a serious person thought of things. It was so self-righteous that I laughed my head off. I definitely listened to it.'

It really does sound like Mum.

She stops and rubs her temple. 'Thing is, we didn't see each other after what happened with Pamela. That was my fault, not hers. I shut everyone out. We went from seeing each other once or twice a week to never at all. There wasn't a chance for her to give me anything.'

It feels so deflating, because I'd convinced myself Vivian would have answers. She isn't only a link to Mum, she's connected to the Earring Killer through her daughter. Much more directly and devastatingly than me.

If there *is* a second cassette, I can't think of anyone else Mum would have given it to. But then maybe it's one more thing I'm wrong about. My mother wasn't saying she made a second version of the cassette, she was saying she recorded over the first because she messed up.

'I suppose...' Vivian tails off as she stares up to a point somewhere on the ceiling. 'I didn't even know your mum was missing until one of our old book club friends told me. I remember I'd had a really bad week. It was still only a year or so after Pamela – and then we had all that rain. I lived down on the river then and mine was one of the houses that was evacuated.'

Vivian is out of her chair, at the window, fiddling with the blind in an attempt to peer into the distance. I think she's the sort who needs to see something to be able to talk about it.

'I lived over there,' she adds, pointing towards a gap in the trees that I know leads towards the river.

'I'm sorry we didn't tell you directly at the time. I wasn't really paying attention,' I reply. We look to one another with a shared understanding. We were both going through different, terrible things. Vivian's daughter had been murdered, and it sounds like she almost lost her home to a flood. I was desperate to find out what had happened to my mother. Or maybe it was simply that I was drinking too much.

Vivian taps a spot on the wall roughly halfway up the window frame. 'The floodwater was up to here,' she says. 'It happened so quickly. In the morning, they were saying they were hoping to hold back the water with sandbags, then, by noon they were saying we had to get out. There was no time to pack; I grabbed a few things and left.'

She's still at the window, and again taps the patch of wall where she says the water reached. I have a feeling she does this often – but then I likely would if I'd been evacuated because of a life-threatening flood.

'Lots of stuff got ruined at the old house...' Vivian says, almost absent-mindedly. It's as if she's talking to herself, before she focuses back on me. 'Your mum never directly handed me a tape but there's a chance that she posted me something and I never got it. Or never opened it.'

A chance.

Vivian keeps talking, explaining. 'The house was almost destroyed. It was more than a week after the flood until we were allowed back. Even then, I was living in a hotel for a while, trying to deal with the insurance company. It was chaos. Eventually the house was rewired and renovated and I managed to sell and move here – but there were boxes of things I never unpacked. The old house was still getting mail that I never opened because I didn't see the point. It's hard to worry about a water bill when your house is wrecked and you've been in a hotel for six weeks.'

Vivian had lost her daughter, then almost her house. Easy to see that she would stop caring about things like mail.

'Have you still got all the mail you received back then?'

A nod. 'Somewhere. Not just mail. There were a few things like fridge magnets and ornaments that were downstairs but survived. I didn't really need them but I couldn't bring myself to get rid of it all. I was focusing on the big things, like replacing furniture.'

The timing might work. *Maybe.* If Mum recorded the tapes a day or two before she went missing, she could've left one for me – and then mailed another to her friend. It would have taken a day or so to arrive, which would have been close to the time Vivian was evacuated.

We're both nodding, having apparently come to a similar conclusion.

'Were you writing the book then?' I ask.

Vivian's sideways flicker betrays her as she glances to the photo of the teenager with the nose rings. 'Yes and no. After Pamela was killed, I kind of only wanted to talk to the other people who'd been affected. There were husbands and boyfriends; parents, witnesses, all sorts. I think it was my way of coping. I didn't feel so alone. Then I started to think that, maybe, I could tell their story. People kept saying Pamela was number eight, and I wanted to say "No, she wasn't." And the more I talked to other families, the more I realised they were the same. They didn't want the victims to be a number.'

She speaks quickly and there's suddenly a gravelly, frustrated tone. Then Vivian takes a breath and starts again. 'I started planning the book and I did ring your mum, for the first time in a long time. I left a message. We'd argued so much about books that, for some reason, I thought she'd want to know I was thinking of writing one. But I never heard back.'

Hardly a surprise, considering Vivian was evacuated not long after – and Mum disappeared. If Mum heard the answering machine message, she could've already stolen the jewellery box with the earrings.

'If she did send you a tape...'

'What's on it?'

I can't tell her it could be the identity of the Earring Killer, partly because I wouldn't want to get her hopes up. And yet, if Mum really *did* hear an answering machine message from Vivian, maybe that explains why she'd send that tape. Who better to trust?

'I'm not sure,' I say. It's a lie, maybe, but I catch Vivian's eye and there's something there. Perhaps she has an idea. Perhaps I'm a bad liar. Perhaps she just wants to make me happy because I'm my mother's daughter.

Either way, it's a long shot. 'Where would everything be?' I ask.

'That's easy,' Vivian replies, peering upwards. 'It's all in the attic.'

I don't have a fear of spiders, as such – but I think anyone would give a little shriek if they lifted their head, only for it to be immediately swamped with a mass of sticky, clammy webbing.

For the most part, I left the spiders to monopolise Vivian's attic as I lifted down six boxes marked 'flood'. The optimistic part of me thought we'd open the first to find a cassette tape, but nothing's that easy.

Instead, the pair of us sit on the floor of Vivian's living room, our joints and limbs creaking to various degrees as we pick through unopened electricity bills; crispy dried-out copies of the *Radio Times* and *Kays Catalogue*, plus things like cutlery and rolls of sticky tape.

'It wasn't me who boxed up all this stuff,' Vivian explains as we pick through it. 'The insurance company had someone who was going house to house. Some sort of liaison person because there were so many of us. She arranged this clean-up squad who went into the house and pulled together everything that was salvageable, while clearing out the stuff that wasn't. I got given those boxes while I was still at the hotel, but didn't think there was any point in unpacking them. I had nowhere for anything to go. By the time I was finally allowed to move back, I was stuck with these boxes.'

I hold up the plastic spatula from one of the boxes. The end is curled from heat and there's a dried egg splatter on the handle. 'I guess that explains this.'

Vivian looks to it and laughs. 'Why did I keep all this stuff...?' She holds up a snowglobe as if to emphasise the point. 'I don't remember ever owning this.'

We unpack but, really, we talk.

Vivian tells me about her daughter, Pamela, and how they

fought over all sorts. The argument on the morning Pamela died that Vivian thinks of every day.

'Do you get on with your daughter?' she asks.

'Usually,' I reply. 'She wants to be an actor.'

'Really?! That's so ambitious. People round here don't do things like that.'

I've never seen it like that before – but Vivian is right. Sedingham is known for one thing, and it's not acting.

'I worry about her,' I say.

'Everyone worries about their children.'

'I know but I worry she'll turn into me. I've had problems. Mum did as well.'

Vivian doesn't ask, even though I'd tell her. 'My daughter wasn't me,' she says. 'I wanted her to be but she wasn't. Your daughter isn't you, no matter how much you might think she is.'

I bite my lip and pull out a pair of novelty plastic sunglasses from the box.

'We have Find My Friends on our phones,' I say. 'She visited me at Dad's house the other day and sometimes I'll look at her dot when she's at college. I worry that I'm spying but I don't mean it like that...'

Vivian pulls a teapot from a box and holds it up, before shaking her head. 'She has the choice to remove you, doesn't she?'

'Yes.'

'So perhaps she likes the idea of someone watching out for her.' There's a flickered glimpse to the photo above the fireplace again.

'Maybe,' I reply.

Vivian places the teapot on the floor and then reaches deeper into the box. It feels as if I've spent the best part of two weeks sorting out things that should have been in the bin years ago.

THE TAPES

When I next look up, Vivian is holding a small, packed envelope.

I know the handwriting immediately – and so does Vivian. She offers it to me, where I turn it over. There's no return address on the back, and it's been sealed with a thin strip of tape.

'It's addressed to you,' I say.

She shrugs. 'You open it.'

And so I do. There's no letter inside, no instructions, or extra information. Simply a cassette box, with 'Viv' written on the sleeve. I pass it across and Viv opens the case to remove the tape inside. 'I don't have a player,' she says.

'I do.'

THIRTY-THREE

Mark presses back in his massive seat until it squeaks. There's a moment in which I think my former boss might topple backwards, however he seemingly knows the spot in which he's perfectly balanced.

'You're lucky I'm giving you this time on a Saturday,' he says. 'You couldn't even have the courtesy to return your keys. Had to drop them in the mailbox and scuttle off.'

If only he knew...

'I'm sorry,' I reply. 'My dad's funeral was the next morning and it was all a bit much.'

Mark nods along, waiting for the capitulation he knows is coming.

'If I could, I'd take back everything I said and did the other day,' I add. 'Putting the keys in the box and not replying to your message was incredibly disrespectful. I should've been much more grateful at everything you've done for me.' I pause and then go for the jugular: 'It's my time of the month and—'

'I get it,' he replies, not getting it. 'I have all this at home. Hormones-this, time-of-the-month that. Women are just temperamental – or, as I always say, temporarily mental.'

I smile while digging my fingernails into my palms, forcing myself not to say anything. I've worked with him long enough to know what to say.

'You're right,' I tell him, even though he's wrong. 'I've learned so much from you. I was upset about my dad and you're the last remaining father figure in my life. I took it out on the wrong person.'

He's nodding along enthusiastically, scratches his balls for good measure, then plucks a cigar from his top drawer. He uses it point at me, before lighting. 'That is very big of you,' he says. The room immediately stinks of that earthy, slightly sweet smell. Mark probably shouldn't be smoking indoors but it's not the time to get all HR about things.

'Lots of people say I'm a father figure,' he says. 'I suppose I was an influencer before anyone knew what one was. I've always been wise for my age but if that's a crime, then shoot me now.'

He has a puff of the cigar and pats his chest. I laugh along, just about holding back the vomit.

'I've always told people you're wise,' I reply – and Mark nods knowingly.

'Of course. Look, I was gonna put up the ad on Monday but, seeing as you're here and you've said sorry, I suppose we can start over.' He nods towards my old office. 'I'll put you back on three months' probation. You can have your old salary and we'll take it from there. How does that sound?'

'Wise...?'

He grins. 'Good girl.'

He puffs on the cigar again as I try to figure out how to twist the conversation the way I want it. 'My missus could learn a thing or two from you,' he says, unexpectedly.

'How?'

'Y'know. Typical woman. Gets all emotional about stuff. You should've heard her kicking off the other night. We were supposed to be at her mum and dad's anniversary dinner – but I couldn't be bothered. She told them I was ill – but then her dad was on a run to the offie and saw me in a beer garden with my mates. It all got a bit... aggro.'

I don't tell him that, in a way, I *did* hear her 'kicking off'. I suppose that's what the 'they can't prove anything – just tell them I was with you' was about.

Mark's still talking. 'Her mum's like you. Hormonal and stuff. Just try not to bring it to work in future, yeah?'

I force away the shudder as I agree that, yes, I won't bring my hormones to work any longer. I don't tell him that I won't be working here for long; but that I need those keys back.

'I've been struggling when I think about Owen, too,' I say.

Mark had been about to inhale from the cigar but a cloud skirts across his face. 'Poor kid,' he says, and some of the bravado has slipped.

'Someone said you played football with him...?'

There's a twitch of the eye, as if he's wondering whether someone's been gossiping – except that Instagram football photo is out there. 'That's why I went to the pub that night instead of the in-laws' anniversary,' he says. 'I'd only been with Owen the night before, played footy with him, and then he was gone. Life's too short for anniversary dinners when you've got your mates.'

I'm not sure whether that's the conclusion most would reach but he probably has some sort of point about prioritising the important things.

'He left his wallet,' Mark says. 'I brought it in to return it, before I knew anything that happened. Can't remember where I put it.' He suddenly spins in the chair, almost overbalancing and nearly stabbing himself in the face with the cigar. Once he's regained some composure, he places the cigar carefully in the ashtray and opens the unlocked safe.

'That reminds me,' he says. 'I let the police into his locker.

They were looking to see if there was a reason he did what he did. They found this in there.'

He passes across Mum's tape. I stare at it for a moment, before taking it, then opening the case to make sure the cassette is inside.

'It has your name on it,' he adds, and I sense him wanting an explanation that, despite my grovelling, I can't bring myself to give. This isn't why I asked Mark to meet me here, nor anything I expected. I thought the tape was lost.

I thank him, then put the tape in my bag, already desperate to listen to it again. 'I know it's Saturday,' I say, 'but I figured I could do a few hours this afternoon to catch up on everything I missed the last few days. It'll get me ahead before Monday.'

Mark waits and, for a moment, I figure he's going to demand details about the tape. Instead, he slowly starts to nod. 'I can't hang around,' he says, while stubbing out the cigar. 'You'll have to lock up yourself — which I guess means you can have these back.' He opens his top drawer and pulls out the keys and fob I left in the mailbox, then slides them across the desk. I catch them a moment before they slip over the edge.

We stay in position for a short while as he probably wonders if I have a bit more praise for him. When he decides we're done, he pops himself up. 'Things to do,' he says.

And then, somehow, I have the office to myself. Mark disappears in his BMW. I wait until he's out of sight before dropping Owen's wallet down the side of the safe. Mark will find it at some point and assume that's where he left it.

He's a creep — but thanks to Mum's tape, I know he isn't the Earring Killer.

The cassette Mum mailed to her old friend sat dormant in a box for thirteen years and, though the contents aren't quite the same as the one I originally listened to, it's not *that* different. More importantly, it doesn't cut in and out.

Together, Vivian and I put the tape in my cassette player. And once we pressed play, everything became clear.

Mum's voice told us how she stole the jewellery box, and found the hidden bottom. How the person from whom she took it would know it was her. That she knew they'd be coming.

She named names.

Vivian discovered the person who murdered her daughter at the same time as me. She would have known thirteen years ago if not for the floods, the boxes, and the fact she had to package up a whole portion of her life. It was the only way for her to cope: to throw everything in the attic and move on.

We both know we cannot take that tape to the police. It's recorded by a liar and a thief. It isn't evidence and – crucially – we don't have the jewellery box. That's what this all hinges on.

Except I have an idea where it is.

So I flit around the office, making sure that Mark doesn't come back, because I can't have him interfering in what comes next. I keep half an eye on the CCTV feed from the adjacent storage facility, waiting until there's nobody there.

It takes almost ninety minutes but, when everything is clear, I move as quickly as I can – first locking the office, then hurrying across the yard and using the master fob to get myself into Mark's other business.

That's the other reason I needed to go grovelling to Mark – I needed access to the computer system to check the storage locker numbers against the people who rent them.

Long rows of roller doors are inside and my footsteps echo as I head along one line before turning to check the parallel one.

And number forty-one is in front of me.

The lock-up rented by the Earring Killer.

The lock-up rented by retired Chief Inspector Kieron Parris.

THIRTY-FOUR

I use one of Mark's master keys to open the locker and then check both ways down the long row of identical doors. There's nobody in sight.

As I move into the gloom, I'm expecting stacks of hoarded boxes and junk. That's what was in Dad's garage, and it's what Nicola told me was in her father's storage locker.

Except it's not true.

The space is around half the width of a regular garage and it's empty. I pace from side to side, confused because I was so certain. There'd been a logic leap – but it wasn't massive. Mum named Kieron on her tape – and Nicola's mum had told me he had a storage locker. He clearly wasn't going to keep anything incriminating at his apartment, or the house in which his daughter now lives, especially after Mum stole the jewellery box. He had to be keeping it somewhere else.

But it's not here. There's nothing here.

I'm about to leave when I realise there's a light switch I missed. Despite dealing with all sorts of admin relating to this facility, I've spent almost no time here. The layout is something of a mystery.

As soon as I turn on the light, I realise the space *isn't* empty, not quite. The wall at the back isn't a wall at all: instead it's columns of identical black packing crates stacked tidily next to one another. There are at least thirty. I check the corridor again, where it's still empty, so head to the crates and lift the top one. It's surprisingly light to the point that I almost drop it. Once I get it onto the floor, I unclip the sides and remove the lid.

There are handcuffs inside, along with a set of keys – plus two barely used rolls of grey gaffer tape.

With the context of everything my mother said about Kieron, I'm overtaken by a shiver, wondering if any of this was used on the women he killed. Whether it was used on Vivian's daughter the day she never made it to her bus.

An old police uniform that I assume is Kieron's is at the top of the second crate. I don't know if it's against policy for former officers to keep their old uniforms, but, even if it is, this isn't what I'm looking for. Underneath the uniform is a solid-looking black police truncheon, as well as some sort of stun gun, or taser. It's lighter than I would have assumed from simply looking but it feels wrong in my hand. I wonder whether this was also used on any of those women and find myself turning it around, trying to figure out how it works.

The third and fourth crates have me wondering if Nicola's mum was correct about her husband being a hoarder. There are old phones, cables, and wires. A classic SCART lead, like those I got rid of at Dad's. There could be evidence on the phones, or perhaps some of them belong to the murdered women. I consider calling the police – but if I'm wrong about the phones, then I've discovered nothing. It's still the taped voice of a thief and liar against that of a very much alive and respected former officer.

I'm having a momentary rest, eyeing the remaining couple of dozen crates when my phone buzzes, Mark's name on the screen.

Where ru?

I stare for a few seconds, wondering what I should do, then make a decision. I race out of the storage unit, close the *click-clack* roller door and hurry back through the various corridors and connecting doors until I make it back to the landscaping yard. Mark's BMW is parked crookedly in its spot and the lights are on inside the office.

I'm out of breath when I reach the door and Mark's going through the drawers of my desk.

'Saw your car on the road,' he says. 'I thought you were catching up before Monday?'

I pat my chest, trying to get the words out. 'I've pretty much gone through the emails,' I lie. 'I was double-checking something next door...'

There's a moment in which I wonder whether Mark's going to want more. I'll have to make up something about a discrepancy over which lockers are occupied – except he never asks.

'I can't find my phone,' he says.

He catches my gaze as I look towards the device in his hand.

'Not this one,' he adds, harshly. 'The other one.'

I spend ten minutes helping Mark search for his second phone, resisting the urge to ask why he has two, while rueing the time I'm wasting.

The phone eventually turns up within Mark's safe. He says he must've accidentally left it there while searching for Owen's wallet. He asks how long I'm going to be, and I say I have a couple more things to check next door. He holds up both phones, says he has to rush – and then I watch him leave for a second time.

This time, I don't hang around for an hour.

I'm out of breath a second time as I hurtle from one business to the other. Kieron's locker opens as before and I head back inside, before getting back to work on the stack of crates. If he took back his jewellery box of trinkets from Mum – if that's what cost her life – then surely it's here?

If it's not, I'm out of ideas.

There are more clothes in the next few crates, some that are clearly Kieron's, others likely Nicola's. It's hard to know why he's kept them but I don't have time to worry over that as I take down another pair of boxes. There are more clothes in the first, but the second has another set of handcuffs, some zip ties, and a police ID card with Kieron's photo.

It isn't his name on the card, though.

It's someone named Keith, which has to be a fraud. I don't know if the taser is illegal but the fake police ID must be – and maybe this is why so many of the Earring Killer's victims appeared to vanish. They were shown an ID from a man who looked like a police officer, because he was one. Except, just in case there was an issue, he wasn't Kieron Parris, he was Keith Jamieson.

I could call the police now – but would I trust them to deal with this, especially as I'm trespassing? Perhaps he'd have a reason for the ID, or maybe it's not illegal anyway? Perhaps that's his real name and I've somehow never known?

There's one more box in the column, though at least another twenty to check. I start to restack the ones I've taken down, then pause for a breath. I had expected the locker to be rammed with clutter but, somehow, the neatness is worse.

And then I remove the lid from the final crate in the stack. There are curled zip ties at the side, and one other item nestled in the corner. The one for which I came.

A wooden jewellery box, with flowers engraved on the sides.

There are scrapes and scratches in the varnish that makes it look as if it's been dropped more than once.

It's how my mother described it on the tape: strangely beautiful from one angle, garishly ugly from others. I can picture it catching her eye and then her bemusement once she got it home.

There's a gentle rattle as I pick it up but, when I remove the lid, seemingly nothing inside. Mum mentioned there was a secret compartment, though not how to open it. It doesn't matter because Vivian and I will figure it out. She'll want to see that jet-black plastic stud for herself before we call the police.

It's over.

Mum was telling the truth about the box; that she was murdered and didn't disappear.

The truth about loving me.

The man who I thought was my saviour, who kept me out of prison, which allowed me to keep custody of my daughter; the father of my friend... he's a monster.

I stand properly, still holding the box as I realise my hand is shaking.

That's when there's a gentle scuff from behind. I turn and Kieron stands tall, a sad, resigned smile on his face. He twists and wrenches the door closed in a single, swift movement that I know I couldn't manage, and then turns back to me.

'Hello, Eve,' he says.

THIRTY-FIVE

We're at opposite ends of the storage unit, maybe five or six metres apart. Kieron sighs, touches his head and glances towards the open crates.

'There's a sensor,' he says, pointing to a small black square on the wall at his side. There's one on the other side too. 'It's sort of an invisible tripwire. The moment anyone breaks it, I get a notification on my phone. Happened last year when there was a mix-up and they accidentally entered my unit when they meant to go into the one next door. I got a free month out of that.'

He blows a low, gentle raspberry as I realise that I would have already left if not for Mark returning to find that second phone.

'Why are you here, Eve?'

I'm holding the jewellery box and he must know. 'Did you kill my mum?' I ask.

I expect a reaction – outrage, resignation, maybe even anger – but there's nothing. I didn't know Nicola's father that well back then. He'd been involved with one of my mother's arrests and helped her out for a while. That's how he knew my parents but it was later I came to know him. He was the officer who sat across from me in the police station when I'd rammed that glass into Jake Rowett's face and almost ruined my life. He finds me a couple of times a year and we have that sit down where he asks how I am. Really, he's asking if I'm drinking again.

Kieron pretended to mentor my mother and he pretended to mentor me. But all this time...

He is the same man now, the one I've always known, yet different. The eyes are dead.

'Why would you ask that?' he says calmly. 'You're the one trespassing.'

'But did you kill her?'

He has a moment, takes a breath, lets me wait and then: 'Actually, I didn't.'

The response comes with such assured calm that I instantly believe him. Why would he lie? Why now? It's only us.

But that has me looking to the jewellery box again, because if he took this from Mum – but says he didn't kill her – then who did...?

Unless...

'Is she still alive?'

And, suddenly, it's all I can think about. Because Mum shot a gun two years ago. Her fingerprints are on it. She isn't dead.

This seems to take Kieron by surprise and it's as if we're having two different conversations. 'Are you drinking again?' he asks. 'You are, aren't you? I knew it the other day.'

There's a stab somewhere between my stomach and my heart and I push a finger into my middle, trying to make it go. 'I'm not,' I reply.

'Why else would you be here, jumping to such conclusions?'

'I'm not.'

There's a flittering murmur of a smile to him now. He knows what he said and why he said it.

'I'm not,' I repeat, talking to myself, more than him. I've changed – and people are allowed to make mistakes. What matters is learning from them.

'Why did you stop?' I add, trying to prevent him taking control of the conversation. In a flash, that wicked suggestion of a smile disappears.

'What?'

'You killed nine people in seventeen years but nobody in the last thirteen. Why did you stop? You obviously enjoyed it.'

Somehow, Kieron has taken a couple of paces towards me and I hadn't noticed. I blinked and he'd moved. 'You don't know what you're talking about,' he says.

I offer up the box, running a thumb across the grooves of the engraved flowers. 'Mum stole this from you. She couldn't help herself. You must have had her and dad over one night and then, after they'd gone, you went to check on it – but it was gone. You knew it had to be her – and she knew you were coming for her. That's why she made the tape.'

There's no acknowledgement but I know I'm right. Not only that, I'm inwardly screaming at myself. When Kieron and I were sitting in the beer garden, I was the one who told him the tape existed. He was sceptical, saying the voice sounded like mine, acting as if it was a cry for attention. But all the while, he knew it was real.

He knew it was real *because I told him*.

I'm so stupid.

I played him the voice note from my phone. I told him Owen had the original.

Oh, no.

'Did you kill him?' I ask.

'I heard he killed himself.'

It takes a second but: 'I never specified the him...'

And we both know now, as if there was any doubt. Kieron

THE TAPES

might have been the person who killed Owen as he went looking for the tape – but *I'm* the reason Owen is dead.

'Where's the tape?' Kieron asks.

My phone is at my feet – but my bag is in the back of my car. The tape is there. I feel Kieron's eyes on me, weighing up whether I have it now.

'He didn't have the tape, so you must have it,' Kieron says. 'Where is it?'

I don't answer because I don't trust myself. I'll accidentally mention Vivian and the second tape.

Kieron doesn't wait long. He scratches his head and sighs. 'I do actually like you,' he says. 'Faith is a good friend for my granddaughter and I'm a family man before anything else.'

'All those women had families too.'

There's a twinkle in his eye. 'I said *I* liked you. But nobody's going to miss you, Eve. Faith's dad is a better parent than you'll ever be. Both your parents are gone. Nobody even knows you're here. Nobody cares.'

He pulls up his top and slips a knife from his belt. The light glimmers from the blade that's as razor-sharp as his words. Both feel too real.

'I wonder if I'm out of practice...' he says.

THIRTY-SIX

Kieron moves slowly towards me, a pace at a time, knife in his hand. His eyes never leave me and I can see the moment of realisation that all those other victims must have had. He would have shown them his police identification, got their trust, and then they would have had this same understanding that I now do.

Almost.

I already knew who Kieron Parris was – because my mother had prepared me.

A sense of calm washes across as I reach into the back of my trousers, and pull out the taser gun. It felt wrong in my hand the first time I held it – but it's right now. Kieron sees what's happening but he's too slow. When the trigger is pulled, wires zip from the barrel, embedding themselves in his neck. I was aiming for his chest but this is better. There's a pop, a fizz – and then Kieron is shaking. He first collapses to his knees as his jaw chatters and then he's on his side, convulsing.

My instinct is to help, to make sure he's breathing – but now's not the time for instinct. I clasp the jewellery box and run for the door. Kieron was able to wrench it down in one movement but it takes me three to lift it enough so I can crouch my way out. I close the grate behind me – and then run. It should be a simple dart through the corridors but, as soon as I reach the first crossroads, my mind is blank. I stand in the middle of the T, looking both ways, trying to remember how to get back to the landscaping yard. I turn back to unit forty-one, expecting the roller door to be up, and Kieron to be on his feet – but there's nothing.

Breathe.

I count to three – and then I know what I'm doing. No point in making my way back through the warren of corridors to the landscaping yard – because I'm parked on the road anyway. I turn in the opposite direction, heading out through the front of the storage centre and following the path to the road.

I see my car and I'm so close. I'll call 999 while I'm driving. Even if they don't believe me, I have the tape and I have the jewellery box. There's no way Kieron can clear that storage unit in time.

My chest is tight and it's more of a jog than a run. I'm balancing my phone in one hand, the jewellery box in the other. When I reach the car, I place those on the back, then fish into my back pocket for the key.

The lights flash orange and the car locks blip open. I'm finally safe.

'Eve...?'

It's not Kieron's voice and there's no way he could've caught me. I turn at the sound of my name – but it's just in time to see something swinging towards me.

Then there's black.

ELEANOR

Extract from *The Earring Killer* by Vivian Mallory, © 2015.

It was nine months later that the Earring Killer struck again. The previous eight victims were women who'd been isolated in various places – but there was something different about Eleanor Beale.

It had been a normal day at the Shell petrol station for Ethan Collins. There had been a rush early in the morning as drivers filled up on their way to work or school drop-offs. After the usual mid-morning lull, Ethan had kept an eye on the tanker refill, though that had gone according to plan. At the end of his shift, his till receipt matched perfectly and he spent five minutes talking with his colleague about the weekend's upcoming football matches.

From there, Ethan drove to the nearby Akbar's, where he ordered a lamb madras for himself, a butter chicken for his girlfriend, and two garlic naans. A curry was their weekly treat, because Fridays was the evening their work shifts matched up, guaranteeing them an evening together. They'd eat from their laps and spend the night catching up on whatever their Sky Plus had recorded across the week.

Ethan parked on his driveway and headed through the side door, as he always did. He called for his girlfriend, only to be met by silence.

Eleanor Beale was dead on the floor of her own kitchen: her throat slit, an earring ripped away.

A little over three years have passed. Ethan never returned to the Shell petrol station, nor spent another night in that house. He is currently working in Hollicombe Bay, where he coaches his niece's football team. They're all under-ten and swarm the pitches in groups, everyone chasing the ball until it breaks to one of the lone girls standing in space.

'It's not really about tactics at this age,' Ethan says. 'I suppose it would be if you were at a big club, something like that, but these are kids. Sometimes you just want to chase the ball at that age, don't you?'

Ethan has spent the past month working five-days-a-week as a part-coach, part-teacher, part-friend, part-parent to a group of a dozen girls who have been ever-present at football camp. We're on the sidelines, watching as the ball bounces erratically around the hard ground. Five or six girls chase as one but the ball bounces off one of their legs, breaking to another girl who was standing separately. She can barely believe her luck as she runs through towards goal, before shooting wide. Ethan claps loudly. 'Next time, Lyla. Next time. That's great positioning. Good work.'

I wait a moment, although I already know the answer. 'Is that your niece?' I say.

'Lyla,' Ethan replies. 'I suppose she's not technically my niece. Eleanor's sister has a pair of girls. Lyla's here for the summer but Maddison's a bit young. Maybe next year – but I don't think football is her thing.'

Ethan jogs on and off, half refereeing, half watching. I do a lap of the field and spend some time watching the older children on an adjacent pitch. It's a little over an hour later that I next catch up to Ethan. He waves off the last of his girls at pick-up time and then kicks the dried mud from his boots, before asking if I'm OK to sit on the floor. I tell him I am, even as my knees insist I'm not. We end up on the edge of the pitches as Ethan does a series of small stretches. He doesn't stop moving as he talks.

'I sort of blacked out,' he says. 'I remember taking the curries into the kitchen and then… They say I called the police but I only know that because there's a recording. I was at the police station and they were asking what had happened during the day. I was talking to them about our curry night and I kept thinking Eleanor would come in and say it was all some weird joke. I couldn't understand what had happened.'

Ethan finishes his stretches and momentarily lies flat on the grass before sitting up, his legs crossed. He no longer works at the petrol station and has started working self-employed as a personal trainer. It was always his goal. He's the sort who'd knock off a 10k in the morning, before heading to the gym to spend the rest of the day helping others do the same.

'We were talking about getting a puppy,' Ethan says. 'We were due to be married in the April and the long-term plan was to have children. Eleanor always wanted girls and I'd joke that I wanted boys but, really, it wouldn't have mattered to me.' He waits a moment, tugging restlessly at his vest. 'I still think about it now: Ellie and me, our puppy, a couple of girls or boys, still having curry night on Fridays. It feels close but I know it's gone.'

Ethan needs a minute and I let him have it. His way of working things out is exercise, so he jogs to one end of the field, turns and then sprints hard for ten seconds or so. He walks for another ten and then goes again.

The killing of Eleanor Beale was a big change from anything that had gone before. She was attacked in her own home, which left the police with many more questions than answers. Had she opened the door for an attacker? There were no signs of a break-in and, though her back door was unlocked, that wasn't unusual. That door opened into a small yard, with an isolated cobbled alley behind, where residents stored their bins.

There were no witnesses to what happened, very little in the way of evidence, and no known motive. There were already eight unsolved killings but this provided even more of a puzzle for investigators. Why Eleanor? Was it random?

The town had gone through so much.

When Ethan finishes his sprints, he returns to where I'm sitting, beads of sweat dripping from his tanned face. He apologises, though there's no need – then he jokes that he's going to have to do his warm-down again.

There are nine named victims of the Earring Killer, all women – but the tendrils of evil stretch so much further into the community. People like Ethan are also victims, yet they've never been acknowledged as such.

Janice McNally is an outreach officer for the local network of churches. Her role encompasses a breadth that includes everything from visiting local schools to helping with a shelter set up to give vulnerable women a place to stay.

'That escalation with poor Eleanor told women we weren't even safe in our own homes,' Janice says. 'We'd already been told we had to go everywhere in pairs or groups; that we could protect ourselves if we chose not to wear earrings; that we should avoid nights outs. But then, even if a woman abided by all that, we were still under threat. If we can't feel secure at home, how can we live our lives at all?'

Janice is a slight woman but she speaks with controlled fury. In the days after Eleanor's death, she led a march through town in which almost six hundred women united to demand police do something.

'We were desperate,' Janice says. 'Maybe we still are.'

Partly in response to that community anger, the police agreed to extra patrols and a more visible presence in town – especially after dark.

But would it be enough?

Seventeen years had passed since the first killing, nine women were dead, yet still the Earring Killer roamed.

THIRTY-SEVEN

I'm a cartoon character as tweeting birds circle my head. There are green and purple stars and, when I try to move, everything spins.

Not that I can move far.

I'm in a sitting position but perhaps it's more of a slump. The cold ground seeps through my trousers, chilling my aching backside, as I fidget to try to get my bearings. My hands are tied to something behind my back, while something harsh digs into my wrists when I try to wriggle free.

It's gloomy, though not quite dark and, as my eyes adjust, I realise I'm attached to some sort of railing. It seems like the sort used to pen in livestock, though it's hard to know.

'I didn't expect this...'

A woman's voice whispers through the dark. I twist against the railing, blinking away the stars as I realise a shadow is sitting on a chair a couple of metres away.

'I knew something was up when you said you'd been thinking about your mum...'

'Nic...?'

There's no reply, not at first. The shadow shuffles a fraction, their feet tapping on the hard floor.

'Where am I?' I ask.

'Don't worry about that,' she replies. 'Who else did you tell about the tape?'

'Nic...?'

This time, she moves, pushing up and out of a chair and stepping towards me, then crouching at my side.

Nicola is grey in the dim light, her hair tied into the tightest of ponytails, stretching her skin.

'You told that idiot at your work,' she hisses.

I sense her more than I see her. It must've been Nicola who hit me over the head at the storage units. I wonder where my car is, where the jewellery box has gone, whether she found the tape in my bag. I can't process what's going on. I tasered Nicola's father back at the storage unit and now...

'Did you kill him?' I ask.

'Well we didn't find the tape at his, that's for sure.'

Nicola stands and shifts away from me, returning to the chair. We've always had an odd friendship that only really existed because of our daughters. Our parents sort of knew each other but we weren't mates at school. After her dad helped get me off those police charges, we shared a bond that was difficult to quantify.

More than acquaintances, not quite friends.

'Does "we" mean you and your dad?' I ask.

There's a long, long pause, broken only by the gentle *tink-tink-tink* of me wriggling against the metal bars. I can't get comfortable.

'I got a flat tyre one evening when I was on my way home,' Nicola says. 'This was before Mum and Dad downsized, before this was my place. I stopped by because I thought Dad could help with the wheel. I didn't know Mum was at the theatre with her sister. No one was home but there was a light in the shed. I came back here – and that was the first time I knew the name Pamela Mallory...'

The gasp that comes from me is involuntary. I spent the morning with Vivian, talking about Pamela. Nicola speaks so casually now, as if that young woman wasn't somebody's daughter.

'What did you do?' I ask.

'What do you mean?'

'What did you do to Pamela?'

I can hear Nicola breathing and then: 'Nothing.'

'What about your dad?'

I jump as a floorboard creaks. Deep in the corner, a second shadow moves as I realise it wasn't Nicola's breathing I could hear.

'That taser really packs a punch,' Kieron says, and there's a surprising croak that undermines his usual assuredness. 'I never *asked* you to get involved,' he adds. I'm momentarily confused but then I realise the second part of the sentence wasn't for me.

'You'd have been caught without me,' Nicola replies.

'Don't be silly.' Kieron's response to his daughter is snapped and sharp.

'The only reason to stop is because you wanted Eleanor,' he says. 'I was fine before you and I'd have been fine without you.'

Nicola puffs an annoyance. 'I *literally* just saved you.'

I can barely see either of them. Is this a family thing? Is Lucy involved as well, or is she a clueless wife to Kieron and mother to Nicola? I strain but there's no sign of anybody else. The tension bubbles between father and daughter. Except I recognise a name. I've spent large parts of the week looking for details of the Earring Killer, and Eleanor Beale was the final victim.

Suddenly, I know where I've heard that name before.

'Didn't Ethan used to be engaged to an Eleanor?' I ask.

There's silence but I can feel Nicola and her father staring daggers through the dark. I don't know the full story of how Nicola and Ethan got together, but I know he was engaged to someone else when they first met. It wasn't long after Nicola had blown up her first marriage. She told me she'd run into someone at a petrol station with whom she thought she had a connection. It was around three years later when she introduced me to her new boyfriend and I realised he was the same person.

'You killed Eleanor because you wanted her boyfriend...?' I say, not sure I believe it. It can't be real.

Except: 'He'd have picked me anyway.' It's a spiteful, furious retort and I know Nicola doesn't truly believe it.

She found out who her father really was when she walked in on him with Vivian's daughter. There was one final killing after that – Eleanor – except that wasn't Kieron, it was his daughter. Or maybe it was both of them?

'Who killed Owen?' I ask.

'Does it matter?' Nicola replies.

'He was going to do me a favour.'

Neither of them answers – but I suppose that's a truth in itself. As soon as I told Kieron about the cassette, he knew he needed it. He killed Owen looking for it, and, once he failed to find it at his flat, he broke into Dad's house to see if it was there.

'Did you kill my mum?' I ask. Kieron told me he didn't and something about the way he said it made me believe him.

'You might as well tell her,' Nicola replies, quieter. There's a silence, still punctuated only by the gentle scratching of my wrists scraping the bars. Neither of them tries to stop me.

'Your parents came here,' Kieron replies. 'This was back when we owned the farm. Maybe a year after one of her arrests, where I'd been trying to help her. It was supposed to be a celebration of her staying out of trouble. My wife loves dinner parties but your mother... well, you know what she was. She took something that wasn't hers and I suppose we both knew what was going to happen from that.'

'So it *was* you?'

'Not exactly.'

'I don't get it. How are her fingerprints on that gun?'

Nicola sighs. 'Just tell her.'

The croak remains in Kieron's voice, a remnant from the taser. He's still shrouded in shadow.

'Your mother came to me after she stole the box,' Kieron says. 'She made an offer: she'd keep the box and keep my secret. In return, I'd leave you, your daughter, and your father alone.'

'You killed her anyway…?'

'I already told you no. But there was no way I could agree to that. She'd be able to hold it over me forever. I think she knew, even as she offered it. That's probably why she left you her backup…'

That's why there's a tape with my name on it. *That's* why another was mailed to Vivian. Mum was planning her visit to Kieron and didn't know how things would go. She needed to leave the tapes behind to tell us what she knew, because she worried it might be too late.

I wonder where mine was left. Likely not in the shoebox with the others – which means Dad probably moved it, likely by accident. Instead of being left out for me, it was hidden.

'When your mother took that jewellery box, it wasn't the only thing she stole. I noticed the box was missing but not the second thing.'

I already know what she must have stolen. 'She stole your gun?'

'At the time I was so furious she'd dare steal anything from me. Especially that jewellery box. When she came to make a deal, I couldn't see past the betrayal. It didn't cross my mind she'd taken more than one thing – plus she came with a plan B. I told her I couldn't agree to her deal, and she told me it didn't matter. That's when she pulled my own gun on me. Like mother, like daughter, I suppose.'

That explains how mum's fingerprints ended up on a gun I knew couldn't be hers.

'Are you *still* pretending you don't need me?' Nicola says, and then: 'I was in the next room. All those times listening to you whine about your mum... you don't know how often I almost told you, just to shut you up.'

I stare. '*You* killed her?'

'She was threatening my dad with a gun. She was extorting my family. What do you expect? I slit her throat the same way I slit that bitch Eleanor's.'

Her words are ice. I finally know what happened to my mother. I'd largely figured it out anyway – but it's still shocking to hear.

Kieron at least sounds somewhat regretful about things but not his daughter. Not my supposed friend.

Nicola and I have never been truly close. But she's still the person I talked to when I thought I might lose custody of Faith; when I thought I was going to prison.

And the whole time, she knew what she'd done.

But there's something else going on here. A seething annoyance in Kieron's tone. 'How were you so careless?' he hisses.

'When?' Nicola replies.

'With the gun. How?!'

'It was buried! I couldn't leave it in the house, could I? You told me to get rid of it after the cinema.'

'So why didn't you?'

'I did! I buried it at the back of the house – but a fox or something must have dug it up.'

'You should never have had it outside in the first place. There are so many times you've almost ruined everything.'

'I told you, I was carrying the gun because it made me feel safe!'

This is a conversation that has probably raged between them many times, likely in hushed, hissed whispers with nobody else around.

'You shot the guy at the cinema?' I ask.

'I was having a smoke and saw some weirdo stab someone. My daughter was inside and he was heading for the lobby. What was I supposed to do?!'

'Let someone else deal with it!' Kieron shouts now and his voice booms around the tight space. Despite Nicola's assertions that he needs her, he wants to be in charge.

Nicola waits a moment for the quiet to settle. 'I ran back through the fire escape. I was so sure someone would've seen and it'd all be over. I thought we'd be evacuated – but nothing happened. We all just sat there watching the film as if nothing happened.'

I know the rest, because we left the cinema as a group that day, to find police tape around the lobby and a bloodstain on the ground. My surprise was genuine but Nicola already knew.

'You should never have been carrying it,' Kieron hisses.

'Did you say that when I saved you?'

'You left it to be found *by my granddaughter.*'

'Shannon's *my* daughter.'

'And you let her find a gun. Anything could've happened.'

Nicola huffs with annoyance. 'Don't talk to me like that. None of this would have happened if you didn't feel the need to steal earrings and keep them *at your house.*'

They're both somehow breathless but perhaps it's their mutual anger. Both seemingly want to be in control; neither seems to be.

'I guess we're lucky the *foxes* didn't dig up Angela's body,' Kieron says – although he sounds cynical about the fox part. 'I did tell you fingerprints can stay on something for a long time. Nobody was more shocked than us when the police came back with your mother's prints on it.'

I only realise part-way through the sentence that he's talking to me.

'I bet I was *more* shocked,' I reply.

There's a scuff and then a scrape of a chair leg, then something skittles across the floor, landing near my foot. I can just about nudge it with my shoe but my arms are pinned and I can't stretch. Nobody speaks but, through the gloom, I recognise the outline of Mum's tape.

So Nicola did find my bag in the back of the car.

'Any other questions?' Nicola says. 'You might as well get them out now.'

'Why?' I ask.

'Why what?'

'Why any of this? What's the point?'

I struggle and strain. Neither of them tries to stop me, even as a metallic *clink-clink-clink* echoes. My shoulders are tight and there's no way out.

'Maybe it's in the genes,' Nicola says after a while. 'Maybe I just like it. Maybe we both do.'

Kieron says nothing to either confirm or deny – and I'm not sure I'm going to get a better answer. There's no mention of Nicola's mum. I sense Nicola moving before I see it – and then she's in front of me. Or, more to the point, her boot is. She stomps hard on the cassette three, four, five times. Something flies off into the darkness and another piece bounces from my chest. There's the sound of splintering plastic – and then silence. She doesn't know there's a second cassette, and I'll never say.

'Will Faith be safe?' I ask: the only question that really matters.

'Henry's a better parent to her – and you know it. She'll be fine.'

Maybe both parts of that are true. Faith is going to have to deal with both a grandmother and a mother who simply disappeared. Will she *really* be OK?

I fell apart after Mum disappeared. Will Faith do the same?

There's another scuff of movement and then I sense a pair of bodies standing over me. I rattle and fight against the railing but there's nothing I can do.

'I think it's time,' Kieron says.

'Me too,' replies his daughter.

SEDINGHAM

Extract from *The Earring Killer* by Vivian Mallory, © 2015.

At the time of writing, there have been nine murders attributed to the Earring Killer in and around Sedingham. Eleanor Beale was the most recent and nobody knows if or when the killer will strike again. Nobody knows if the culprit will ever be found.

This is a town whose residents take pride in the history of their home. There's the annual summer street fayre that draws tens of thousands; the winter market, which dates back to the eleven hundreds. This is the town that accepted more than four hundred evacuees in 1939, many of whom set down roots that still bloom today.

Sedingham is eight miles from the coast and surrounded by rolling, emerald hills. Its first known settlement was somewhere around 700 AD.

But there's a worry that everything this town has been built upon is in danger of being replaced by the notoriety that comes from nine unsolved killings. Nine women who should still be a part of this community have been taken, and nobody appears to have answers.

Its people are living through an ongoing trauma that has festered through generations.

It is exactly seven o'clock on a Tuesday evening when the bells of St Mark's Church chime. There's a six-minute chorus, as there is every week. Afterwards, community outreach officer Janice McNally joins me on a bench at the front of the church.

She looks up to the church and it's as if the sound of the bells still hang on the breeze. 'I started ringing when I was only nine,' she says. 'Dad had been doing it his whole life – and he picked it up off his mum. It's a family thing.'

There's a hint of a smile as we look out to the wash of green beyond the church walls that stretches to infinity.

'This church was built almost a thousand years ago,' Janice says. 'There's a floor panel inside with the date. We have a stone mason come in every year or two to clean and maintain it. The stained-glass windows came around a century later, and we have a specialist who looks after those, too. There have been problems with the roof and the stairs. We've been working with a charity to help with accessibility issues. It's this monolith that's been here a thousand years, and could be here for another thousand.'

Janice speaks passionately, drumming her fist gently into her thigh as she speaks.

'That's how I think about this town,' she adds. 'It's easy to feel disheartened – but Sedingham isn't one person. It's not this monster looming over us. It's the community and the people who live here. When we had the march in town, it came from a place of anger. This burning, furious rage at what had been done to us. But there was beauty there, too. Solidarity with hundreds of women, saying we were going to stand up for ourselves and each other.'

I tell her it's inspiring to hear such things, given what the town has been through.

'I don't think we have another choice. I'm obviously not saying there's a positive to this but I do believe it should make people appreciate others in their lives. How much we should be looking out for them. I think there will be a time we all need to stand up and say we're not going to accept this any longer. This person has taken so much – but that doesn't mean we're defined by this evil. I firmly believe that, one day, you, I, or someone in our town will have a moment to stand up and say we've had enough.'

THIRTY-EIGHT

From nowhere, swirling, spinning blue light floods the space. I'm blinking through the dark, getting my bearings, suddenly able to see that we're in a shed with a rail bolted across the width. Nicola is standing over me, the crushed remnants of Mum's cassette at her feet. She looks to her father, eyes wide – though he is only watching me.

'Dad...?'

I guess, in the final seconds, it's clear who's in charge. There's fear in Nicola's faltering voice – but Kieron's expression doesn't change. He peers down at me and there's a merest hint of a nod that's caught in the whirling spirals of blue.

'Dad...?'

Nicola speaks with half a gasp and, when another second passes without response, she turns and bolts. A wooden door flies open, giving the merest hint of something green, before it clangs closed again. Somewhere in the distance I hear heavy bootsteps, and a bang.

Kieron glances behind him – but it's only us. There's a knife on the ground, though I'm not sure if Nicola dropped it, or if it was always there. Kieron glances towards it and, for a second, it feels as if he's about to pick it up. Instead, he lowers himself to the ground, until we're sitting a pace apart.

'I sometimes wondered who it would be,' he says.

'How'd you mean?'

There's a smile but the wickedness from the storage locker has been replaced by exhaustion. He doesn't reply – and perhaps it's because there's no time – but maybe it's because he doesn't need to.

The door sounds again and there are new silhouettes. Someone shouts 'Down' and then 'Show me your hands'. Kieron never breaks eye contact with me as he stretches his arms backwards, before lying on the floor. A man asks if I'm OK but it's hard to hear, let alone reply, with the thunder of heavy boots.

Then, from nowhere, there's hush. I realise my eyes have been closed and, when I open them, Detective Sergeant Cox is standing in front of me. She also asks if I'm OK, and I'm fairly sure I say yes. The door is wedged open and the spinning blue lights have been replaced by a slice of daylight.

'This might hurt a little,' she adds, showing me what looks like a pair of garden clippers. I tense as she stretches behind me but then my wrists are loose. She holds up a pair of clipped cable ties.

'Can you stand?' she asks.

'I think so.'

She squats and lets me use her shoulder to help pull myself up. 'Where am I?' I ask.

'A shed at the back of your friend's house.'

I know the place. This is at the edge of Nicola's property, close to where the gun was found a few days before. This is where she said she stumbled across her father with Pamela Mallory.

My head's cloudy and I take a step towards the wall, using it to hold myself up as I realise I'm standing on a reel of broken tape.

'You can take as long as you need,' Cox says. 'You're safe now.'

There's a sound of shuffling, more footsteps, softer this time – and then a new figure appears in the doorway.

'Gosh,' Vivian says – which is quite the understatement.

Sergeant Cox looks between us. 'You have a guardian angel,' she says, talking to me.

'It wasn't my idea to set up Find My Friends,' Vivian replies. She's right but not completely. When she said that Faith might have liked the idea of someone watching out for her – of *her mother* watching out, I realised that I'd like someone to be watching out for me. Especially considering what we both found out about Kieron.

'She insisted we come here,' Cox says. 'We probably wouldn't have listened, except it's hard to argue with a person who literally wrote the book on a subject.'

Vivian is quiet at that. Quite soon, it will be confirmed that she's standing in the place where her daughter died.

'He's got a storage locker,' I say.

'We'll get to it.'

'Did you find my phone?'

'I'm not sure it's the time for—'

'If it's somewhere around here, I've had voice notes recording since the moment I walked into Kieron's storage locker.'

Vivian holds the door wider, sending more light into the space as Sergeant Cox looks around the floor. 'Like mother, like daughter,' she says.

EVE

Extract from *The Earring Killer* by Vivian Mallory, revised edition © 2025.

It had been over a decade since the Earring Killer had last found a victim and yet, in the space of a week, there were funerals for two more.

Owen Jefferson was a recent graduate, working at a landscaping firm while figuring out what to do with his life. He did part-time shifts at a podcast studio, where he'd agreed to try to clean up a spotted, damaged audio cassette.

Ultimately, it was that which made him the first male victim of the Earring Killer. No trophies were stolen from him, though that doesn't make him any less a casualty.

The other funeral was for Angela Falconer, who was killed shortly after Eleanor Beale. For those who insist on counting, she was the tenth victim; Owen was the eleventh.

The sound of Slade's 'Merry Xmas Everybody' bleeds through the too-thin walls as Eve Falconer points to the strip of tinsel that's pinned to the wall in the corner. 'That's not from this Christmas,' she says, before taking a seat on a squishy chair that has yellow foam bleeding from the side.

We're in the function room of Sedingham Labour Club; the same one in which Lorna did shifts after leaving Prince Industries. It feels like a throwback to another time, with posters advertising tribute bands like Pet Store Boys and The Strolling Stones.

'I dread to think how much money Dad spent in here over the years,' Eve says. 'He'd call me and said I'd missed a cracking night watching Kiss, then it'd turn out it was some tribute band called Snog, or something like that. He found it hilarious.'

There are a few reasons why the Earring Killer was finally caught – and Eve is primary among them. Previous chapters describe how a cassette tape finally led to justice – but the final word has to go to Eve herself, no matter how reluctant she was to be a part of this book.

'Mum was the reader in the family,' Eve says. 'But she was never really a writer. She liked to talk, which is where all the tapes came from. She left about three-dozen cassettes with her thoughts on life, and everything. I listen to snippets here and there, almost like it's radio in the background.'

Eve and I have been in one another's lives ever since that afternoon in the shed. We speak most days, even if that's one of us texting the other to ask how things are.

'I blame myself for Owen,' she says. 'It was me who involved him and it was me who told Kieron what was going on.'

I tell her she had no way of knowing that at the time – but Eve simply shrugs that she should have known.

'When I heard Mum's fingerprints were on that gun, there was a part of me that wanted to think she was alive – except I also knew she wasn't. I sort of believed two different things at the same time and wasn't sure how to handle it. I was surprised at how much I *wanted* it to be true.'

I wonder if there's any consolation or comfort in knowing that the final thing her mother did was bargain for the safety of Eve, plus Eve's own daughter.

'Some comfort,' she says. 'But was it the right thing to do? Would Kieron really have stopped? And it doesn't bring her back. I think family is a complicated thing for me. There's my daughter at number one and then everyone else. I have a brother but we aren't close. There were times in that week I was suspicious of him for no reason, really. We're very different people – but maybe that's all right.'

After the arrest of Nicola and Kieron Parris, the police discovered the jewellery box containing the stash of stolen earrings in Nicola's car. Further evidence was found in a storage unit in Kieron's name. There was also long, sometimes muffled audio recorded on Eve's phone. It might not have been enough in and of itself – but, together, the police were able to build their case.

Nicola's daughter remains friends with Eve's, despite everything. 'I'm trying to be there for her,' Eve says. 'She's gone through a lot, with her mum and her granddad.'

Was she worried after waking up, cuffed to that rail in the shed? Eve thinks for a surprisingly long time about this. She sips from a mug, then tells me she doesn't even like tea. 'I wasn't worried for myself,' she says. 'I was for my daughter. I think you can cope with a death – but not knowing is worse. I wouldn't have wanted to leave her another question.'

It's apt, of course, because there were dozens of people from Sedingham and beyond left with only questions when it came to the fate of their loved ones. They now have answers, albeit perhaps not what they might have expected.

'My daughter thinks I've lost it,' Eve says after a while. 'I've been recording voice notes of myself going about my day. Little memories here and there. She says talking to myself is a sign of madness.'

I ask Eve what she thinks and she has a moment, taking in the tinsel and the posters. 'I remember the first time I heard Mum's voice again after all those years. The way the tape crackled and then she was speaking. It was…' Eve stops, smiles and shrugs, unable to put it into words, before she makes her conclusion.

'I think my daughter will change her mind one day.'

PUBLISHING TEAM

Turning a manuscript into a book requires the efforts of many people. The publishing team at Bookouture would like to acknowledge everyone who contributed to this publication.

Audio
Alba Proko
Sinead O'Connor
Melissa Tran

Commercial
Lauren Morrissette
Hannah Richmond
Imogen Allport

Cover Design
The Brewster Project

Data and analysis
Mark Alder
Mohamed Bussuri

Editorial
Ellen Gleeson
Nadia Michael

Copyeditor
Jane Eastgate

Proofreader
Tom Feltham

Marketing
Alex Crow
Melanie Price
Occy Carr
Cíara Rosney
Martyna Młynarska

Operations and distribution
Marina Valles
Stephanie Straub
Joe Morris

Production
Hannah Snetsinger
Mandy Kullar
Nadia Michael
Ria Clare

Publicity
Kim Nash
Noelle Holten
Jess Readett
Sarah Hardy

Rights and contracts
Peta Nightingale
Richard King
Saidah Graham

RAISING READERS
Books Build Bright Futures

Dear Reader,

We'd love your attention for one more page to tell you about the crisis in children's reading, and what we can all do.

Studies have shown that reading for fun is the **single biggest predictor of a child's future life chances** – more than family circumstance, parents' educational background or income. It improves academic results, mental health, wealth, communication skills, ambition and happiness.

The number of children reading for fun is in rapid decline. Young people have a lot of competition for their time, and a worryingly high number do not have a single book at home.

Hachette works extensively with schools, libraries and literacy charities, but here are some ways we can all raise more readers:

- Reading to children for just 10 minutes a day makes a difference
- Don't give up if children aren't regular readers – there will be books for them!

- Visit bookshops and libraries to get recommendations
- Encourage them to listen to audiobooks
- Support school libraries
- Give books as gifts

There's a lot more information about how to encourage children to read on our websites: **www.RaisingReaders.co.uk** and **www.JoinRaisingReaders.com**.

Thank you for reading.

Printed in Dunstable, United Kingdom